On The Wild Coast

by Patrick J. Lee

for Sandi and Sara

ISBN: 978-0-9894588-1-8

Note to readers

On The Wild Coast is set in southern Africa, where many different languages are spoken and mingled together. Below are some of the common words, colloquialisms and slang used in this book.

Aikona   *I-corner* (Zulu). Negative, No.

Boers   *rhymes with "Coors"* (Afrikaans from Dutch). Literally: farmer. Commonly used to describe white settlers of Dutch descent in southern Africa, or all white settlers. Sometimes used as derogatory reference.

Bonsella   *bon-seller* (Zulu). A bonus or gratuity.

Broer   *brewer.* (Afrikaans from Dutch). Brother, ally.

Dagga   *say "duh" and clear your throat.* Marijuana.

Durban Poison   Marijuana grown or sold on the east coast.

Gwellie   a ball of spit.

Kak   shit.

Klap   *klup.*   A blow with the hand. A slap.

Kwaai	*kwhy.* Versatile slang. Meanings include: cool, impressive, angry.
Moer	*m<u>oo</u>-er.* ditto. Meanings include: assault (v), superlatively large (a), idiot (n) .
Moffies	(colloquial) Homosexuals.
Naai	*rhymes with "sky".* Literally, to sew. Colloquially: have sex with (derog.).
Nkosasana	(Zulu) Young woman, princess.
Okes	(colloquial from Afrikaans: ouens) Guys.
Sjambok	*<u>sham</u>-bok.* long rubber whip.
Slapgat	*<u>slup</u>-ggut.* A sloppy, lazy fellow.
Voetsek	*<u>foot</u>-sak.* get away, scram.
Wena	*<u>wear</u>-na.* you.
Yebo	*<u>yeah</u>-bore* Yes. Affirmative.

PART ONE

Mendi Mkhize knew little, and cared less, about Port Victoria when he set out across the African veld to investigate the murder there. Mendi had been in a two-year sulk which was today focused on the fact that his car was not air conditioned. He was wearing a black Armani suit and tight Italian shoes, part of a large consignment of executive clothing he had bought on his credit card while in New York as a guest of the United States. He was hot.

When the Government of National Unity came to power a few years earlier, the cascade of political reward created an entire new class of black people from coast to coast. Men who had once been in jail claimed high political office and their relatives and friends were catapulted up the economic ladder. But by the time it reached Mendi Mkhize—who had labored long and hard, he felt, in the Freedom Struggle—the cascade had become a dribble. Mendi's reward was a post as chief magistrate of an area on the eastern coast. His parish was substantial in geographical extent but economically backward and politically worthless. The provincial capital, a filthy truck stop between the industrial hinterland and a major port to the south, was overflowing with grubby prostitutes and abandoned vehicle carcasses, and haunted by a chemical smell no one could trace. Gunfights were commonplace at its many filling stations as disputes arose over the trade of petrol, drugs, stolen credit cards, sex, and any other merchandise that the truckers might be buying or selling. The rest of Mendi's domain was scarred with soil erosion and forlorn mud hut villages, depleted over a hundred years by the migration of all able-bodied men to the gold and diamond mines on the highveld.

When Mendi's car hissed to a stop some seven miles short of its destination, his disgust with the whole damn business was complete. He was driving an old Toyota on a work assignment across treacherous roads to a remote and godforsaken dump. And were his leaders in the capital making the journey from their state homes to their state offices in cars like this? *Aikona*. They had appointed themselves to the *Wa-Benzi*—a class who traveled exclusively in black Mercedes Benzes. Mendi was sure that not only his leaders but his leaders' spear-carriers and praise-singers were driving around in Mercs with their smart phones buzzing importantly (Mendi's domain was not considered worthy of cellphone coverage).

He got out of the car and looked both ways along the road. It was otherwise deserted and could remain so for the rest of the day. He was calculating whether to walk back or onward, when a car heading toward the coast came into view. Mendi stepped into the middle of the road and raised his hand. He was a tall man with the spreading girth of a respected elder. He had complete confidence in his leadership demeanor.

Alice Burley, recently arrived from London, had been warned not to stop for anyone who was black. A black clerk had conveyed that to her at the car rental office, without the word "black" ever being used. In fact, Alice had been warned not to travel on these roads at all, much less alone. She had been left in no doubt as to the dangers to a single white woman in this country, where suburban housewives exchanged horror stories of violent crime in the way they might swap the names of recommended yoga studios. Alice had arrived at the bottom end of Africa with a momentum strong enough to carry her through those fears, but the appearance of a black man blocking the road ahead snapped the earlier warnings sharply into focus.

She slowed down. The man in front of her looked too well dressed to be a highwayman, but she had also been warned not to take anything at face value. He was not waving a gun, but then he wouldn't, would he? She slowed the car to a crawl, unsure what to do. The man waved her forward impatiently. She knew what he was thinking: this white woman doesn't want to stop for a black man. She knew he knew she was probably thinking that.

She lowered the driver's window and put her head out.

"Don't be afraid," he called with brisk authority. "My name is Mendi Mkhize. I am the chief magistrate for this area. My car has broken down and I have urgent business in Port Victoria."

It was an authentic performance. Alice drove forward and stopped the car next to him.

"Actually, I'm going there myself," she said.

"Of course you are," he said. "This road doesn't go anywhere else."

Not waiting for her invitation, Mendi stepped around to the

passenger side and opened the door of the compact rental car. He pushed the passenger seat all the way back and squeezed his large frame in beside her.

"Let's go," he said.

She looked at him for a moment, which was his opportunity to thank her, but instead he took a white handkerchief from his pocket and leaned forward to dust off his shoes. Alice put the car in gear and drove on.

"Where have you come from?" said Mendi.

"London," said Alice. "In England."

"I know where London is."

Alice chastised herself silently. "So what is taking the chief magistrate to Port Victoria? I was told nothing ever happens there."

"I have to conduct an inquiry. A man has been killed. Murdered."

"Good God! Who by?"

Mendi turned his eyes on her. "That's what I'm supposed to find out," he said.

"Of course. What about the police? Didn't they find anything?"

"Port Victoria has no police presence. In any case, my purpose is not to investigate the murder as such, but to establish whether it is a crime against a tourist. This province has a Commission of Inquiry into Crime Against Tourists. It's not good for the industry."

"Or the tourists, presumably."

"Most of them are just careless," said Mendi. "Like you. You should never have stopped for me back there. Didn't they warn you about that sort of thing?"

Alice couldn't tell whether he was serious or not. His manner was gruff, but that might have been the heat. She had taken the cheapest of the rental cars available in the capital, and it, too, did not have air conditioning.

"It certainly is hot," she said. "You must be feeling it in that suit."

"I'm an official of the government."

Alice decided to give them both some relief, so she used the electric buttons to lower the rear windows. The wind compression into the car created a thudding vibration that eliminated the possibility of conversation.

The road decayed progressively as it loped across a barrier of hills so tight they seemed packed there for storage. The tar surface crumbled and eventually gave way to gravel or compacted dirt. Stray goats and barefoot children occasionally blocked their way. They passed two women carrying firewood on their heads and an erect old man on a limping horse who refused to give way until he had delayed them to his satisfaction.

An hour later, the car crested the final hill and the Indian Ocean came into view. Alice let the car coast to a standstill on the side of the road.

"Why are we stopping?" said Mendi.

"Just to look. Isn't it beautiful?"

Port Victoria is located at the mouth of the Umzimvubu, a river sufficiently muscular to have cut a deep ravine through the barrier of hills. Finding itself abruptly at the Indian Ocean, the river is reluctant to give up its journey so suddenly and flattens out across the narrow plain into a massive lagoon. It was just the kind of place, in Mendi's opinion, that white people would choose to build something. Pretty but useless. You couldn't grow anything or raise cattle there. The lagoon was too wide and shallow for anything useful. It was a nightmare to get to, and when you got there all you had was a perpetual sea breeze laden with salt, which corroded anything and everything. Mendi did not think it was beautiful—it made him think again about how he had been tossed a dry bone from the last pickings of the political carcass. But it seemed to completely transfix Alice—even the small village center below them, which was unkempt and inglorious.

Finally, Mendi got impatient. "I'm staying at the Cape Hamilton Hotel," he prompted her.

"So am I," replied Alice.

"Follow the telephone wire." Mendi pointed to the line of poles that ran alongside the road. "The hotel has the only phone."

Alice enjoyed this example of local expertise and turned her best smile on Mendi, who consequently assessed, for the first time, her carnal possibilities. Some of his friends regarded white women as trophies, but reports on their actual performance were mixed at best, and this one was at the top end of Mendi's age range. Still, he thought, the pickings might be slim here. So, he smiled back at her. Then Mendi and Alice bumped down the steep and somewhat terrifying road through the ravine into Port Victoria.

2

Tribes fleeing from Shaka Zulu crossed these hills and valleys and gave it a name that sounded like distant drumming and expressed the sound they feared: the bare feet of Shaka's warriors pounding on the hard African earth behind them. Some didn't stop running until they were a thousand miles away. Later Shaka's men ran back the other way, ahead of the guns of the British colonial infantrymen. The latter paused only momentarily to overwrite the onomatopoeic Zulu name of this place with one of their own construction: Port Victoria, in honor of their queen.

Since then, Port Victoria has not warranted attention by historians, policemen or officials. Occasionally, an ambitious minor politician would arrive with the intention of pulling the place into formation, but quickly found there was no traction for a political career here. Port Victoria was believed to be not only ungovernable but not worth governing.

The blessing upon this place is that it has no blessing. There is no harbor, no gold in the hills, no diamonds or titanium in the beach sand, no arable land, not even a fashionably threatened sensitive ecosystem: none of the things that have created so much misery elsewhere in southern Africa.

A place so remote develops in abnormal ways. Unrinsed by the general stream, it can be dominated by the peculiar. Those who end up here are the discards, people who have evacuated themselves from previous lives filled with trauma, people running so hard they could get through the barrier of hills and are stopped only by the wild ocean and the hope that even the sternest demon would hesitate to follow.

The naked body had been found on the rocks at low tide two days previously by ten-year-old Temba Xhosa, whose mother, Mama, ran a restaurant on the beach at the mouth of the lagoon. Port Victoria lacked not only a police officer, but also a town clerk, postmaster or indeed any bureaucratic figure. So Temba ran to fetch Johnny Fourie. The victim was white. Johnny Fourie was white. Temba didn't think his mother, or any other black person, would want to spend any part of their day on the problems of a dead, naked white man.

Johnny Fourie was de facto head of the community at Port Victoria. He lived alone in a cabin up on the hillside and fished for a living from a ski boat. He rounded up his bait man, Woodstock, and Clive Gilman, who owned the Cape Hamilton Hotel, and together they carried the body up from the rocks. After a brief objection from Clive, they made space for the body in the hotel's old supermarket display freezer, moving aside the frozen steaks and Clive's fishing bait. Then they studied the body.

"Good teeth," observed Clive.

The deceased, a male of about forty, had dental work of a standard that implied wealth. Also a neat haircut and well-kept nails.

"Not a fish from these waters," said Johnny.

"Check out the watch," said Woodstock.

Johnny pulled the watch off the man's wrist and held it up. "Gold Rolex." He weighed it in his hand. "Five thousand US dollars, minimum."

"Let's play sticks for it," suggested Woodstock, which earned him a look from Johnny.

"They took his clothes and left a five thousand dollar watch?" said Clive.

"Sending a message," said Johnny. "You know, *Goodfellas* Mafia kind of thing."

Goodfellas was one of the half-dozen videos that were repeated often on the VHS player in the "Ladies Bar" of the Cape Hamilton. They all knew it by heart.

"But we know everyone here," said Clive.

Johnny Fourie gave no reply, but stroked his chin as if pulling on an imaginary beard. The others got the gist immediately.

"Dom Marais," muttered Clive.

Johnny raised his eyebrows, not even wanting to speak the name. Johnny Fourie was tough. He had once been swept off his ski boat while fishing alone and was presumed drowned after the empty boat washed up near the lagoon. That evening, a wake was held at Mama's restaurant on the beach. By ten o'clock, most of the mourners were stretched out on the sand, either passed out or stupefied by drunken sentimentality, while Johnny's favorite Bob Dylan album played. Johnny walked out of the sea and up the beach to the bar, where he ordered a double brandy and Coke from Mama. He had survived in the water for fifteen hours, on a coastline that regularly lost surfers to sharks. But even Johnny Fourie did not want it to get around that he might have accused Dom Marais of anything.

Clive phoned through to the provincial capital to report the dead man. Then he turned the refrigeration up to high, covered the body with a canvas siding from the marquee that was occasionally used on the lawn, and everyone went about their normal business.

Alice's room at the Cape Hamilton Hotel was spacious but crestfallen. The wallpaper was either peeling or sliding off the walls, the victim of irredeemable damp. The bathroom mirror offered Alice a cloudy and whimsical version of herself. The bed linen was hospital or military issue, laundered to oblivion and held together by starch. The carpets smelled, the taps dripped, every door was out of alignment. The windowpanes were so salt-saturated they could never be wiped clear, the steel framework crusty with painted-over rust. Another visitor from London might have found this disconcerting, but Alice did not. Once she had forced the window wide open, it gave her a good view of the south hill facing onto the lagoon, which was what she wanted.

On the hillside was a big old house with a corrugated iron roof. Situated to take advantage of the view of the lagoon, it was double-storied with verandahs upstairs and down—verandahs so deep that even windblown rain would not reach open windows. Alice felt a transport of recollection envelop her. For although she had a home and a family in London, half an English accent and a degree in media studies from the Open University, thirty years ago Alice had known this house, this village, this brown river and its wide flat lagoon.

She decided not to go up to the house immediately. She was exhausted from the flight and the long drive, and it was already four o'clock. She knew she was finding a reason to postpone a difficult moment, but she forgave herself that. She lay on the bed without unpacking and fell asleep to the sound of the waves.

News of an unaccompanied female staying at the Cape Hamilton was sufficient reason for Clive to expect brisk business at the hotel that evening. He fired up the two rusty barbecues made from old 44-gallon drums and defrosted some steaks. Then he, Johnny and Woodstock took up position at a table at the end of the verandah, where they were soon joined by Bob Peace.

Bob Peace had come from California to Port Victoria for an exotic sabbatical ten years before and had never gone back. He was a radio man, hired to train the staff of Radio Freedom, an independent radio station which had been located in Port Victoria against all economic, technical and common sense; that is to say, for political reasons. After a fanfare opening, the impracticalities of running a radio station from a remote and harsh location quickly became evident, and operations had steadily migrated to the provincial capital. But Bob Peace had a contract, and the best ratings on the station, and used these to persuade Radio Freedom's management to allow him to continue his own show from the studio at Port Victoria.

Bob had found in Port Victoria something that made it difficult to leave. For it's a fact—although not mentioned in official agricultural or economic bulletins—that a fine and potent strain of marijuana flourishes in the creases between the claws of these hills, along the river bank in the ravine, and inland for several miles. Since the early 1960s this superior produce has been known as Durban Poison, Durban being a harbor city some several hundred miles away where the dealers take their bulk buy and bundled it for street distribution. In this land, marijuana is called dagga, and it has been smoked by the people of the nation, black and white, for as long as anyone can remember. Railway workers and young men doing national service in the army; rebellious, wealthy teenagers—English, Afrikaans, Jewish, Indian; hobos and coffee-house intellectuals...all had used that blessed weed to loosen the dull grip of reality upon their lives. And now it was the force holding Bob Peace far from home.

"Check it out," yipped Woodstock. He was positioned at end of the table with his chair turned sideways so that he could cover the whole verandah, his role that of the watch baboon who gives the sharp bark.

Alice had stepped out onto the verandah. She saw the three white men but glanced away quickly, as if unprepared for the frankness of appraisal that she was getting from Woodstock, or the shock of his appearance. She turned away from the men and walked to the far end of the verandah, where she was seated at a table by Darlington Dlamini, a Zulu in a shabby but clean waiter's uniform.

"Shit, you've scared her already, Woodstock," said Clive.

Female tourists had been known to jump up and run when Woodstock snuck up on them sunbathing on the beach. There was something atavistically cautionary about his appearance. His legs were short and bandy and misshapen, as if broken in childhood. His skin was abrasive and stubble grew in patches on his face. His hands were large and extremely powerful but did not close completely, with the effect that small things fell from his grip, while larger items tended to get crushed. He looked like he had developed from a contaminated embryo, which possibly explained why he had been abandoned into an orphanage as an infant.

11

Then, at age nine, Woodstock had been delivered to an adoptive family where he became younger brother to Gerrit, who nicknamed him after the faded logo on his T-shirt.

"She's no spring chicken," said Woodstock, watching Alice take her seat.

"Yeah," said Bob, "but she's got that something."

"What?"

"The good-in-bed look," said Bob, his eyes not straying from Alice's profile.

"Wedding ring," remarked Clive.

"That's fucked," said Woodstock.

"Not necessarily," said Bob.

"If she's looking for a screw," said Woodstock, "she's going to take off her wedding ring, so the guys can know."

"Chicks don't think like that," said Clive. "What you scheme, Johnny?"

"Probably bangs like a shit-house door," said Johnny. This was Johnny's invariable and undiscriminating judgment on all females from puberty to middle age.

"You'd like to know," said Clive.

"Nah, broer," Johnny retorted, not one to be caught acknowledging the power of any woman. "I mean, I might fuck her if she asks for it, but I'm not going to go out of my way for it."

"Brandy makes old Johnny randy," offered Woodstock.

"Watch it," said Johnny, "You'll catch a klap."

That was not a real threat, just a cuff to remind Woodstock of the established pecking order. The veneer of civilization upon Johnny Fourie was thin, and it did not take much abrasion to expose a child whose father had directed him to the recommended choices in life with stabs of pain. Up to five beers, Johnny was fine. The fifth was a switch that opened up a well of aggression within him. His drinking buddies had learned to count carefully and disperse in good time, leaving Johnny alone at the bar with his own resentment, like the victim of a cruel flirtation. Violence upon an unsuspecting party usually followed within hours.

What made Johnny so dangerous as an alpha male was the fact that he was only a provisional holder of the title. He knew, and he knew everyone else knew, that when Dom Marais came to town, Johnny was moved down a notch. And Dom Marais's sovereignty was quite different from Johnny's. Dom Marais had never fought anybody but had attained legendary status through a number of other acts. When the small bridge had washed away at Second Beach, Dom had, without assistance, positioned a fallen tree from bank to bank as a temporary bridge. When he had started sculpting, Dom cut his own marble right out of the cliff faces near Lusikisiki and rafted it downstream himself. Dom Marais grew a good crop of marijuana each year and it was popularly reported that he never lost a single plant to theft. But Dom Marais was not at the Cape Hamilton that night, so Johnny Fourie was top dog.

"You go talk to her, Bob," said Johnny. "You've got the chat."

"Tune her to come play sticks," said Woodstock.

"You just want to see her bend over the table," said Johnny.

"Like you don't," said Woodstock.

"She doesn't look the snooker type to me," said Bob Peace.

That was accepted as wisdom. Coming from California, Bob Peace was acknowledged to have an insight into women, in the same way that some men could find fish and others comprehended lion behavior.

"I don't think she's the type for fishing, either," said Clive.

"So what's she here for?" said Woodstock.

"Maybe it's something to do with the dead guy," said Johnny.

"Shit, then she's a write-off," said Woodstock. "I mean, she's not going to want to screw around if she's, you know, upset or that kinda shit."

"That's where you're wrong," said Bob. "Women are most available when they're emotionally charged." The others drew closer, concentrating. "She's come here, maybe she's in grief, or shock. In the presence of death, women want to feel life. She knows she'll never come here again, so her reputation's not at stake. I think she could be very susceptible. We just need to create a climate of reassurance."

"Jussis," said Woodstock, his face knotted as he milled this complex information.

"Maybe we could all reassure her," pondered Johnny, "you know, one after the other."

"But it'll be no good if we all rush her straight off," continued Bob. "If she gets the idea she's being thought of that way, she'll go into her shell. What we need to do is make contact, make ourselves accessible to her, in a friendly way but not pushy. Open up a path for her and let her choose. Then if she wants it, she'll come ask for it. The modern woman knows how to do that."

"Fuck me sideways," said Woodstock, gazing across at the tableau of Alice studying the immense quantity of barbecued meat that had been put in front of her by a perspiring waiter. "Check. She drinks beer. Chicks are supposed to drink vodka or wine."

"That's because she's from England," said Clive.

"How can you tell?"

"She signed the hotel register. Home address, somewhere in London."

"Shit," said Woodstock, losing enthusiasm. "I'm not sure I want to naai an English chick."

"What's the difference?"

"You know, sanctions and all that. They scheme they're so much better than us."

"That's why we should fuck her," said Johnny. Woodstock grasped this quickly and it changed his expression. The beer can in his hand cracked as he constricted it involuntarily.

"Go on, Bob," said Clive. "Free case of beer if you score first night."

Bob Peace pushed back his chair and ran his fingers through his hair. Then he rose and made his way through the rusted old steel furniture that was arranged haphazardly along the verandah to where Alice was sitting. She had plenty of time to watch his approach.

"Excuse me," said Bob, "but I can see you're a stranger here, and I thought I would introduce myself. I'm Bob Peace."

He extended his hand, which she took.

"Alice."

"It's a bit of a strange place, Alice. You have to know the ropes here."

She smiled. "You don't sound like you're from here either."

"California. I came to help set up the radio station. But that was quite a while ago. I'm just like a local now."

Her eyes flicked with apprehension and Bob turned to see that Woodstock was approaching the table, his face rent with a terrible grin.

"Hi. I'm Woodstock. Bob's buddy."

"Hello," said Alice.

"Not really," Bob muttered.

"You know, Woodstock—like the festival?" Woodstock's face was throbbing with effort. "Jimi Hendrix?"

"Yes, I understand," said Alice.

"Have you come to identify the body?" Woodstock continued.

"What?"

"We thought," Bob interceded smoothly, "you might be connected to the deceased. There was a man killed here the other

15

day."

"Oh. No, I heard about him. But I've nothing to do with him."

"That's good," said Woodstock. "Because that steak you're eating comes from the same freezer."

"Same freezer as what?"

Bob closed his eyes. But Woodstock was delighted to have hit on his own vein of conversation.

"They're keeping him in the bait freezer. The dead guy. That's also where Clive keeps the meat that comes from inland. Most of us have been eating the fresh fish the last few days."

Alice seemed to take a moment to arrange the information into a coherent image. When she had, she stood suddenly.

"I have to go now," she said, and walked away from Bob Peace and Woodstock, across the verandah and toward the stairs to her room. Bob watched her go, but Woodstock trotted after her. He caught up with her on the first landing.

"Ma'am," he called. She was obliged to stop and face him. "Would you like me to come and check your room for spiders? We get them bad around here."

"No, but thank you for offering."

"Even snakes. Snakes come into the rooms."

"It's not necessary, really. I'm going to have to ask you to leave me alone now, please. I'm very tired. Good night."

She fled up the stairs.

"So did you score?" jeered Clive as Woodstock returned to their table on the verandah.

"I told you she would be a fucking bitch." Woodstock's face was distorted with humiliation. "I wouldn't fuck her with yours."

"Actually," said Clive, "I got the impression she wouldn't be inviting you to fuck her with John Travolta's."

"Don't worry, Woodstock," said Bob. "Deep down inside she's

probably quite shallow."

"You've fucked it up for everyone now, Woodstock, you cunt," said Johnny. "Now she'll think we're all baboons like you."

An apt metaphor. Baboons, like lions and many other species, maintain a sharp distinction between who is accepted within the troop or pride, and who is outside. To be within is to share food and protection. To be an outsider is to be driven off or ripped to shreds. Surveying the liquor-swollen faces arrayed before him, Woodstock knew again the feeling of living right on that dividing line. When he had joined his adoptive family, Woodstock had survived by cleaving to his older stepbrother Gerrit, who apprenticed him in truancy, small time theft, and violence against the defenseless. They lived on the railway compound, among the working-class Afrikaners whom apartheid had been designed to protect. Their aversion to black people came with their religion, part of the shape of the world. Woodstock had made his way under Gerrit's patronage until he was sixteen, when an unhappy incident separated them forever. Gerrit had been a crane driver at Durban docks. He sat all day high up in the steel cab, controlling the levers that swung large cargo pallets off and onto ships. Through those long, baking subtropical days, Gerrit would drink quantities of warm mqombothi (a Xhosa beer that looked like milk but was rather more potent), smoke dope and masturbate over pages torn from girlie magazines. Accidents were common, but Gerrit and his colleagues were remote from the dockside in their aeries and protected by the union, which existed to make sure black workers did not replace them.

Gerrit hated the black dock laborers inconsolably. And he hated one black man in particular, his dealer, the man who sold him mqombothi and marijuana. This hatred derived naturally from the circumstances; Gerrit was dependent for the fulfillment of his illegal weaknesses on a man he considered inferior to him.

He thought the dealer smiled knowingly at him when he handed over the stuff. Each time he received his goods, he threatened the dealer with betrayal to the police. The nonchalance with which the dealer received these threats infuriated Gerrit. So, Gerrit's idle mind evolved a plan to kill the black man by accidentally loosing a pallet onto him from the crane. But this required the man to be carefully positioned on the dock, which required an accomplice.

Woodstock received his curious instructions without question. Gerrit did not mention the purpose. Woodstock was to pretend an interest in purchasing some marijuana from the black man, and to draw out the negotiations for a long time, while standing on a designated spot on the dock at exactly ten past three in the afternoon.

But Gerrit's geometry was rudimentary and the possibilities for errors of parallax were multifarious; the outcome was that a pallet of eighteen-inch cast-iron pipe joints exploded onto the dock about four feet behind Woodstock. His reaction was to piss himself with a force that expressed all the pent-up fear of childhood nights in the orphanage, where unspeakable horrors were visited upon the sleeping inmates in the dark.

The dealer howled with laughter. People came running, mainly black laborers. The laughter spread like the dark stain on Woodstock's denims, and became instant legend all along the docks and into the brothels of Point Road where Woodstock liked to go just to look. A week later Woodstock walked out of the adoptive family home with his toothbrush and Gerrit's portable radio. He signed up for the army. This institution was wise in the deployment of people like Woodstock, who found himself in a small protected niche, running the guard duty roster at the empty oil storage tanks. Here he could terrorize the conscripts doing their nine months of basic training—English-speaking liberal types destined for university. But when the prospect of black officers came onto the horizon, Woodstock resigned from the army by walking out the gate. They did not come looking for him.

And here he was again with the other baboons arrayed against him, their teeth catching the light from the pool room. Woodstock did what he always did. He got up and walked without a word. They watched him go. Something in them had been satiated by this process.

"It's a good thing Woodstock doesn't have a dog," Clive mused, "because that dog would get the shit kicked out of it tonight."

"I can never get over how he walks," said Bob. Woodstock's retreating figure did seem to convey the whole story about him, the congenitally resentful soul who, when the dust settles, crawls out from under the bodies of dead heroes and hobbles away with their wallets.

Alice studied herself in the bathroom mirror. It was a long time since a man had crossed a floor to try and pick her up. Not because she was not still attractive, she thought, but because the codes of conduct that applied at her stratum of social life in London prohibited it. And although Bob was not a man whose attention she might have wanted, she had nevertheless responded to the interaction with a heightened self-awareness.

She was still slim and had retained a wiry strength in her frame. The imperfectly healed cut on her lip was a minor, but alluring, deformity which, coupled with her level gaze, suggested an uninhibited woman who had played rough and fearlessly. But middle age had seeded its insecurities. She had color highlights in her hair which she knew were going to betray her quickly in this climate.

In London, Alice was self-conscious about her skin. When you grow up in Africa the sun marks you every day, while many of her English contemporaries had skin that was pale and flawless. The woman she saw in this mirror seemed entirely suited to this place. She knew how to walk barefoot on African soil.

Alice switched off the light in her room and stood at the window for a time, staring out into a blackness that was hot and palpable, layered with the sound and salt of the sea and the odor traces of decaying material that came off the dune bush. The sensations available from that window were a theater to her.

Alice was in Port Victoria as a wife without her husband, a mother without her child. She had done a deal with her family when planning the trip. To Julia, her ten-year-old, she had presented it as a growing-up challenge—Julia was old enough to check her own school timetable, pack her own bag each day and show her dad the ropes of the domestic routine. Mum, who had always been as constant as oxygen in Julia's surround, was going for a few weeks to one of the remotest parts of Africa where there might not even be a phone. It would be fun for Julia to manage herself and her pet lizard, Alice told her.

To Philip, her husband, Alice had made a somewhat less generous presentation. She started by boxing him in with *a fait accompli*, having sold it to Julia as an adventure before consulting him. When he asked for time to consider, she came home with an air ticket.

"I guess you're going, whatever I say," he'd said.

Standing at the window of the hotel room, she couldn't pick out the old house from the dark bulk of the hillside—no lights were on. In fact, the only light beyond the lawn in front of the hotel was the flicker from an open fire, which seemed to be on the sea, but Alice judged it to be on the point across the lagoon. She assumed it was built by night fishermen and enjoyed a sudden vision of the contrast between such a world and the regimented lives packed around her in London.

Walking home along the beach at about the same time, Bob Peace also saw the fire across the lagoon, but he knew exactly whose fire it was, and it reminded him again of a morning several years earlier.

Bob Peace and Johnny Fourie had been walking along the rocks at sunrise after a night's drinking at the studio with two women who were staying at the Cape Hamilton. It had been Bob and Johnny's intention to destroy the women's resistance with drink, but the women had proved more artful and sweet-talked Bob out of four ounces of prime Durban Poison from his personal stash, against nothing more substantial than a promise to return some day. The girls had driven off with the rising sun, and the men had set out across the rocks to try and persuade Mama to open early for breakfast.

Ahead of them on the rocks, they saw a familiar figure. He had the lean and powerful physique of a Zulu warrior, but not the demeanor. His head nodded and tilted and twitched on his neck, as if unseen insects were bothering him. Bob Peace himself once described this man as looking as though he was having a continuous epileptic fit, but it was not Bob who gave him his name. This man had been called Breakdown since before anyone could remember. People claimed that as a child he had fallen off Bird Rock and the surf had bounced him against the rocks for a good while before ejecting him up onto the beach and since then he had been a creature of a different plane of consciousness. But no one really knew, because no one laid claim to any family connection with Breakdown. He had rolled down the hills from one of the villages or fallen off the back of a migrating family, or been spat out by society like Woodstock. No one knew, perhaps not even Breakdown himself. But he had somehow survived and slowly scrounged himself a habitat in the tidal zone between the ocean and the town, between civilized and wild. He lived as if by special decree in this community. Everyone respected the spot where he slept and ate at the end of the point across the lagoon as if he held the title deeds to it.

Breakdown was a familiar figure to Bob and Johnny, and they would have paid him no particular heed that morning. He was traversing the rocks with his usual bobbing gait, moving and then stopping, moving and stopping, looking down at his feet. The receding tide had left pools of trapped water among the rocks, and Breakdown was meticulously inspecting each pool in turn. Johnny saw Breakdown pause, slowly kneel next to one of the pools, and become quite still. That's when the two men stopped to watch.

Breakdown had positioned himself facing out toward the sea, so that the sun threw his shadow behind him and not on the surface of the pool. He extended his left hand to the rim of the pool and held it there. All motion ceased. Bob and Johnny would argue over this for years to come, because the concept of Breakdown being even for a moment utterly still was a challenge to the laws of nature. Yet, the recollection of both men was that Breakdown reduced his body to a rock-like immobility for fully a minute, his eyes steady and his left hand poised at the rim of the pool. Then there was a blur of movement, and the next thing they could report was that Breakdown was on his feet, chaotic again as he danced along the rocks, chasing after the fish he had plucked with his bare hand from the pool, and which had escaped his grasp. They held their breath as the frictionless fish skated wildly across the rocks until Breakdown pounced successfully a second time and whacked its head on the rocks. He looked up and, seeing them, raised the dead fish above his head in a wordless victory salute, then turned away and loped toward his campfire at the edge of the dune bush.

Breakdown lived as though he had grasped only every third or fourth lesson of childhood, but had learned those in fine detail. He was unable or unwilling to hold down even the simplest job, but he was keenly aware of the mechanics of his society. His level of poverty seemed to be voluntary, but he insisted on dignity. He never asked for anything for free. If he needed something that cost money—which wasn't often—he bartered his labor for it.

He was unembarrassed to forage in dustbins in full view of the populace. He would sit on the dock of the lagoon and pick his nose with an entrancing thoroughness while life continued around him. He had his own moral code, the ferocity of which had been quickly made known to anyone who had ever cheated him on an exchange of food for a chore, or impugned his dignity in any way.

Breakdown's method of dealing with those who transgressed against him had two key elements. The offenders were always called to account in public view; and this was never done immediately, but at some later time when it was most embarrassing. So, anyone who made an enemy of Breakdown could expect not only vivid retribution but an agonizing delay of execution. Clive had once forgotten to reward Breakdown for a day's work and three weeks later, when Clive was cooking steaks for a party of tourists on the lawn in front of the hotel, Breakdown burst out of the dune bush. To this uncomprehending audience, he held forth on the shortcomings of Clive's mother, father and reproductive equipment. In the rising intoxication of such occasions Breakdown could not get his declamations out fast enough and would collapse sentences down to their essence, mixing Zulu, Pondo and English. These invariably culminated with the phrase, "You bloody fucking!" For his own rhetorical purposes, Breakdown had converted the word "fucking" into a noun, understood throughout his community. Johnny Fourie, who sometimes used Breakdown to help load his ski-fishing boat on its trailer, said he was sure Breakdown was a genius at something, like Dustin Hoffman in *Rainman*. On his radio show at one in the morning, Bob Peace sometimes rapped about Breakdown's biblical outrage.

Never in any of Breakdown's outbursts had there ever been the hint of violence. He seemed to be unaware that other members of his species used force and not just invective on their enemies. But after that morning on the rocks, Johnny would say that any guy who picked a fight with Breakdown was in for a shock because Breakdown, he said, had the reaction speed of a leopard.

Breakdown was a regular on the rocks at dawn. Some mornings he was after fish, but he went out even when he wasn't hungry because he could never sleep once the seagulls started. He had a quick eye for what was useful in his world, and two days earlier, when he had seen the flash of bright color among the rocks, he first thought it to be a child's toy, useless to him. But he went over anyway. Breakdown had no idea of the value of things in the commercial world, so he did not know that the brightly colored Hawaiian-style shirt and denim jeans he saw before him were of the best quality. To him, they just looked useful. Breakdown was blissfully clean of guilt or sentimentality; he could see that the man wearing these clothes had died very painfully, but he felt no emotion about it. All he thought was that the man no longer needed these items and life was presenting them to him. Ignoring the gold Rolex watch, Breakdown carefully removed the clothes which he hung to dry on the dune bushes around his campsite. The idea of reporting the body did not enter his head.

3

All along this sub-tropical coast, the indigenous foliage is mixed with prosperous interlopers. The Brazilian bougainvillea drapes itself in regal purple on any available shrub. Hydrangeas from China line many winding driveways. Madagascan flamboyants, locally known as flame trees, cast their boat-like seedpods at the base of gaunt but laden mango trees from Indonesia.

Walking up the hill to the old house in the hard morning sun, Alice's mind was recovering a torrent of images and cross-references, none of which could be individually examined before being overridden by the next. For a moment, she experienced herself simultaneously in childhood and adulthood. Minute detail and panoramic overview elbowed each other for her attention. She stopped and studied the ruts in the stony dirt road, convinced that the erratic path chosen by the small course of water running down was exactly as it had been three decades ago.

Structurally, the old house was unchanged: the deep verandahs, the tall chimney for a fireplace—superfluous in that climate—the narrow gutters that always overflowed copiously in summer thunderstorms. The house was still white but the paint was peeling everywhere, the woodwork unprotected and rotting. The house wore the same heavy wooden door she remembered, but an ugly steel retracting security trellis, locked with a heavy padlock, had been installed to protect it. As Alice stood at the door, she was a woman of some experience and aptitude with the world. Yet there was a flush on her cheeks, and she needed a momentary loosening of the shoulders before pressing the bell.

After a delay, the door opened and an old woman glared at Alice through the trellis.

"Hello, Phyllis," said Alice.

The woman gave no sign of recognition. She was using both hands to hold a revolver but it was still too heavy for her, so the barrel meandered, picking out random targets at knee height.

"Phyllis! I'm Alice. Len's daughter."

Without responding, the old woman took several slow steps to a sideboard and placed the revolver on it. The barrel tinked against a heavy goblet.

"So," said Phyllis. "You've come for your house."

This remark had the effect of a pre-emptive military strike; it took out so much of the intermediate territory between them that for several seconds Alice was left without a response. She remembered that Phyllis had always had this fastidious separation of signal from noise.

"I've come to see you," Alice offered.

"About the house," replied Phyllis.

"About all sorts of things. Really. I haven't seen you for years. I've come all the way from England."

"I know where you live. We all know that."

Phyllis made no move to open the security door. "Abigail's not well. I don't want you upsetting her."

"I'm not here to upset her. May I come in?"

"I'm just going to ask Abigail."

And with that, Phyllis left her niece standing on the far side of the security trellis and proceeded up the carpeted stairs at a leisurely pace.

Alice let out her breath. She stood there in the doorway at the point where the smell of Africa outside met the smell of the heavily polished colonial furniture and moist rotting carpet from inside. A capsule of memory burst upon her: a cricket commentary, tapestried in shortwave radio static, South Africa playing in Australia. Her father and uncle, sitting on this verandah at five in the morning, following the last session of play on the other side of the world. Six-year-old Alice concentrating hard on carrying a tray of tea out to them, barefoot on the reed matting the Pondo women made. Two long-haired Alsatian dogs, flattened, taking up the residual night cool from the polished concrete floor.

Without any awareness of why she was doing it, Alice knelt in the doorway and ran her fingers down the edge of the doorframe. Those fingers retained a knowledge of the past she herself had forgotten; they found the scar in the doorframe at knee height to an adult, softened by many coats of paint, but remaining still in the geological record of this house. Her fingertips recalled those times in ways her mind could not deal with. It occurred to her that she had walked backwards out of her childhood, sweeping her footprints. She now lived in another culture, so different it could be a distant universe. And all that time, this life lay here; coiled, little changed, quite unresolved, its potency undiminished.

Phyllis returned tediously out of semi-darkness: the curtains were heavy on the windows and the light so bright outside. Alice stood up quickly. Phyllis looked her in the eye as she said, "She's not well at all. And we haven't been able to get the medicine she needs. The Sammy at the trading store forgot to order it. You'll have to come back tomorrow."

The security gate between them was finished in white super-gloss paint. The rivet heads on the moving joints were stainless steel. But the washers were not, and rust had already attacked them. Thirty or forty rusting washers in the security gate—soon it would be immovable, certainly in Phyllis's arthritic hands.

"Surely you're not serious, Phyllis? You're not going to let me in?" Disconcerted, Alice's brain was collecting small details: two of Phyllis's fingers were curled in against her palm in a half-claw, her skin was a mass of liver spots and the knobs on her wrists were like saddle hitches.

27

"Abigail says come to tea tomorrow afternoon," said Phyllis. "She's sure she'll feel better then. We'll ask the Sammy to bring up something nice from the store. If he's got anything."

Alice had prepared herself for many possibilities but this was not among them. She was completely nonplussed.

"Where's your family?" Phyllis said.

Again: signal from noise.

"I left them behind," said Alice. "In England."

"You haven't changed."

The eye that Phyllis trained on Alice challenged her to rebut. Alice, who seldom shrank from confrontation, dropped her eyes.

"I'll see you tomorrow, then."

"That will be nice," said Phyllis and closed the door.

As she turned away, Alice's over-exercised memory squirted out the soundtrack of an event otherwise unrecalled. Something full of pain. One sharp cry breaking over the house, like the shriek of a hadeda bird in the early morning. That was all. Unconsciously, Alice fingered the scar on her lip which she had had since childhood. Walking back down the hill under the blazing red canopy of flame trees, she silently wept.

4

Two women walked up the main street of Port Victoria, carrying on their heads buckets of fresh cow shit, to be used in daubing the walls of new huts. Western anthropological researchers have shown scientifically that the practice of African females carrying substantial weights on their heads can be severely crippling, but aid agencies have yet to carry this revisionism to Port Victoria.

Suddenly the two women started grinning, then laughing, then ululating—that curious bird-like tongue sound which stirs in the belly like no other. In Africa, this sound heralds the sighting of a person of eminence in the community, or of someone whose fortune has changed, or has the power to change the fortune of others. It makes all within earshot stop and pay attention. When Nelson Mandela swore the presidential oath there was scheduled ululating, while heads of state from around the world looked on.

The subject of this day's ululating, however, was merely Breakdown, who was strolling along the very middle of the main street, secure in the knowledge that few vehicles would displace him. The vivid Hawaiian shirt and designer denim jeans may have lost some of their quality after several hours immersion in seawater, but on Breakdown's figure they nevertheless attracted attention. Breakdown had gone up in the world by several rankings. He acknowledged the ululating women—it was a fluorescent moment for him. At the end of the street, he turned and walked back again, lord of all he surveyed.

Johnny, driving past in his lopsided Land Rover, slowed down and called out.

"Jussis, Breakdown! You're looking kwaai today!"

Breakdown gave him a grave nod.

Entering Sammy's trading store, Alice had to pause to let her eyes adjust to the dimness. The windows were tiny and so heavily barred that it would be simpler for a burglar to knock the walls down. She was still feeling like a survivor of a minor car accident after her encounter with her blood relative up at the old house.

Alice watched an old black woman buy two loose tea bags and three cigarettes, methodically isolating the necessary payment from a large collection of copper coins. Although Sammy's Trading Store had been unable to provide Phyllis with what she wanted, its merchandise was astonishingly diverse. Motor oil stood beside Chivas Regal twelve-year-old premium Scotch whisky, a staple of the colonies. A brand new imported fishing reel, heavily greased against the salt-laden atmosphere, kept company with a skin-lightening cream bearing a label that anywhere else in the world would be hanging on a gallery wall. There were no prices displayed. The price of everything was in Sammy's head, and had been since he worked in the store as a nine-year-old. Sammy's real name was Govender, but he was known, like his father and his grandfather before him, as Sammy, or "the Sammy" to the most ancient white settlers. His forefathers had been shipped to this coast from Bombay to cut sugar cane. In less than a generation, they had turned in their machetes and become traders and shopkeepers. They found a niche between the indigenous blacks and the colonial whites of the country. Sammy was a non-practicing Hindu, slim and wiry with a neat moustache and the tang of after-shave.

Alice asked, "Is there a pharmacy, or a clinic, or anywhere around here I could buy prescription medication?"

"What do you need?"

Alice hesitated. "Just my, you won't know it, it's an anti-depressant."

"You feeling blue?" he asked, blinking behind his glasses.

"Unfortunately I forgot it when I was packing." This was not true. Back in London, Alice had impulsively thought that this trip might be an opportunity to take a break from her medication. But now she was so shaken by her encounter up at the house that she felt the need to have the medication at hand, like a protective weapon.

Sammy stepped away from the counter and started searching through the over-crowded shelves behind him. He returned with a plain white cardboard box which he placed on the counter. Alice could see it had "Prozac" written on it in ballpoint. Sammy opened it and handed her one of the blister packs of pills inside. Alice examined it skeptically. There was a long chemical name

30

which she didn't recognize.

"Generic," he said. "But exactly the same thing. This is state hospital bulk consignment."

She pointed to the stamp on the pack. "It's past the expiry date."

"Well, you're not taking it for the taste. Have you taken anti-depressants before?"

"Yes. Not this. Something else. But I didn't bring my prescription with me."

"No problem," he said. "People here can't get prescriptions. No doctor. I keep everything. Antibiotics, heart pills, blood pills, fever pills."

"How do you know what to give them?"

"All the medicine has a leaflet with it, tells you what it's for. I have to keep everything. People depend on me. If I don't have it they get angry with me. Try it. I'll make a good price for you. If it doesn't work, we try something else."

Alice was groping for a polite refusal when Breakdown entered the store. Sammy eyed him sharply. Owning the largest repository of visible, portable wealth in this community, Sammy had learned that preventative policing was better than curative, of which there was none.

"What you want?" his voice contained all the contempt that the industrious have for people who make no provision. Sammy was sure Breakdown had no money and if he did, it was ill gotten. The Hawaiian shirt was itself an alarm bell. Sammy had a hygienic and rational view of the world and no tolerance for the disorder represented by Breakdown. But Breakdown did not want to buy anything. He had no money. He was simply carrying the vision of his resplendent self to all corners of his domain.

Breakdown's wild-horse eyes snapped a quick shot of Alice, took off over to Sammy, then returned to Alice. The output of

Breakdown's chaotic being passed across Alice like a pulse. Even when silent he seemed to give off a howl. She could not hold his eye. It was impossible to say what Breakdown made of Alice, but perhaps he felt in turn, from her, a message not unlike his own, because he eyed her deeply and said, "Sorry."

"You go out!" ordered Sammy. He said it with an edge of fear, like a groom dealing with an unpredictable racehorse. Breakdown drew off a further sample from Alice and savored it. Then he turned and walked out. The room changed.

"Who's that?" asked Alice.

"Homeless guy. He lives on the beach. No money. You want the pills?"

Alice paid Sammy for the pills and a bottle of water. She spotted a flashlight on the cluttered shelves and bought that as well. She stepped out of the small shop into the devastating brightness of the day.

When her eyes had adjusted, Breakdown was standing in front of her. He spoke a rapid sentence in Zulu or Pondo which she didn't understand. Alice had known some Zulu when she was growing up, but lost it once she went to boarding school. And Breakdown's machine-gun style of speech did nothing to aid interpretation. The perpetual movement of his head was both transfixing and difficult to watch. She didn't know where to put her eyes.

"I'm sorry, I don't understand," she said.

"Nkosasana," he said. And for a brief moment his eyes rested on her.

"Hey, voetsek wena!" It was Sammy shouting at Breakdown from the door of his shop.

Breakdown wheeled around.

"Don't bother the lady."

Breakdown muttered something unintelligible at Sammy and

32

then turned and shambled away.

"It's okay," Sammy said to Alice. "He's not dangerous. Just a nuisance. Was he begging?"

"No," she said.

Alice walked through the town to the wooden dock on the lagoon, where she sat with her feet over the edge. She studied the blister pack of pills, then pressed one out and examined it more closely. She tossed the pill into the water, returned the strip to the plastic shopping bag Sammy had given her and placed that in the trashcan chained to the rail of the dock. Then she walked down onto the beach and was immediately gratified by the give in the sand, an absorbing surface she could push against. She tilted forward into a long walk, washed with sea air.

5

"That's fucken outrageous!" bawled Johnny.

"Can he do that?" said Bob Peace.

"This is why the rest of Africa is such a fuck-up," was Clive's judgment.

Chief Magistrate Mendi Mkhize had made his mark on the Cape Hamilton Hotel. He had changed his room from a sea view to an inland view, because the sound of the waves was too loud. He had demanded, and got, the only room service meal Clive had ever served. He had sent a bottle of wine back. And now he had decreed that he required the billiard room to be converted into an operations center for his inquiry. The billiard room was, to the white men of Port Victoria, their officers' club. The fact that they might not use it more than twice a month was irrelevant.

The billiard table, when boarded over with chipboard from Sammy's, made an impressively large surface on which to display a map of the area, sundry brightly colored map pins, index markers, and other paraphernalia necessary to give the appearance of a dynamic investigation.

Mendi Mkhize had not wanted to come to Port Victoria, but now that he was here, he was enjoying himself. The position of chief magistrate could not be described as exciting or even challenging. The work involved reading huge quantities of poorly written material; the office politics involved people above and below him who were just as resentful about the measure of their status as Mendi was about his own. But here, things were different. Here he was not inhibited by shabby police work and constraints of procedure. The Commission of Inquiry into Crime Against Tourists had been hastily invoked and its terms broadly written. Mendi could do pretty much anything he pleased, especially here, where he was the sole public official of any kind. Mendi had no particular interest in influencing Crime Against Tourists one way or the other, but he did see this case as an opportunity to do a bit of real investigative work. Like most lawyers, Mendi believed he could do much better police work than the police.

Mendi often thought back to his stay in New York as the high point of his career. It had been soon after the transition to democracy, and the election of the first black government, a time when Mendi still held hopes of high office. The US government had invited a group of fifty potential new leaders to make a three-week tour of the democratic institutions of that country. There had been intense competition to get on the trip, not because anyone in the party believed that the US government could teach them about governance, but because it would undoubtedly be the ultimate freebie junket. Mendi had gorged himself on the hospitality at his disposal, making phone calls of several hours to everyone he knew in Africa, signing bar checks to his room, racking up implausible hours on the premium adult TV channel. In the United States, many people had pressed Mendi for accounts of his role in the freedom struggle. He soon learned that a few carefully constructed allusions left them with the impression that the nature of his role had been so secretive, so deadly, and so effective that it had to go to the grave with him. They spent the last two days in an uptown hotel in New York, where Mendi was particularly enthralled by the Executive Services Suite on the mezzanine level, which he visited often to fax photos of gift options to his mistress. There was always activity in the suite and yet it was always immaculately tidy. Wealthy, powerful people of all descriptions came and went at all times of the day. Platoons of mineral water bottles stood everywhere.

Clive was hot and irritable when he arrived to deliver the mineral water bottles that Mendi had ordered for his new office in the billiard room.

"When are they going to come and take the body away?" said Clive. "It puts people off coming here. It's unsanitary."

"If you're concerned about the sanitary level of your establishment," Mendi said, eyeing Clive steadily, "I could ask the health inspector to come down here and do a thorough audit. Or you could just be patient. I booked a mortuary van before I left the capital. It should be here tomorrow, which is why we need to make our preliminary forensic examination of the body now. You will help me."

They went down to the old freezer, which stood in the corridor behind the kitchen. Mendi examined the body thoroughly and without reluctance. He had no medical expertise at all, but he had watched many hours of television. He looked for bullet holes, stab wounds, impact traumas, evidence of restraint and evidence of identity. At the end of this study, the body looked the same as it had at the beginning: a naked white man who had gone into the sea and been mashed against the rocks. Mendi had never seen a completely naked white person before, and he found this the most distasteful aspect of the lot. When alive with their clothes on, white men looked sick and incapable enough, but like this, they looked absurd. It amazed him that the race had been perpetuated at all, considering what an unattractive spectacle the naked male presented. His skin was so white, forming a stark backdrop to the extensive black body hair. His penis was a cowering little snail. The whole experience was more likely to induce pity than lust, in Mendi's opinion.

"He wasn't a guest at this hotel?"

"No," said Clive.

"You've never seen him before?"

Clive shook his head.

"If he was a tourist, where else could he have stayed around here?"

"There's a campsite about three miles south that's used mainly by fishermen and surfers. I doubt he would have been staying there."

"Why?"

"Very good teeth, very good watch," said Clive. "Just not the type to be staying around here."

"But he *is* here," said Mendi. "He got here somehow."

"Maybe he fell off a yacht," Clive suggested. "That's an expensive watch. If this was a crime, the watch would have gone. I think it's an accident."

"A body with clothes is an accident. A body with no clothes is a murder. I want to interview each and every white person in this town. Get them to come and see me, one by one."

"I've got a hotel to run!" Clive protested. "This is a small place. We know who all the cowboys and hoodlums are. Nobody around here would have killed him."

Mendi simply eyed him silently, and Clive's indignation dribbled away.

"I'll see what I can do," Clive said.

Mendi shook his head briefly as he watched Clive spreading the canvas siding back over the body in the refrigerator. It was hilarious to see how white people responded to the change of power in this country. Those who had once considered black people to be an inferior species were now quite without a clue as to how to behave. They cringed like dogs, no doubt expecting that at any moment all the accumulated hate and resentment of the apartheid experience would be unleashed on them individually.

At quiet times in his store, Sammy did bookkeeping. No computer. He preferred a traditional bound ledger which he kept in immaculately neat handwriting, entries made provisionally in pencil until everything had been checked and balanced, and then written over in ballpoint. Sammy had no wish to expand his business. He derived all the satisfaction he needed in life from the steady rotation of money into a little more money over the years, all perfectly recorded. Sammy's wife and two children lived near her parents fifty miles up the coast in an orderly community with schools. Once a month he returned home for a long weekend, when his brother would travel down and keep the store open. Disorder made Sammy unhappy, and events following the discovery of the dead body represented the most potentially severe disorder he could remember.

Anyone who knew him understood Sammy's entire modus operandi in life was based on the maintenance of good trading conditions. Sammy could overlook anything except shoplifting. He did not concern himself with people's private lives, sex lives, source of income, creed or hygiene. He was not a gossip. He needed to be trustworthy in the community. Normally, he would not volunteer information about anyone, but a dead man on the rocks was far from normal, and the coincidence of Breakdown's sartorial upliftment was impossible to ignore. Sammy did not like Breakdown. He represented disorder.

When Mendi and Clive returned to the billiard room, they found Sammy there, studying Mendi's large map.

"This room is closed to the public," Mendi told him.

Sammy blinked and stepped away hurriedly. "I have some information," he said.

"Speak," said Mendi.

"Breakdown is walking around town wearing a Hawaiian shirt and jeans."

Mendi looked at Clive. "What's he talking about?"

"Breakdown is a homeless man who lives on the beach," said Clive. "He doesn't own any kind of shirt and jeans, and doesn't have the money to buy them. Breakdown has new clothes. The dead guy is missing his clothes."

"You call this person Breakdown?" said Mendi.

"That's what he was called when I arrived here fifteen years ago."

"Would this Breakdown be so crazy as to rob a man of his clothes and then parade around in them in public?" asked Mendi.

Clive hesitated to pass judgment on Breakdown's degree of craziness, but Sammy spoke up readily.

"Yes," he said. "The man is retarded."

Mendi turned to Clive. "You will help me arrest this man."

Clive said, "We need to get Johnny Fourie."

"Why?"

"Johnny gets how Breakdown's head works."

"Where do we find this Johnny?"

6

Out on the water, beyond the breakers, a solitary surfer sits on his board, his back to the shore. The swell lifts and lowers him gently, like a mother soothing a child. His eyes read the swells rolling toward him. From a snapshot of the depth of color in the reflection off the surface, he computes a wave outcome two minutes hence.

The sea can be treacherous on this coast, where the southbound warm Mozambique current runs close inshore against the southwesterly prevailing wind, a perpetual state of conflict that can produce a mountainous swell. The original Portuguese seafarers died on this coast seeking a sea passage to the east. Before them, Phoenicians and Zanzibaris turned away, finding the coast unwelcoming.

No one surfs at the beach in Port Victoria where the waves are sloppy and often muddy from the river mouth. But thirty minutes' walk to the south is a wide bay framed by a long promontory into the ocean. That promontory provides the pivot around which the wind and current can cooperate to refract a rhythmic swell into the bay. As it approaches the shore, that swell will reliably produce the smooth late-cresting waves ideal for surfing. And when the wind and tide are in harmony, there can be an hour of the deep green tube rides every surfer dreams of.

When the time is right, the lone surfer flattens onto the board and with a few strokes, takes himself with precision to the point and moment at which the wave's angle steepens and its energy sharpens. His board comes to life as it takes up the energy of the wave. The surfer rises to a standing position, pauses a moment, then sends the board on an arcing inscription across the face of moving water.

Alice's body responded as she watched the surfer—she came up onto her toes slightly, as though she was traveling with him along the wave.

She had walked south from the village, hesitantly crossing the mouth of the lagoon. It was low tide and the water was running fast in a shallow sluice. When the beach ended she continued across the rocks. She watched a group of women from the huts above the village move methodically along the tideline, harvesting mussels from the rocks with screwdrivers and tossing them into a hessian sack. She watched two small boys slice up a dead fish for bait, using the edge of a broken bottle. She came to a second bay, where the coastline cut away to the southwest so the breeze came onto her cheek at a new angle. She was thinking about what the man called Breakdown had said to her. *Nkosasana.*

As a child, Alice had known enough Zulu and Xhosa to conduct simple conversations. Those mellifluous languages had been all around her as she grew: the nouns and place names, which often began with the resonant "um" sound, as if saying "regard this item." *Umzimvubu*: the name of the river that cut a thunderous path through the barrier of hills before flattening into an agreeable lagoon around which Port Victoria had taken root.

Alice knew that *Nkosasana* meant young girl. And she could think of no reason Breakdown would say that to her.

She had been watching the surfer on his board out behind the breakers. It seemed like he was never going to take a wave and was just there to feel the ocean beneath him. His patience detained her and she sat on a rock on the promontory, waiting with him. Alice knew nothing about surfing but she caught her breath as the surfer turned his board into the wave. As she watched him write his long sweeping signature on the wall of water a sigh of emotion passed through her.

7

Johnny was servicing one of the outboard motors on his boat when Clive came to recruit him for the magistrate. The news did not make him happy. Firstly, the idea of arresting Breakdown fell into the same category as pulling a live shark into the back of his fishing boat. Things could get broken. But there were bigger issues as well: Johnny's best interests lay in the maintenance of the status quo in Port Victoria. He did not like outsiders meddling in that equation. The magistrate with his shiny shoes represented an unquantifiable threat.

"Why did that stupid prick have to get himself killed here?" Johnny complained as he scrubbed the engine grease off his hands with turpentine. "You know that first day when we found him? I thought then I should just put him in my boat and take him a mile out and drop him in the Mozambique current. Then the sharks would have got him or he would have washed up three hundred miles down the coast."

Clive nodded in agreement. "But if we don't do it, then maybe the magistrate will call cops from the capital to come down here, and we don't want that. You need to make a plan, Johnny."

They walked to the hotel where Johnny put a proposition to the magistrate.

"Instead of trying to arrest Breakdown, let's just walk over to his camp on the other side of the lagoon and talk to him."

Mendi shook his head. "As magistrate, I am not going to visit the accused at the convenience of his premises. Things must be done properly. He must be arrested and charged and interrogated."

"But we don't have anything," said Clive. "There's no police station, no cell, nothing."

"Don't you have a gun?" Mendi demanded.

"No," said Johnny. Of course, Johnny had several guns, but he had no intention of using one in a situation as delicate as this.

"You're the magistrate," said Clive to Mendi. "Don't you have handcuffs or something?"

Mendi had no handcuffs. He had in his briefcase the necessary stationery to convene an inquest, process an arrest, evict a transient, declare a curfew and record the findings of a postmortem. He had a silver Parker pen presented to him by a Danish aid agency and several dozen laminated business cards with his name and title in relief. He had three condoms, extralarge. But he had no handcuffs.

"Anyway, it'd take more than the three of us to get handcuffs on Breakdown," said Johnny. "Listen, I've got a plan. I'll get him in a room where you can talk to him." He turned to Clive. "That room next to the store—get the key from Sammy. I'll go get Breakdown."

"How are you going to restrain him?" asked Mendi.

"I'm not," said Johnny. "But you'll be okay while you talk to him."

After his ceremonial tour of the town, Breakdown returned to his camp and removed the new clothes. He found them restricting and uncomfortable compared to the tattered cast-off T-shirt and shorts he normally wore. An hour later, when he saw Johnny approaching across the dunes, Breakdown assumed there was work for him on the boat, so he pulled his new clothes on again. They exchanged greetings and then Breakdown followed Johnny back towards town without concern. They said nothing on the walk and when Johnny led him toward the main street instead of his house, Breakdown thought merely that there was something for him to carry from Sammy's.

Before the budget cuts, the room next to Sammy's store had been used as a post office. It was divided down the middle by a counter with bars, and there were bars on the windows and good locks on the door. Sammy used it to store excess stock from time to time, but it was currently empty.

Johnny and Clive ushered Breakdown into the room. When he saw there was nothing to carry out, Breakdown's mind went in search of possible explanations. In Breakdown's version of the world, there was direct cause and effect. The only change in his life recently was that he had acquired a new shirt and jeans. Now leading members of the community had called upon him and were inviting him to view a room. A single explanation presented itself: those who acquired smart clothes were given rooms. All the evidence supported that. Breakdown was touched. He turned and beamed at Johnny and Clive. Breakdown had no wish to live indoors, but he embraced the human kindness of those who offered it.

"Just hang five here a while, Breakdown, okay?" said Johnny, and he and Clive shuffled out of the room. Johnny closed the door behind him and turned the key—which might have alarmed many people, but Breakdown had never had his life modified by a door before, so the sound meant nothing to him. Then Mendi entered from another door, on the far side of the bars. He sat in a chair which had been provided by Sammy. Breakdown beamed at him. Mendi opened his briefcase and took out the appropriate stationery and the Parker pen. Breakdown was deeply impressed.

8

Alice got up to leave when she saw that the surfer was coming in to shore, but he called after her, so she waited.

In the shallow water he pulled the Velcro leash off his ankle and carried his board across the sand towards her. He limped slightly, which she thought was a curious contrast to his grace in the water.

"That was beautiful," she said.

"Wind's changing," he said. "Are you the English woman?"

"The English woman?"

He grinned. "Sure, the English woman was top of the news this morning when I went into the village. You knocked the dead naked guy off the front page. I'm Simon." He offered his hand.

"Alice," she said, "and I was actually born near here. But I've lived in England for a while now."

"You sound English."

She shook her head. "Not to the English. Over there, some people hear me and my daughter together, they ask me if she's adopted. I'm stateless. People in Britain think I'm a foreigner, and everyone here thinks I'm English."

"Holiday?" he asked.

"And a bit of family business to sort out."

"How are you handling the Cape Hamilton? It can be a bit rough when Clive takes his eye off the ball."

"The room is fine. I'm not sure about the food."

"You eat lobster?" he asked her.

"Not often. They're very expensive in London."

"I'll feed you one straight out of the ocean. Or two if you like. Have to be tomorrow night because the tide's done today."

She hesitated. "Do you live alone?"

"I do." He turned and pointed at a house on the rise behind the beach. "That's my place. I put the big window in so I can check the swell without getting out of bed in the morning. Come on. Don't be nervous. It wasn't me who killed the dead guy. Ask anyone about me. I just surf."

44

"Okay," she said.

"I'll fetch you from the hotel, you don't want to be crossing these rocks on foot after dark. Six o'clock?"

"Fine." She turned to leave, but stopped. "Can I ask you something? *Nkosasana*—it means young girl, right?"

"Yeah. Or princess. Treasured young girl in the family. Why?"

"Someone said it to me earlier. I would have thought I was too old."

"Who said it to you? Was it a much older man?"

"No. Well, I don't know how old he is. He's weird. The shop owner said he's homeless."

"Breakdown?"

"What?"

Simon mimicked Breakdown's head movement.

"Yes, that guy," said Alice.

"Breakdown. That's his name. He lives on the beach at the end of the lagoon."

"Is there something wrong with him?"

Simon shrugged. "I guess there is, medically, if he was ever examined. But he's not stupid. I think he's a good luck charm—like a community asset. He's here to teach us something."

"What?"

"I haven't worked that out yet. You want me to drive you back to the hotel?"

"No, it's okay, thanks. I need the exercise. I'll see you tomorrow."

9

On the verandah of the Cape Hamilton, Clive and Johnny had started drinking at pace right after discharging their duties as

Mendi's deputies. Bob Peace found them when they were on number three. Woodstock arrived on number five and was disappointed to have missed all the news. He was eager to re-establish himself in the troop.

"So what happened?" Woodstock asked.

"Fucken Breakdown didn't get the point. At all," said Clive.

"Poor bastard thought he was being offered a free room," said Johnny.

"What about the murder?" Woodstock asked.

"He admitted it."

"Why did he do it?"

"I didn't say he did it. I said he admitted it."

"There's no difference," said Woodstock. "He did it. He's a retard and he should be locked up even if he didn't do it. We should go up there and give him a smack so he understands it's not a hotel."

"Fuck off Woodstock, jou slapgat moer," said Johnny.

"Hey, fuck me!" Woodstock yipped with indignation.

"Breakdown's a free spirit," said Bob Peace.

"He's a fucking baboon!" Woodstock was hopping.

"You're the fucking baboon." Johnny's voice had a tone in it and Woodstock skipped back in alarm.

"Breakdown didn't murder that guy," said Johnny. "He may have killed him, accidentally, but he didn't murder him. Murder requires..." he groped for the phrase, "malice aforethought. Breakdown isn't capable of aforethought. Any guy who comes to this part of the world wearing a Rolex is basically committing suicide. It's a suicide, this."

"But the watch wasn't stolen," said Bob, "so in fact that wasn't what got him killed."

"That's how life is," said Johnny. "You're supposed to die for one reason, but you die for another. It doesn't alter the fact." He subsided, content with this logic.

"That black magistrate's just pissed off because there's another black guy being so stupid," said Clive. "Breakdown embarrasses him. For his own people, like."

"And he's gonna take it out on us," said Johnny. "Woodstock! Go get us some chips from the kitchen. Where's that little bastard?"

But Woodstock had absented himself from the bar. The alpha member of his troop was angry and the best course of action was not to be in the line of sight. Passing through the hotel reception, Woodstock asked what room the English chick was in. Kwela, the ancient Zulu clerk, told him room 13, but the madam was not in at the moment. Woodstock walked out the main door, doubled back around the building, and went up the back stairs.

Room 13 was locked. Woodstock examined the lock without any particular intention. He could have broken it without much trouble. He didn't know if he wanted to get into the woman's room or what he would do if he did. He just knew that this secret act gave him a sense of purpose and a thrill, and it made him feel some power over the woman. His mind leapt with possibilities. Something told him that Alice's panties would smell of perfume. Typical fucking bitch. Emotions that Woodstock could not define swept him. They were sexual in nature, but not about sex. They made him feel afraid and excited and provoked. He slipped unseen out of the hotel and merged into the dune bushes, where he masturbated quickly before limping home with semen caking on his hands and jeans.

10

After midnight a vindictive southwesterly came skating up the coast. For two hours it scrabbled at every window in Port Victoria, tested every roof. It stripped water off the surface of the lagoon and flung it at Bob Peace as he stumbled home after his show. It brought Johnny cursing out of sleep to go tie down his boat on the trailer. On the verandah of the Cape Hamilton Hotel it swept up all loose items—ashtrays, candleholders, forgotten sandals, potted plants, a chess set, three small speakers—and stacked them against the north wall. Out on the point of the lagoon, the most exposed place in Port Victoria, it searched for Breakdown but didn't find him, but satisfied itself by blowing every trace of his camp halfway to Durban.

The wind woke Alice and blew her a childhood memory of looking out of the window of the big old house at banana plants gesticulating crazily in a similar wind. That long-ago wind had rattled the old house on the hill so that Alice could not hear what was being said in the next room. The memory left her with an itch—how she had desperately wanted to hear what was being said, but the wind had obliterated the words.

Alice was up early. The wind had died in the night and the heat was returning. The electricity was out and there was no hot water. She considered it was possible that there was no edible food in the entire village. She also found that she was shrinking from the prospect of going up to the house for morning tea. She decided on a long walk. She would walk through the town, up across the bridge and into the ravine along the river. In the main street she found herself quite alone, except for wildlife. Indian mynah birds were noisily driving the pigeons away from the litter scattered by the wind. Feral cats, also scavenging, skittered at her approach. In this state, Port Victoria looked very much an abandoned town; every pressure point buckled, every surface corroded.

Perhaps it was because of the cats that she ignored the noise at first. A keening noise, easily taken as animal. She heard it, but did not process it. However, as it persisted, she took notice, and walked toward Sammy's to investigate. She stood at the door of the post office for a long time before deciding that this noise was human.

"Hello?" said Alice.

The sound stopped. She waited.

"Are you okay?"

Nothing.

Alice found a box to stand on and peered through the window. The tableau within provoked a visceral feeling she had never known before. Breakdown was crouched in the corner of the room. His face and his arm were cut. The Hawaiian shirt and denim jeans had been ripped off. There was blood and shit on the walls and floor. The slim metal bars that had divided the room were twisted out of their moorings—a sight that would give Mendi a bowel spasm when he saw it later.

Breakdown and Alice eyed each other.

"What's happened?" she said softly.

Breakdown's wild eyes told her a story, but he uttered nothing. His lips were crusted with dried foam. There was a trauma at the edge of his left eye socket.

"Who locked you in here?"

"Bloody fucking," said Breakdown.

Then he came up close and examined her face. They looked at each other for a long time.

She said, "I'm going to sort this out. I promise you." She waited. "Do you understand? Wait. I'll be back."

She turned from the window because she could not hold his gaze any longer, and got down from the box. Sammy's store was still locked, but she could see him approaching on foot, enjoying the morning in a neatly pressed white lounge shirt. The best possible master—a television foreign correspondent—had coached Alice in righteous indignation. She descended on Sammy.

"What the hell do you think you're doing?"

Sammy blinked at her.

"Do you think you can just take the law into your own hands?"

She waited for his answer, twitching.

"The pills not working?" This was the only construction Sammy could put on Alice's behavior.

"Do you think you can just lock that man up because you're afraid he'll steal from you?"

"Oh! I didn't lock him up!"

"Isn't that part of your shop?"

"It's the old post office! The magistrate locked him up!"

"What for?"

"For murdering the dead man."

"That's rubbish."

"No, it's true! He confessed."

Who knew what thoughts occupied Breakdown's mind the evening before as Mendi had questioned him? Mendi had studied law at Fort Hare—a second-class university for black people when Mendi was a student. His instructor in courtroom strategy was a lean, unhappy white lawyer who had missed the coveted professorship at Stellenbosch and thus transferred his knowledge to black students with a certain vindictive satisfaction: "Ask questions in an ever-diminishing circle. Build a cage out of the simple answers. By the time you ask the final question, the suspect must be in a situation where the only answer consistent with the evidence he has already given is the answer that incriminates him."

Mendi had loved that sort of lawyerly cunning, but it was entirely superfluous with Breakdown, who contributed readily to his own incrimination, culminating with a nod and a firm "Yebo" when Mendi asked him if he had killed the tourist.

"Why?"

"It's a sin," Breakdown had explained.

"It is a sin, yes, but why did you do it?"

Breakdown had rolled his eyes as if to indicate an inability to comprehend the mind behind so diabolical a murder. Then he said, "I don't want this room."

"Did you want those clothes?"

Breakdown nodded and grinned. "Yes! Beautiful clothes! You like the clothes?" In an impulse of goodwill, Breakdown stood up and quickly stripped off the shirt. He offered it to Mendi.

Mendi rubbed his eyes with frustration and thought back to the immaculate plans for universal and equal justice in the New Democracy. Then he walked out leaving Breakdown without an explanation.

When Alice found him, Mendi was enjoying a leisurely breakfast on the verandah of the hotel. Her face was flushed and her eyes sharp as she pulled out the chair opposite him and sat down. The effect was provocative to Mendi and sexual implications came to his mind before judicial, but he was quickly disabused of this fantasy.

"You've locked up that retarded man!"

Her tone lacked the groveling Mendi had come to expect from whites subjected to his whim. His manner changed instantly and wickedly.

"How is this your business?"

"He's not the kind of person you can just lock in a room! He's very unstable. He should have proper guidance and representation! I doubt he even understands the crime or the charge!"

The fact that Mendi had the same doubts made him all the more determined not to hear it from this woman. She needed to be brought up to speed on the state of the nation.

"Thank you ever so much for your advice—" This phraseology came to him in a flash of satirical brilliance, which he admired as he spoke it. "I'm sure that in England you do things differently. We have had some experience of receiving counsel from Europeans on how to run our affairs, but if you know your history, that didn't turn out well…"

"I'm South African," she interrupted him. "I grew up right here in this town. Which I think is more than you can say. So don't patronize me."

This revelation jarred Mendi, but he recovered quickly. "Are you a lawyer?" he asked her.

"No."

"Do you represent the accused in any way?"

"No, but—"

"Then I don't think we have any business."

"You've got to offer him bail!"

"He's not going to make bail. He hasn't got ten cents!"

"You've still got to offer it."

"All right, he can have bail of five hundred rands."

Alice took out her purse and counted off five one hundred rand notes and handed them to Mendi.

"I shall want a receipt."

Mendi was furious with himself. "No, I won't take it. You can't just pay his bail!"

"I can and I have and I want him released."

"No. I have reason to believe he will abscond." He stuffed the bank notes back at her.

"Have you looked into that room? There's not even a toilet! What you're doing is barbaric! This man hasn't even had a charge brought against him!"

"He's admitted the crime."

"I'm going to phone your superior officer."

Mendi clicked the twin combination locks on his briefcase, opened it up and handed her a laminated business card. "His name is Mr. Zondi, and you can reach him on that number."

Mendi knew that Alice would have to spend hours hanging on the phone before she got through Mr. Zondi's barrier of bureaucratic underlings. Should she succeed, that worthy gentleman would give her an experience of being patronized far beyond anything to which Mendi could aspire. He picked toast crumbs from his sleeve. "Don't forget to mention that you grew up here. I'm sure that will influence him."

Alice walked straight back into town. She did not try to phone Mendi's superior officer from the hotel phone. With that irresistible parting shot Mendi had not only tipped his hand, he had motivated Alice beyond what she might previously have been capable of. Besides, the humidity was driving her insane; she had a deodorant rash and a stiff neck from sleeping badly. She was pissed.

She confronted Sammy again.

"I need access to the prisoner. I'm going to represent him."

Sammy twitched. "The chief magistrate—"

"I've just spoken with the magistrate at the hotel. He has authorized me to speak with the prisoner and communicate with his boss." She handed Sammy the business card Mendi had given her, identifying Mr. Zondi. "Could you let me in, please?"

Alice turned the key in the lock and entered slowly. The rising heat and humidity of the day had multiplied the olfactory horrors of that little room. Alice had to control her breathing. Her heart was thumping as she stood in the doorway. He was still sitting on the floor at the far end of the room, unmoving. She stayed where she was, watching him nervously. But he made no move, other than his eyes, which followed her.

"Come out."

She beckoned. She moved to the side, out of the doorway, so that he could see it wide open and unobstructed.

He studied her face without moving.

"Come on," she beckoned, "come out of there."

Then he moved quickly and she stepped back instinctively. He was right next to her in the doorway, rank and overpowering. Alice imagined she could detect his body going to battle stations, the production of adrenaline, the dispatch of oxygen to the muscles. His eyes swept across the world outside the room. He gave Alice a look that she would own forever and then streaked away in a straight line toward the dense bush behind Sammy's store. When Alice was five she had seen a dog hit by a car. It had run just like Breakdown was running, for a hundred yards to its safe spot under the house, and it had never walked again. Her uncle shot it a few days later.

She bought a can of Coke from Sammy's cooler and set off up the river. She found a path leading away from the lagoon into the ravine. The canopy of foliage quickly drew her in and the path became a cocoon of sensation—the hum of bird and insect sound, the air viscous and textured.

11

Made by feet unrecorded, the bush path leads eventually to the bank of the river. Here the water is brown from erosion in the inland hills, but salted by the high tide, and carries the grunter and kabeljou from the ocean. The fish feed where seawater meets fresh water; the path knows this and so does the fish eagle, perched high on a shelf on the ravine side. The bird knows every permutation of air current on the steep journey to the river's surface. Gathering speed, he slows time and moves about within roomy microseconds, drawing in a precise moment when he thrusts forward his talons to meet the soft back of the fish.

Alice is seven years old, standing on the bank of the river. She traces the bird's path with her eye, standing on the bank of the river in the possessing heat. Staring out across the river, she sees on the opposite bank an African child, a boy. They are of an age. The river moves between them. They are both radiant, in their way. They stare across at each other for a while, and then Alice's uncle steps out into the light on the bank, and the boy steps back and is absorbed into the shadows of the thick bush around him.

Time waves a hand and thirty years pass like vapor. The river is unchanged, the path unchanged. Port Victoria seems little changed to Alice. Her aunts seemed changeless in the large house on the hill. Yet Alice is changed, and across the barrier of hills, there has been change: not quite a revolution, not quite a civil war. For two decades it was called "unrest", though the term does not convey the image of children shot in riots, an image with which Alice was particularly familiar. At the point where the forces equalized, unrest became transition, and in a poorly ventilated conference center near the international airport, leaders met and planned a new society across cups of tea. It was a miracle, a conquest, or a conceit: the final judgment still pending.

Alice remembered watching her country's first democratic elections on the TV from her sofa in west London. Mile-long queues of people snaked through high-rise buildings and across the dusty veld, filled with hope. After the change in power, there were several years of hope and flurry and wrenching transformation. Some changes that might take a generation elsewhere were effected overnight, while other things did not change at all. Vivid stories were commonplace, small tragedies went unchronicled. The country seemed full of the jumbled traffic of those going upwards to power and wealth bumping into those tumbling down. New dynasties were born overnight, the old flung off the roller coaster. Yet, in Port Victoria, behind the barrier of hills, the change was different. It was as though the present had arrived without completely displacing the past, and the two were wandering around in a blend.

Alice knew the road ran next to the river at the far end of the ravine, so if she walked all the way up the ravine, she could come back down the road. But she underestimated the distance and the path seemed to go on and on, climbing ever more steeply. Her head started to spin. She had eaten no breakfast and now realized she was dehydrated and probably heat-stricken. The rock faces of the ravine bounced fragments of memory and far off voices to her as she walked—voices from women walking the hillside paths, or a man in a narrow field of corn calling to his home. Vocabulary dormant for half a lifetime returned to her as she walked through the landscape. *Nkosasana.* She remembered the two boys she thought of as her elder brothers, long-boned and tanned and wide-grinned, teasing her.

When she finally reached the road, she slid to the ground in the luxuriant shade of a flat crown tree. She remembered how the tiny, tender leaflets of the flat crown fold away at night; how she had watched the chameleons draw up the slate gray of the bark onto their bodies. She lay under the flat crown for a long time until the sound of approaching vehicles roused her. Alice stood up and stepped into the road, just as Mendi had done to her.

The leading vehicle was a police van with a prisoner cage behind the driver's cab. A grand but exhausted hearse with a collapsed rear suspension followed it. Alice was a sufficiently exotic sight to bring them both to a halt.

"Can you give me a lift to Port Victoria?"

"It's not allowed," said the police constable driving the van. But he was grinning at her agreeably.

"I'll give you a *bonsella* if you take me to the hotel," she offered. "My money is there."

Underway again, the constable was chatty. "We're coming to fetch the murderer. You heard about him?"

"I heard there was a dead person," Alice said.

"Now they caught the man who did it. You ever been in one of these?"

"Actually I have," said Alice. "I was arrested once, in the old days. I worked for the foreign press. We were taken to John Vorster Square in a van just like this one," she said, running her fingers on the swollen and decaying plastic of the dashboard.

The constable was in his early twenties and Alice doubted whether the world raised by her recollection meant anything to him. But his grin was a gift to her on this day. Her country may have been irretrievably divided, but in that moment, she and the young man thought only the best of each other and delighted in the bumping of their worlds. They chatted easily as they made the long slow downward curve into the village. Alice didn't mention that she had deprived him of his intended cargo.

Back at the hotel she ate and then slept, waking in perspiration in the damp, clammy room. She had itchy abrasions on her arms and shoulders where overhanging foliage had scratched her on her walk. There was barely sufficient water pressure for a shower, but she felt somewhat restored by the time Simon collected her at six. His old Land Rover bounced slowly along the dirt road back to his house, where he had a fire going and a large pot of water standing by. The lobster were still alive, in water in a metal bathtub that stood under a downpipe from the roof guttering. He gave her a beer and then set the water to boil and started cleaning greens for a salad.

"So what did you do today?" he asked.

She told him about her walk and how it had precluded the agreed visit to the aunts. As soon as she permitted this thought, it pleased her—a small revenge for yesterday's treatment. She confided that thought too, while her eye followed the economy of his movement as he worked.

They consumed a huge quantity of lobster, eating like cave dwellers while Simon's two cats circled. The night came suddenly and encased them, and the surf sounded closer and the smell of the dune bush seemed stronger. Flying insects patrolled around Alice's head.

"Can I ask you something?" she said. "You have a limp. Is it from a surfing accident?"

"No. I had polio."

"Didn't you get the vaccination?"

He smiled and shook his head. "I went surfing that day."

It had been a hot day. Classes at school had been suspended for the vaccination process. Simon had no particular objection to the vaccination, which was just a sugary pill, but the queue was long and slow and full of childish noise, while Simon could feel the breeze on his cheek, a steady westerly, which he knew would be banking the surf perfectly. He felt the ocean beneath his board.

He made no decision. His body simply left the school and went to the beach. This was a time when twelve-year-old boys went out on their surfboards among the sharks while their mothers were at the store and no one thought much about it.

Simon cleared away the lobster shell. "You feel like a joint?" he asked.

"I remember the dope from here—Durban Poison?"

"That's right. I don't have any in the house, but we can walk up to the radio station and score some from Bob."

Alice had a brief apprehension that her abandonment of her depression medication, without medical supervision, should probably not be combined with marijuana, but she was charmed by the idea of this transaction, and they set off with a lantern.

The Radio Freedom building sat on the south shore of the lagoon, on the same road that led to Simon's house. More ground had been cleared than had been finally used. An architect who knew neither the climate nor the workmanship of the area had specified the cladding. After fifteen years, it suggested the remains of a bunker on the atolls where nuclear weapons were tested. Simon did not knock before leading Alice inside. The interior was instantly stifling. The air conditioning had failed several years ago and windows were sealed shut, the wood salted and swollen. The acoustic paneling had absorbed so much moisture that blocks on the ceiling occasionally detached themselves and fell on passing heads. The odor was a distillation of the years of dope, ozone, undercooked meat, and three electrical fires. The studio warning lights still worked, but someone had stolen the red and green filters for a home disco, or possibly to replace the rear lights on a car. In any case, the door was standing open, and Bob Peace could be observed in the gloom, crouched over faltering dials and sticky control slides, like a veteran pilot nursing the last old airplane full of refugees out of some ill-advised adventure.

Bob was evidently unsurprised by night visitors—though he did flinch when he recognized Alice. He motioned them to be silent while he spoke into the microphone. Bob's signature style was a close-to-the-mike drawl with a whispery, conspiratorial sibilance. He spoke in an elegiac rhythm full of obscure references. Altogether, it was a performance reminiscent of the sixties, when hippies talked in code. Then he faded the music up and flicked off the microphone and turned his attention on Alice.

"So, you've had a busy day, I heard?"

Alice just smiled.

"Can we score?" said Simon.

"Is the pope a Catholic?" said Bob, and walked to the corner of the studio where he knelt down and lifted the aluminum ducting which carried cable around the walls. From beneath the cable, he produced a plastic bag of the resealable type used by banks for coins. The bag was full of dope.

"That's a rather obvious hiding place," said Alice.

"As manager of this station, I conduct regular searches for illegal substances," said Bob, "but I never find anything."

Hiding the dope was quite unnecessary, but Bob enjoyed his dope more in a context of illicitness. Already his fingers, seemingly working independently of his brain, had located the paraphernalia necessary to roll a joint and were busy with it.

"I assume you'll be wanting to sample the merchandise before you buy it?"

"Oh sure," said Simon.

Bob kept at his elbow a special stack of very long tracks of music, which he called on when he wanted to go out for a joint. He selected a Jackson Browne album where the first track segued into the second without interruption, giving him a good long time away from the controls. It was a matter of great pride with Bob that he still used turntables and records. No carts or CDs here, much less hard drives. They walked outside and sat on the grass under a clear southern night sky, passing the joint. A Californian song of the sixties traveled up the cable to the transmitter on the hill and was lobbed out into the atmosphere over southern Africa, newly liberated. Quite possibly, not a single soul was tuned in, but Bob Peace was utterly content with his turn on this planet.

"It's amazing, isn't it, how life is?" Bob was staring up at the stars. "How did I get all the way to this paradise from the shit-hole that is Barstow, Nevada. I feel truly blessed."

"Truly guilty is what you should feel," said Alice. "This ridiculous non-radio station only exists because some apartheid nut thought up the homeland policy. This was never about broadcasting. This was about a bunch of accountants contriving something to satisfy the criteria for the tax incentives."

Bob Peace remained peaceful. "Yes but those nuts weren't me. I am just a dolphin moving through the ocean. I didn't make the ocean, nor did I pollute it. I merely exist."

"Barely exist," Alice muttered.

"Whoa," said Simon, "we're smoking the man's dope."

"I'm sorry. I'm not used to this stuff."

"Absolutely no offence taken," said Bob. "My serenity is inviolate. I've heard all this before from the earnest white liberals who have journeyed here for the purpose of berating me. Oddly, none of the local black people seem to mind me."

"I'm sure they have no concept of the swindle," said Alice.

The original white entrepreneurs who had started Radio Freedom chose its location wisely: it was true that the transmitter on the peak of the highest of the surrounding hills sent a tolerable medium wave signal into the hinterland, but the real strategy lay in the fact that the remoteness of Port Victoria discouraged government inspection.

Radio Freedom had enjoyed a cult following when it was launched in the early 1980s. Against the banal output of a repressive state broadcaster, Radio Freedom was exotic. Bob Peace's show, which went out from 10 p.m. to 2 a.m., five nights a week, had been the apotheosis of this cult. Bob professed to use drugs in the great tradition of Samuel Coleridge and Ken Kesey. Listening to his show had become an accompaniment to drug use across the limited listening range. But Radio Freedom had started running out of budget about a month after it was launched, possibly intentionally. Now it stood as a unique kind of monument to the disaster of social and economic engineering in Africa, with Bob Peace as the forgotten museum keeper.

As Alice and Simon walked back along the dark road, he took her hand.

"I'm high," she said, "or something."

Back at the cottage, she walked directly inside, saying, "I need to lie down for a while," and feeling a pleasure at trusting that she knew Simon well enough already to know he would not take this as an implicit invitation. She hit the bed sleeping.

12

In the lounge of the hotel, Mendi could not sit still long enough to enumerate the items he was furious about. He knew he was already way outside the boundaries of action he could reasonably take under the Commission of Inquiry into Crime Against Tourists. But he was determined not to back off in the face of a retarded tramp and a tricky white woman. He had a couple of enemies back at the office who would not hesitate to turn on him if he made a mess of this. The whole motivation for the

Commission of Inquiry into Crime Against Terrorism was to avoid negative publicity.

He got up and walked around the table again, watched by an unhappy band of community leaders and public deputies. Johnny and Clive were there. So was Sammy. Constable Phosa and Constable Makwena, who had driven the police van and the hearse from the capital, were also present. Clive had abandoned good business practice and was allowing everyone to help themselves from an array of bottles on the table. The situation seemed to demand it. Every ten minutes, Mendi strode through to reception to check whether Alice had returned to her room yet. Giving her a piece of his mind was the single pleasure on his immediate horizon.

Mendi was, of course, furious with the interfering woman for liberating his suspect. He was also furious with Sammy for being conned by her. He was furious with the constable and the driver for arriving promptly, instead of being a few days late as usual and thus multiplying the appearance of disaster. He was furious with Johnny and Clive and anyone else from around there for not having the wherewithal to catch a tramp with no shoes.

"We must organize a search party for the morning," said Mendi.

"Forget it," said Johnny. "You wouldn't catch him with an army now. He knows the bush, he'll survive."

"This town is like a lunatic asylum," said Mendi. "It needs proper administration. I'm going to appoint a commission of enquiry."

The three local men were too alarmed to even risk responding to this, and there was silence in the room as, from the beach door, two white men entered the lounge. One of the men scanned the room and spotted Clive.

"Hey, Clive," he called out. "Can we buy a bottle to take back to the house?"

Clive looked flustered. "You know I can't do that, Andries. It's outside off-license hours."

Both the newcomers laughed as if they genuinely thought Clive was kidding; alcohol licensing restrictions had never been known to be applied in the Cape Hamilton Hotel or anywhere else on that coast.

"We've got the chief magistrate as a guest tonight," said Clive.

The two newcomers ran their rusty eyes over Mendi, the humor gone from their faces. Mendi stared back. Before him were two men each past middle age, with old sandals, soiled shorts, wispy gray hair and bellies that represented over a century of charred meat and alcohol consumption. One was tall and bony and weather-beaten. The other was powerful and squat, selectively bred to play prop in a rugby scrum. Two men you could have seen in any farming town, at any rugby match or *braaivleis*, from Cape Town to Phalaborwa. They gave Mendi no greeting, but sat down in chairs at the far end of the lounge and ordered drinks from Darlington Dlamini.

"Who is that?" Mendi said to Clive.

"That long one is Andries Kromhout. He's lived up the beach for ages. The other guy I don't know what his name is. We hardly ever see him."

"Couple of *moffies*, you see," said Johnny.

Everyone except Mendi sniggered. "Homosexuality is not a crime in the new democracy," he pronounced.

"Kromhout came here fifteen years ago to count people for the census," said Johnny, "and he never left again."

Johnny explained that Kromhout had arrived with a VW Kombi full of crisp yellow government stationery. As with so many others, when he saw Port Victoria, he recognized it immediately as the place where he would die. He expressed it as the closest he had ever come to a religious experience. He ceased to be a census official at that moment, although it took several months to dispose completely of his supply of shrink-wrapped papers from the Government Printer. Some were stacked along the east wall of his remote windswept cottage beyond the northern promontory where they proved effective at absorbing the persistent damp, before being thrown into the sea. Other pieces lit beach fires, wrapped fish or served as toilet paper when Kromhout couldn't be bothered to walk all the way down to Sammy's for supplies.

"And the other man?" said Mendi.

"He just came a few years ago."

Word was that Kromhout and the other man had found each other in a dark, putrid, dangerous bar in the capital and were able to achieve mutual recognition despite the insistent attentions of the prostitutes. It was an encounter that had the ring of destiny.

"Listen," said Clive to Mendi, "please don't make an issue about the bottle. This whole thing has screwed up my business enough. I'm asking you now."

"They might be suspects in the murder," replied the chief magistrate.

Clive gave up. Looks were exchanged between the two tables. Kromhout's companion raised his glass in mock toast then turned his back.

"Does anyone know anything about the other man?"

Sammy shuffled.

"I'm sure he's not involved," said Sammy. "He's an ex-government employee, he's retired here."

"How do you know this?"

"He's asked me to clear his post box in the capital sometimes, and put his pension check in the bank and bring some cash. You know, I have to go regularly to collect supplies. And he doesn't like to go into the capital. He's got arthritis. The long car trip is painful for him."

"So what's his name, then?" said Mendi.

"Van den Heever. Really, he's just an ordinary fellow, I'm sure. Zacharias van den Heever."

At the sound of that name Mendi rocked in his chair as though the earth had moved. The Commission of Inquiry into Crime Against Tourists vanished totally from his world. He sat for a moment, checking that life was proceeding as normal, that the only changed element was an old Afrikaner named van den Heever sitting at the far end of the damp old colonial lounge, drinking the brandy that was paid for by his state pension. Of course, Mendi couldn't be sure—there might be more than one Zacharias van den Heever. But everything about that man, and that moment, converged perfectly.

"What's up?" said Clive, noticing the change that had come over Mendi.

"Constable Phosa," said Mendi, "go over there and tell those men to join us, I would like to buy them a drink. I want to know if they can throw any light on the murder."

Clive glanced nervously at Johnny as the constable made his way across the lounge. They all watched the constable talking to the two men, whose reluctance to get out of their chairs was evident. They turned in their chairs and stared across at Mendi's group. Mendi smiled back.

Clive called out to Darlington, "Bring a bottle of KWV."

Perhaps it was the prospect of this premium brandy that caused the two Afrikaners to rise from their seats slowly, in their own time, to indicate that the black magistrate had no power over them—they were cooperating voluntarily.

Mendi stood to receive them. "Thank you for your time," he said, "but we are trying to get a grip on this case and I must speak to everyone in the area, and this seems like a good opportunity."

Darlington returned with the fresh bottle and Clive poured generously.

"I will be happy to buy your drinks," Mendi added. "Please sit."

"I prefer to stand," said van den Heever. Unfazed, Mendi stayed standing as well. He handed Kromhout and van den Heever each one of his embossed cards. Without even glancing at the card, van den Heever placed it face down on the table and put his brandy glass on top of it, using it as a coaster.

"What case?" asked Kromhout.

"A man was murdered here a few days ago," said Clive. "Didn't you hear?"

Kromhout and van den Heever shook their heads.

"Who?" asked Kromhout.

"We don't know. Nobody seems to know him."

"Nobody told me," said Kromhout.

"Any visitors recently?" asked Mendi.

Van den Heever's line went tight instantly. "Are you suspecting us of murder?"

"No," said Clive quickly. "The magistrate is pretty sure that Breakdown did it. He's just trying to gather evidence."

Mendi's manner approached the obsequious. "You see, when we gather evidence, we get it from people who don't even understand the relevance of what they've seen. It's routine investigative procedure."

"Sounds like a TV show," said Kromhout, pouring himself further brandy.

"A piss-poor TV show," said van den Heever.

Mendi laughed agreeably.

"So did Breakdown murder a black or a white?" Van den Heever's face was corroded with years of exposure to the sun and obvious heavy drinking. His eyes were deep in swollen sockets.

"A white guy," said Clive. "Nobody knows him."

Mendi addressed the tall man, "Meneer Kromhout, I believe you are retired from the census department?"

"Ja. A long time ago."

"We gave up counting you buggers," said van den Heever. "Couldn't keep up."

Mendi turned to him, smiling at the joke. "And you, sir?"

"I'm also retired. As you can see."

"Yes, I can. Retired from what?"

Everyone could tell that this was the step from polite query to interrogation, and no force on earth would make van den Heever submit to interrogation by a black man.

"Listen," he said, standing, "I don't give a shit about this. Get to the point. Am I suspected of killing anyone?"

Mendi found this cue irresistible. "No, no, no! I don't suspect you, Mr. van den Heever. I know you've killed people. Lots of people. At Pretoria Central. Am I right?"

All that existed in the world was the look that van den Heever gave Mendi. It evolved into a gruesome smile. Van den Heever pulled back his shoulders, stood erect, and acquired the look of a man listening to his national anthem.

"Ja," he said. "So you're a political. The ones I didn't get to, they're the ones running the country now."

"Mr. van den Heever here," said Mendi for the benefit of the rapt onlookers, "had a long career in the prison service under the apartheid regime. As a hangman. He was the best. He was so good they gave him a special nickname." Mendi looked at van den Heever. "Slipknot."

For thirty years, Zacharias "Slipknot" van den Heever had been the principal hangman at Pretoria Central Prison. Slipknot had single-handedly eliminated a significant proportion of the black male population of the country—and a fair crop of whites, too; even a few women, including the notorious scissors murderess in 1964. But Slipknot made his reputation with the efficient dispatch of a steady stream of black men harvested from courts across the country, men guilty of anything from forgetfulness to treason. Because he was so good, they sent him all the special cases. The politicals.

Hangmen do not tie slipknots; on the contrary, strangulation is considered bad form among hangmen. An efficient hanging snaps the spinal cord with a knot that holds, not slips. But Slipknot's nickname had emerged from the rumble of rumor around his reputation, and he had the good sense not to meddle with the power of a popular myth.

"Ja," said Slipknot. "I served my country. None of those buggers ever came around a second time when I was in charge. You know, if you're going to do a good job, you have to manage every detail yourself. I oiled the trapdoor hinges myself. I checked the electrics. There were no kickers or twitchers on my rope."

Slipknot paused to toss some brandy down his throat. Then he eyed Mendi. "They used to ask for me, you know—your comrades. If you're going to get hanged, you want the guy who does it properly." The alcohol had reddened the veins in his face and his head seemed to swell slightly.

"It was a mistake to give up the death penalty," he continued. "If we were still hanging people, there wouldn't be all this raping and bank robbing and car hijacking. And I'd be rich, man! Hanging could have become a privatized industry, like the airways and the cell phones and all that, and I could have become an entrepreneur, listed on the stock exchange. I could have produced one of those instructional videos."

"You know," said Kromhout, "he was so good, that when he was made redundant, Swaziland offered him their top job in hanging. It's true. With a car and everything."

"Ja," said Slipknot, "but I didn't have the motivation for it. What's the point in hanging a bunch of people from another country? It doesn't mean anything. In my time, I was a hero. In the seventies when I was doing all the politicals, when I used to pitch up at a *braaivleis* or a school rugby match, people would clap."

Mendi had listened to all this with the serenity of a Buddha. Now he spoke quietly. "Did they clap when you hanged my uncle?"

Complete silence fell.

"October 16, 1979," said Mendi. "Matthews Mkhize."

Playing prop for the Prison Rugby Club, Slipknot had taken plenty of punishment. To him, an unexpected blow was merely vindication for returning with something worse. "I remember him," said Slipknot. "He went smoothly."

He sidled up next to Mendi as though they were old rugby buddies and put his arm fondly on the magistrate's shoulder. Constable Phosa's hand twitched near his police weapon, but Mendi's continued serenity stayed him.

Slipknot's stubby, powerful fingers found the flesh above Mendi's collar and closed on the joints in his neck. He said, "I mastered every kind of neck there is. Fat, thin, long, short, thick layers of protective muscle. I was like a surgeon."

He closed his hand tighter and produced a minor spasm from Mendi. Holding him in suspended animation, Slipknot raised his other hand in front of Mendi's face and clicked his fingers. Then he let him go.

Slipknot looked away from Mendi. "Thanks for the drink, Clive, but we must waai now."

Kromhout got up to accompany Slipknot. Mendi turned to Constable Phosa. "Constable, please place these two men under arrest."

Slipknot grinned. "Sorry, comrade. I didn't have anything to do with your murder, and you won't be able to pin it on me, even though you'd love to."

He turned his back on Mendi and the two men started walking away without haste.

"On a charge of trying to buy liquor for consumption off the premises outside of trading hours," said Mendi.

"Hey, Jesus!" objected Clive.

"Don't worry," Mendi assured him, "probably nothing will come of it. But we'll have to take them back to the capital and hold them while we investigate. The cells are very crowded at the moment, but it can't be avoided."

Slipknot van den Heever turned back and looked at Mendi. "I remember your uncle. Stupid shit. He wasn't even worth hanging—he was a courier or something, not one of the real ones. He was no Nelson Mandela, your uncle. And he pissed himself before I even put the noose on him. That was his contribution to the struggle—a white man had to clean up his piss. And I'm not going to the cells."

He turned and continued walking away.

Mendi fixed an unblinking eye on Constable Phosa.

"Proceed with the arrest."

This is a country where hundreds of police officers die every year as a result of armed attack upon their persons. As a result, the demand for police officers was always way ahead of supply, basic training was consequently truncated, and police officers were inclined to shoot first in any routine inquiry.

When Mendi ordered Constable Phosa to arrest a gray-haired man in a hotel lounge, the constable did what he thought was appropriate in these circumstances—he drew his service weapon. Hearing the sound, Slipknot turned on him like a buffalo.

"Hey, I also got one of those, you moegoe!" he shouted.

If there had been an investigation into the events that followed, it would have turned on whether Slipknot raised his loose shirt just to show the 9mm Parabellum automatic pistol in a holster on his belt, or whether he was drawing the weapon. Required to make a split second judgment, Constable Phosa shot Slipknot van den Heever in the chest.

13

This was what Alice remembered from that first night with Simon: she rose from the bed some minutes or hours or lifetimes after walking back from the radio station. It was completely dark. She walked out of the open front door. Simon was sitting in front of the fire, watching the last embers burn down. She could see moonlight on a small piece of the ocean through a notch in the dune bush. The air around her was so thick it could not mingle with itself, and zones of varying temperature touched her skin. She was asleep and awake and both and neither, in that gorgeous zone where subconscious and conscious briefly permit mutual coexistence, a zone in which anything was possible. Surviving shards of dream took up texture from the real world around her and made short cameos that dissolved quickly. A nearly full moon was slathering down light; the silver coated her skin like a fluid. The night was dense with information, delicious but optional, it would be there forever.

Simon said he was going down to the river mouth to fish mullet for his cats. She used the bathroom and then followed down the path through the dunes. This river—much smaller than the Umzimvubu—met the ocean in a shallow stretch of water too small to qualify as a lagoon. Simon was walking knee deep into the water with his fishing net. Alice would remember this: in slow motion the net flowered as the heavy sinkers on the perimeter pulled it open, and it drifted down onto the water's surface. When the sinkers met the water, the moment was suspended, and she had time to observe every indentation as the surface tension of the water held briefly against the weights. The surface of the lake was silver with moonlight, but where the lead sinkers depressed the water, they produced a circle of dark points. The net itself descended onto the water and printed a black mesh on the silver before sinking through.

Alice took off her jeans and walked into the silver water. She had the sense that this was a moment slipped to her illicitly, not really a part of her life.

Their figures converged in the silver lake. Simon watched her approach. She got to him and put her hands on his sides. He drew up the fishing net and the small vibrating fish sent angles of light off in all directions. He passed the net to her to hold, then dipped his hands into the water and collected a double handful, which he dripped onto her head, fat droplets like mercury in the moonlight, a baptism.

In the inkiness of the bush cover on the edge of the lagoon Woodstock squatted, watching them in the heraldic landscape of the silver water. He felt extraordinarily capable at this—as though he had accidentally stumbled on his life's calling. Preparing a fate for Miss Smelly Pants gave him a serenity unobtainable in any other way of life. It gave him patience and tolerance. It was like discovering a destiny after a life of meaningless indignities. He watched them kiss and licked his own cracked lips.

14

In the course of a restless night, Constable Phosa considered running away into the bush. There was really no knowing what was in store for him in the police force after last night. But he was a township kid with no skills for surviving in the bush and the villages. The chief magistrate had been curt and businesslike as he directed the cleaning up after the shooting. They loaded the dead hangman into the freezer along with the naked white guy for the night. Then the chief magistrate informed the constable and the hearse driver that they were to set out for the capital at first light, to avoid the heat. Both bodies would be in the hearse. The magistrate himself would ride with the constable in the police van.

In the morning, after they loaded the bodies, the hotel manager gave them coffee and toast. The chief magistrate was dressed in a suit and a tie, his black shoes shining. He wiped down the passenger seat of the police van before climbing in. They set off up the difficult road into the hills with the sun rising behind them. The magistrate remained silent as they crawled along behind the old hearse, watching the suspension sag and sway under the double load like a cow that needed to be milked.

An hour later, when they were on the flat road and the drone of the struggling engine had abated, the chief magistrate turned in his seat.

"Constable," he said, "listen carefully to me."

And for the next thirty minutes, the magistrate explained, in lawyerly detail, the true legend of what had been achieved the night that Slipknot van den Heever was brought to justice and how he, Constable Phosa, was a hero of the Struggle.

Alice woke to sharp sunlight bouncing off the ocean surface. She was alone in Simon's bed with a rough, noisy surf framed in the large window. Gulls swooped in and out of the picture. The steady gaze she was getting from one of Simon's cats made her wonder if this animal had seen a succession of women from the hotel in exactly this situation.

She pulled on her jeans and walked outside just as Simon's truck bumped into view.

"I went to the village to get some breakfast," he said. "There was a shooting at the hotel last night."

While he prepared the food on a rickety gas range, he recounted the story to her.

"So the magistrate has headed back to the capital, I can't imagine he's going to be back. Breakdown's probably off the hook, if we can find him to tell him. Do you want eggs?"

"No, thanks. Would you mind driving me back to the hotel?"

"No problem. What are you going to do?"

"What every wife does after she's slept with another man. Phone home and check that everything's okay."

Saturday. The first weekend of her absence from home. No nanny. Julia had ballet at 2 p.m. Homework and playdates had to be kept on schedule.

Clive allowed Alice to use the hotel phone on the strict understanding that she would get her family to call her back immediately. The connection was poor and the conversations short. Philip was relaxed and businesslike; Julia excited about a friend's party upcoming that afternoon. When the call was over, Alice was first relieved that there had been no long discussion into which her guilt might leak. But that relief was quickly overtaken by a feeling of loneliness. Her family in London could carry on in her absence. If her body turned up on the rocks next to the lagoon mouth, Philip and Julia would survive. They would have a crisis of grief, but as the years flowed on they would have full lives. Neither of them knew anything about the life she had had here, nor did they want to.

She bought a bottle of water and returned to her room. She went into the bathroom and cleaned her teeth ferociously. She knew what was happening. Years of consistent medication had abruptly been ceased. Certain chemicals were draining from her mind and body. She had a metallic taste in her mouth and an excess of rapid hand movement that she knew from way back. The urgent need for behavior change pressed on her. She promised herself she would smoke no more dope. And not mix it with wine. And she would stay away from Simon's beach and Simon's house. She lay in the bath for half an hour while the anxieties thrummed in her ears. She dried herself and fell on the bed.

At four o'clock she woke, dressed and walked up to the old house.

15

"You've made Abigail sick with worry."

Alice and Phyllis with the security trellis between them again.

"You don't let me into your house and then you miss me when I don't come?" replied Alice.

"You said you would come!"

"I got involved in something."

"Yes, you've been busy. You let the madman escape and then you spent the night with the surfer." Phyllis leered at her in open triumph. "Your old aunts aren't as stupid as you think."

"Are you going to let me in, or not?"

Abigail was in the lounge. The African sunlight had been defeated here. Alice had grown up in rooms like this, but now she recognized it as a colonial thing: to take themselves seriously, they banished the uncivilized light. And color. The paintings were all dark, Thomas Hardy-style agrarian scenes, dramatically framed. Lugubrious furniture that Alice remembered still lurked against heavy drapes. There was dust on all the shelves. Comfortable topics of conversation evaded Alice.

"You should have dogs," she said. "I thought you would. For security."

"I can't be bothered with dogs," said Phyllis. "I have a gun."

"You'll shoot yourself, most likely," said Abigail. "It's five o'clock. Shall we have a spot?"

At a grandiose liquor cabinet, Phyllis measured gin into heavy crystal glasses with quivering hands. Phyllis and Abigail had been having a spot at five o'clock since 1934. The steady trickle of gin through the filter of their bodies might have been one of the profound constancies of their lives. Gordon's Dry Gin. Rose's Lime Juice. Tap water. There was no ice. The drink was the temperature of bath water.

"Cheers," said Abigail, her eyes fixed on the glass as it approached her mouth slowly. Abigail was reed-thin, painfully drawn like a bow that has dried to brittle. Her whole body contorted around the act of harvesting oxygen via the small portion of her lungs that still functioned. Lifting the gin was a complex task. Abigail had started smoking back in the days when a cigarette in the fingers of a young woman was an act of sexual defiance, and she had found in tobacco the sensual companion she would never find in bed.

Phyllis and Abigail had been young in one country and old in a different one without emigrating. As the rolling stock of colonialism, they had played tennis and gone to horse races and spent days and nights at a time working in the soup kitchens in Durban harbor during the war. Now a different country came at them through their TV screen.

"How is your daughter?"

Alice told them Julia was fine, but the aunts clearly considered that a demonstrable improbability.

"Philip's got an executive position now," she said. "He's not doing news anymore."

"Not going around the world," said Phyllis, "telling people how to mind their business."

"I heard he nearly got arrested before," said Abigail.

"Before you ran off with him," chimed Phyllis.

"Of course, this new lot would love him. He'd do very well here now."

"Except he's white."

Alice paced her breathing. "What I meant was, he doesn't have to travel any more. He's not a correspondent. He works normal hours, and comes home every night. It's good for Julia."

"Especially seeing you're not there."

"Couldn't have both of you gadding off around the world."

"Or maybe you could. Maybe that's how you bring up children these days."

They were the perfect double act, with a co-ordination honed over decades.

"I'll tell you what," said Alice. "I'm going to behave like family, even if you don't treat me like family. I'm going to assume I am welcome to come back to the house of my childhood and visit my aunts." She stood up. "I'm going to have a look around."

They watched her with the grim resentment of a subjugated population watching the army of invaders take over the best restaurants. Alice strolled through the old house. It was laden with scraps from lives long ago run out. Clothes hangers with knitted woolen envelopes over them, grubby for twenty years. A record player in an ornate polished wood cabinet. All the wood was distorted by the climate, bulging at the dovetails, and all the metals were corroded.

At six o'clock they turned on a radio to listen to the news.

Alice left them and went out to take in the sunset on the verandah. She knew they would be agitated because she left the security gate standing open, but she did it anyway.

Five-year-old Alice used to lie on that verandah with the dogs, watching for the moles to push up soil in the kikuyu grass of the lawn. The dogs would pounce and dig furiously, their paws spewing up grass and soil. Mostly the moles escaped, but occasionally one would be too slow and find itself yanked into daylight and heat, squealing and confused in that incomprehensibly vivid world, before it was torn to shreds. Alice as a child on the hot-night verandah, the flying ants coming up to the light like hopeless refugees, the Alsatians' wet jaws snapping on them. Lightly fried, the flying ants tasted like butter—so said Robbie, Alice's uncle, teasing her. As she remembered that, it came to her where one of the Alsatians was buried—not the one hit by the car, but the one that later died terribly of distemper, maddened and chewing through its metal drinking bowl, watery eyes a threat where once there had been total trust. First death. She remembered her father talking to her about it. Across the soft membrane of time, there came to her memories of beer in tall fluted glasses. Talk of racehorses and second-hand petrol-driven pumps, suitable for powering boreholes for fresh water, the value of scrap metal and Bedford trucks.

In the dark, the aunts came at her, issuing from the house onto the verandah, dispersing her reverie.

"Well...?"

"You've had a good look around."

"Decided what alterations you want to make?"

"When are you going to throw us out?"

"We have plans to make, you know."

"If we're going to end up in some old age home."

"You can't just sit here and tell us nothing."

"It's falling down anyway."

"You'd be welcome to it if we had anywhere else to go."

Alice led them back inside and replenished their gin drips. "Why did Uncle Robbie leave me this house?"

"Well, if you can't work that out you must be awfully dull."

"So, I'm awfully dull. Tell me."

"Robbie always felt guilty because of your father. Because of what happened to him."

"Being crippled in the war?"

"Yes. And everything."

"What's everything?"

"You don't know what life was like. It was tough. You people today take everything for granted."

"What's past is past."

"There's nothing to talk about."

"Don't you have any interest in me, at all?" said Alice. "Just as a family member? Aren't you at all interested just to talk to me?"

"Oh, excuse me," said Abigail. "We had forgotten how much family means to you. Since you walked out of Jerry's home. Since you cut off all contact with your family... "

"Since you married that liberal reporter and took off to England and never saw anyone again."

Abigail was running out of oxygen, but Phyllis was standing by eagerly, like a relay runner.

"Not even Jerry, who gave you a home for ten years. You didn't even come back for Felicity's funeral. She was like a mother to you."

Alice could have contested this with a quantity of evidence, but did not. "Shall I make us some dinner?" she asked instead.

"Well—" said Phyllis

"We don't really eat dinner," said Abigail.

"Just some toast and cheese. There's probably not enough. We had food ready the day you were supposed to come."

"Haven't you paid for dinner at the hotel anyway?"

So Alice walked back down the hill with only the flashlight she had bought at Sammy's to make her way in the darkness. There was no one else on the hotel verandah, so she thought it would be a good opportunity to enjoy a glass of wine there. No staff were in view, but she found Clive alone in the kitchen. He told her to take a seat on the verandah and a few minutes later delivered a bottle of cold white wine and a glass.

"Do you want to eat?" he asked her.

"It didn't look like you were making dinner tonight."

"I'll rustle something up for you."

"Just a salad," she said.

"That's not the easiest choice. We're short on fresh stuff. Bacon and locally laid eggs?"

"That's fine, thanks. Do you run this place on your own?"

He nodded. "I bought it with my wife way back, but she only lasted a year."

"I'm sorry."

"No need. It was our way of disentangling from each other."

He walked away. Alice poured a glass of wine. Philip would have said it was too chilled, but she guzzled it. The hostility she had unearthed in her aunts was still ringing in her head.

PART TWO

16

Alice sits in a house in the affluent northern suburbs of Johannesburg with the history and the future of South Africa alive in her hands.

On the television monitor in front of her, a group of black teenagers roll a car onto its side and torch it. Alice's fingers on the dial of the videotape edit console control the speed of playback action—freeze-frame, jog forward or back, frame by frame, or she can scream through the tape at speed. The dial is made of notched non-slip rubber and has a satisfying soft click in its action. She can pick through the record of any number of horrors with great precision.

At real-time playback speed, the flames spread quickly on the car. These rudimentary revolutionaries do not seem to realize they will be in mortal danger when the flames get to the fuel tank.

They stay close, performing for the camera, dancing in the manner that news correspondents from Japan and California learned to pronounce: "Toyi-toyi." By swaying the controller back and forth, playing and rewinding at real-time speed, Alice can produce a rhythmic rise and fall of the flames while the revolutionaries dance, so it looks like they are extracting fire from the car and pushing it back with their arm movements.

She has two videotape players and one recorder, a screen for each, and an edit console controlling them all. Fast-forwarding through the tapes, she notes the time codes of shots that will serve the story. When she has chosen all the elements, she punches in the time codes and the edit machine automatically compiles a montage of short visions. At the climax of that, she adds the shot of the foreign correspondent giving his closing statement to the camera.

When it's done, the tape will be rushed to the broadcasting center and satellited to London. Within twelve hours, it will be on the TV screens of cottages in Cornwall and hotels in Dubai. Every day Alice makes the history of this country on her edit desk and then goes out drinking with the crew.

Alice told Simon all this in response to his question about how she met her husband.

Her resolve to stay away from him lasted one night. Then she walked down the beach again to his surfing spot. Wrong wind, no waves and no Simon. So she walked up to the house. He was on a ladder, repairing a gutter. He stopped doing that and they went into the bedroom, where they spent much of the next two days. In between, they walked the beaches and climbed on the rocks and talked.

"The producer for Independent Network News picked me up in a bar. I started as a runner, a gofer, a dogsbody, going for pizza and rushing tapes for satellite. Then I graduated to logging tapes: sitting at a video tape player, going through the video cassettes that came in from the cameramen in the field. It was different in those days, you didn't need a degree and a resume. All you had to do was be best at the job."

Soon she was assisting the producer in compiling; before the year's end, she was editing final programs. She immediately recognized this was the business for her. It required quickness and endurance. On a story, they could be twenty hours a day, but stories were complete in a week at most, often no more than a day, building to an absolute deadline at satellite-feed time, and then it was done; no hangover, no stultifying routine. Alice had quickness from childhood, she was equipped for compiling a story under pressure.

Alice just had that knack for picking, first time, the exact moment at which a shot was exhausted of meaning, and knew exactly what—from hours of tape—should come next to keep the story ticking. Sometimes, when they were really late on a story that could compete for top of the news in London, she would red-button cutaways straight onto the master tape without even trialing them first. It was on such an occasion that the correspondent first put his hands on her shoulders, standing behind her as she worked, granting her the power to make the story as she saw fit, giving her his blessing. Everyone noticed it.

The INN bureau operated from one of the large stone-base mansions of the early Randlords—pale Englishmen who were drawn to the bottom of Africa to make money from the gold and diamond mines. They built grandiose English country houses in the scrubby veld on the ridge north of the main gold seam; the Witwatersrand. Within a century, urban sprawl consumed them. Those houses with their large rooms, rolling lawns, swimming pools and tennis courts became popular as offices for small businesses, and most suitable for the unconventional business of the foreign news crews, who could afford to pay any rent with their networks' dollars or deutschmark or sterling.

Alice's station in that production run of instant history made her the person who saw it all. Often, the cameraman did not fully appreciate what he was shooting—too busy trying to run and shoot and check the remaining tape at the same time, tripping over sound wires and competitive crews and fleeing civilians. And the producer and the correspondent never looked through the whole tape; there wasn't time. Only Alice got everything, the multiple stray details in shots, the expression of a young mother as the camera passed over her, the curse hurled by an unseen bystander on the sound track. She saw white policemen carrying the long rubber whips called *sjamboks*, policemen with grenade launchers used for teargas, policemen in camouflage, policemen with riot masks and automatic weapons, sitting on top of military personnel carriers, sharing chocolate and talking about rugby, waiting for the day's revolution to get under way. She saw black children without weapons, often without shoes, lining up in ranks against those white policemen. She saw the political funerals where personal sorrow, genuine outrage and cool political orchestration combined in a cauldron.

The correspondent talked to Alice about truth and democracy and representing the view of the disenfranchised and creating change in the country by triggering the outrage of the world community. Tony overheard that and took Alice out for a drink and said to her, "Leave the ideological bullshit to him. You concentrate on making movies. Go for the heart."

In that, Tony understood the convergence of news and technology better than any foreign correspondent and he conveyed it to Alice. She had clear intuition on how the most casual TV shot teems with detail and symbol that no written report can ever match. With a juxtaposition of images, she could set in motion a train of emotion in the viewer which was independent of any analysis of the facts.

"Being posted to Johannesburg is a career godsend for a guy like him." The cameraman gave Alice his opinion of the correspondent. The cameraman may have noticed the correspondent's proprietary hand on Alice's shoulder as she worked.

"Here, he is the world capital of moral evil. He gets to represent sanity and goodness for the world TV audiences. He's an angel." The cameraman made a jerk-off gesture with his hand.

The cameraman's name was Hugh, but he preferred to be known as Tango after his old military radio call sign, Tango-Two-Zero. Before he carried an ENG news camera into townships around Johannesburg to record the progress of the revolution, Tango carried an automatic rifle in the bush war for Rhodesia, fighting for the continuance of white rule. Tony met him on a story in Rhodesia, seen him in context. Tango had led a stick of six soldiers on helicopter drops into the bush on the Zambian border, where they waited to ambush the teenagers who'd received sixty days of training in guerrilla warfare and were returning to die for their country.

Tony recognized that Tango would be good at this job because he had been good at that job. "There's no take two in news," was one of Tony's key guidelines, and he needed a cameraman tough enough to carry a 45-pound camera all day and get the shot that would pay back his massive bank loans.

That fact that Tango, the ex-colonial soldier, could serve as a cameraman for the foreign news crews covering the last colonial regime in Africa was only one of the ironies he embodied. Tango also waged a war of contempt for the people who paid him handsomely in US dollars. Alice was too new for that, her only reflex was the obvious one, her lines borrowed: "But the regime is evil. What they do should be shown to the world."

"Not the point," said Tango. "Why are these guys actually here? What's their true motivation? Justice? Bullshit. They're in a movie and they've been cast as the good guys. And they've got these wonderful bad guys to work off—these big ugly white policemen firing teargas rounds into mobs of fleeing blacks, mostly children. When they're on TV, the correspondents put themselves on the same team as the black kids. But off-screen they're actually living in the best houses in Johannesburg, driving BMWs, having their clothes washed by black maids and fucking only white chicks. Everything they put out from here is a judgment on the white way of life, but they're queuing up to come here and share it."

"They couldn't very well produce news TV from a shack in Soweto!"

"Why not?" said Tango. "They only need electricity and telephones, both of which are available in the townships."

Alice didn't have the information to contest that.

"I'll give you an even better measure of them," says Tango. "That shot you used the other day of the kids torching the car. You know those kids were performing for the camera. There was actually nothing happening there that day. We were at the wrong place. They saw us with the camera. They started on the car. Because we were there."

Alice could not deny that. It was obvious when she saw the whole tape, not just the selected cuts, that a portion of the material presented as live, squirming, just-born news was actually choreographed. But Alice believed she had the right answer to that—she had heard the correspondent on the subject.

"But logistically it's impossible for us to capture accurate images of the revolution, so it's legitimate to use some constructed one," she argued. "The overall picture we send out is still representative of what's going on here."

"Does His Smoothness ever mention that in a report? Does he ever say, 'The scenes you're watching now took place because and only because a foreign news crew stopped here for a Coke?' Does he ever share with his audience the information that some of what they're looking at is phony? Have you ever left in the shot the part where the producer gives the thumbs-up sign to the kids afterwards?"

"But these kids are fighting for their country, for very good reasons, against an oppressive regime."

"That's a given. I'm not arguing that. This discussion is whether these correspondents are glory seeking, cynical bastards. And whether they've taught you the same thing. You were the one who thought of cutting that scene tight up against the shot of the prime minister babbling about crushing anarchy."

"Hey, you're doing the same thing!"

"No fucking way. I'm working for the cash-dollars rate and I'm not pretending otherwise. You don't see me pretending to care about any of this."

Alice's edit suite had once been a bedroom, complete with a slow-rotating ceiling fan. Beyond the TV screen, through the open French doors, Alice had a view of the pool, a holding pen for young women collected by the correspondent and crew at restaurants. A particular type of young woman was attracted to the foreign news crews. Alice called them Bimbos Deluxe, because they had a sheen of intellectualism.

"We're all here for a reason," she heard one say as she moved the shoulder strap of her bikini an inch, to tan the pale area. They were social science students and NGO researchers and the daughters of white liberals who had grown up in a mix of idealism and privilege. Tony and Tango went through those women with the impersonal reflex of sperm whales filtering plankton. But the correspondent kept himself aloof.

"You're underestimating the sexual attraction of danger," replied Tango one day when Alice wondered aloud why women came at the news crews in such a torrent.

And of history making, she thought. Alice loved the sense of power, of creating history. Whenever there was a rumor that Mandela was about to be released, Alice would be delegated to booking the private jets and the suites at the Mount Nelson Hotel in Cape Town, near the prison where he was held. And she would have the sense of riding the wave of history.

17

An afternoon up at the old house. The aunts are asleep, or pretending to be, in the humid, heavily draped rooms upstairs. Alice is wandering time and space, simultaneously an adult and a child running through the house with the dogs. The kitchen floor is lined with linoleum on which rubber squeaks—the tires of her father's wheelchair as he turns it sharply, or tries to position himself closer to the table. The wheelchair has no brake on it and Len always has trouble keeping a fixed position when exerting power through his arms—slicing kudu biltong on the kitchen table, for example. Len keeps one special knife particularly for biltong; sharp and heavy. It can take a thin shaving off the stick of uncooked, dried black meat—a shaving so thin that the center of the slice is a translucent red, suggesting a trace of life retained. But to achieve that he has to press down firmly, and when he does the wheelchair tries to roll away from the table, and he grabs the wheel quickly and swings it back, making the tires squeal on the linoleum. Decades later, Alice knows that sound intimately, remembers those wheels. The axles on the wheelchair had no hubs, just steel pins holding the wheel in place, sharp edged pins that nicked wood out of the doorframes at knee-height when Len passed too close. Every downstairs doorframe in the house was scarred; Len marked his territory thus.

18

When a man makes love to a woman, he tells her his story, he sings her his song. It cannot be otherwise. Should he attempt to pretend or conceal, these artifices are his song, the truth of him. It is a song written and performed afresh each time, addressed to that woman alone, more eloquent than the spoken word, and certainly more true.

Rocking on Simon in a sheen of afternoon sweat in the house by the ocean gave Alice a reprise of youth. Though younger than Alice, Simon was no kid himself, yet he had the life and outlook of an adolescent. He had simply failed to show up for adult life, gone surfing instead. Making love with Simon, Alice temporarily reclaimed a part of her life from the devouring empire of middle age.

Alice was a decade into upper-middle-class west London parenthood. That meant her heart pumped blood in order for her to report daily to the school gates at 3:30 p.m. with a smile in place and something neutral but not boring to say to the mothers of her daughter's friends. Philip had fixed notions about how successful, well-balanced English children were brought up. They were funneled through the private school system toward the best universities, in the select company of similar children and families.

In this ideal, each child is like a prizefighter—a high performance organism with a demanding schedule of achievement targets. These children are administered expensive education, transported to extra-curricular activities and sleepovers with friends, dentistry, ballet, piano, swimming, extra French, horse riding. They need to visit museums and cultural events, and are monitored for a host of possible health calamities—crooked teeth, nut allergies, asthma, dyspraxia or low performance in reading possibly caused by a rare eyesight condition. They need to have hamsters admitted to, and removed from, their lives at key points, including a sad funeral and a review of the meaning of life and death. The prospect of not achieving entrance to the desired private schools haunts the lives of these families.

It is inconceivable that a wife and mother might willfully deviate from this program. The only thing which is feared—so feared that the children are shielded from even the thought of it— is that the breadwinner might lose his grip on whatever source of income he has secured, and the whole chandelier of privilege will come crashing down.

Here on the hot, pungent coast, a totally different version of Alice walked Simon's house, brilliantly awake in the middle of the night, naked in the dark. She could hear everything. Simon's house above the beach seemed to be convivially shared with many small living things and she felt their proximity through the thrill in her feet. She walked with his touch on her skin. She felt every movement, felt the subtle temperature change as the breeze swung around to come off the ocean. She knew she was feeling also the centrifugal force of swinging out of medication, everything was amplified by added sensitivity and nagging undercurrent of alarm.

In London she had lived in one life, so delineated she lost feeling along stretches of her being. There in Simon's house Alice found and re-found herself again and again in small moments, so many unlived lives, a universe and just a touch away.

Simon lived in his life every day, without reviewing it and re-casting it. He caught fish for them, and taught her to make a fire that consumed no more wood than was required to cook what they had. He had the habit of going absolutely still for a moment while he considered something. Yet, his hands were always there before you expected them, but not abruptly. He never preened. He spent time examining his own feet.

He listened to the BBC World Service on shortwave and had a great number of books. She enjoyed small things about him—his habit of watching the sea and the horizon for a moment to make a judgment about surfing conditions six hours hence. He asked her nothing personal but was interested in anything she offered, and she found that so agreeable a method of conducting a short intense relationship that she adopted it herself. She asked him none of the big questions. She just let him talk. What he chose to talk about was his childhood, time on the ocean, that host of solitary hours that shaped him. And Alice, who had been marinating in her own story so intensely since deciding to return to Port Victoria, was pleased to have the diversion of someone else's story.

There were raised, rough points on his skeleton where it had been in contact with the surfboard over twenty years—calcium deposits known as surfers' knobs. She liked to seek those out with her hands during lovemaking. She loved to feel the muscles in his back as he moved on her. When Simon made love to Alice, he sang a song of aloneness that is not loneliness. His rhythm told her of the long hours on the ocean, not the surfing, but the waiting, chest on the board, the board like an aerial taking up the transmission of the ocean. The pulse of the deep ocean was his rhythm, his intuition of forces that brush us without our being aware. The surfer knew the enduring caress of a wave of energy generated far away in water two miles deep and eight thousand miles across, energy traveling in its own time and finally presenting itself as an exquisite equation out of disorder, the immaculate moving face of the wave. And just when he thought there could only ever be one of those, there came three more in a perfect set—beneficence casually awarded and just as casually withdrawn by a ten-degree change in wind direction. Simon was no prophet, no genius, but he was gifted, and gifted also to know that he knew those few things. Simon made love with all that knowledge in his bones.

"I came from the long board era," he told Alice. "When I carried my board down to the water at dawn, my shadow on the sand was shorter than the board." The longer, heavier, less versatile board imbued in Simon a certain style, a languidness; a longer, larger stroke of the arc on the wave.

The polio he remembered as a time of faded flannel pajamas, which came back from the wash heavily starched. Slow days. The crucifix on the wall of the hospital which was an adjunct to the monastery at Mariannhill in the hills inland of Durban. The bell. The quietness of the sisters. Returning to school a year later, he had quickly come to know the barrier that rose up between children who are healthy and those who are not. The healthy had a herd reflex that came unheralded from within and drove the others away, coated the healthy against any involving sympathy. Somehow the wounded one had become other, he was no longer recognized as of the species, and his survival was not critical to the group. In an animal pack he would have been left out of the feeding; in nomadic tribes he would have been abandoned. Simon saw it all, recognized it although he had no reference to work from, and went surfing on his own. It kept him different.

When Simon came back to surfing, the short, competitive, easy-to-ride board had driven out its primitive ancestor. Simon adapted to the new equipment, but he kept his long board state of mind.

Simon's polio hit Simon's father in quite a different way, though just as hard. Albert Scully had been ambitious for his son and the polio seemed like a targeted judgment on him. A competitive swimmer in his youth, Albert had trained by swimming out beyond the breakers and then a mile up the beach against the current. Albert had the will and the commitment; he simply didn't have the ability. Transference of ambition to his first son was an obvious consequence; Albert had Simon in the surf by the time he was five, and it soon became apparent that Simon did have ability.

Soon after Simon got out of the hospital, Albert took him down to the beach again. That began as a shared father and son healing. Then Albert realized something; the polio gave Simon a point of distinction. Without it, he would be just another sunburned kid on the waves, a "grom" as they were known. But the disfigurement, the handicap, gave him dignity and gravitas.

From that moment, Simon as world champion surfer was an image that Albert clung to as a talisman for both of them. The ocean would give back to father and son what the world had taken from both of them. Every morning before school, Albert drove his son down to the beach and made him surf. It was much the same as before, but completely different. The difference could be seen in Albert more than in Simon. Albert would patrol up and down the shore as Simon surfed. The man who had never surfed would shout coaching instructions at his gifted son.

But Albert Scully was due to be disappointed. The greatest surfer ever produced in these parts, Simon never won a contest.

His father drove him to achieve, and that produced in Simon the reaction of being constitutionally incapable of achieving. Everyone could see he was the best; but in any contest, Simon found a dozen ways of losing. He would cruise through the early rounds, and then he would screw it up. Late arrival, falling at critical moments, poor wave selection, broken leashes, cramp. On the beach Albert patrolled and seethed, cutting a swathe through the surfers and bikini girls and other parents, cursing.

Simon had needed a reason to fail in surf contests, and he found it. He expressed it once in a remark to a friend that was quickly circulated, pressed into metaphor and even became the title of a record album released by a local band. What Simon said was, "I can't surf slop." Commercial arrangement required that surfing contests be planned in advance, but the weather and the condition of the surf seldom cooperated. Most days the surf was not good. Winning surfing contests is about surfing poor waves—slop—and Simon could not surf slop. Simon could only produce that awesome grace when he was in the right state of mind. Competition was anathema to the right state of mind. Simon traveled once to Hawaii to compete in the Pipeline Masters, and lost, as usual, in the third round. Later, Simon went to contests but did not compete. It thus became a standing fixture after a day of competition that the cognoscenti would gather and watch Simon surf. He was an eccentric celebrity in communities from Bondi Beach to Waimea, yet still marginalized.

He was the uncrowned champion of world surfing. In that perverse manner, Simon actually achieved the level of distinction his father had sought for him. He became a cult figure. There were the professionals, the contestants, and there was Simon. He was the paradigm. He was muscle memory. Simon had been moving away from society ever since the polio marked him. It was as if he sensed that his relationship with human affairs—family, community and humanity—would be disastrous, so he simply backed away. When he had seen the gift of wave sets in Port Victoria, he had known that was home.

All this, Simon told Alice in their long days and nights together. He told her in words and in his lovemaking, a download of person, one to the other. He did that without the slightest query into her life in return. And because he asked nothing, she would feel free to tell him.

19

The only mirror in Simon's house is a hand-size shaving mirror hanging on a hook above the bathroom sink. In it, Alice examines the lively tangle her hair has become, the dusting of freckles across her nose to match those she has already seen on her shoulders.

"I was anointed the day that the Minister of the Interior got the freedom of Soweto," she tells Simon.

There was an unofficial ranking among the foreign correspondents and their crews. The guys who had seen the most, been through the most, had the respect of the others. It was acknowledged in short conversational reference; Barry was the first to see the bodies in Richmond ... Andy was right behind the cops when they set the dogs on those students.

For crew-level people, the rite of passage into the academy was to be tear gassed. It was not official policy for the riot police to tear gas the foreign press corps, but somehow the latter found themselves downwind more often than not when rioters were dispersed. Some of the American networks issued their staff with gas masks and bulletproof vests, but it was considered not cool to wear them. It separated you from the oppressed. You could not be separated from the oppressed while covering the story, even though at the end of the day you drove an air conditioned Mercedes back to the white side of town.

Alice's role never took her into the field. She had to be waiting at the edit desk, receiving the first cassettes out of Tango's camera, rushed back by a runner, cutting the platform for the story even while it was going on. Alice had received Tango's footage of tear gas canisters fired from grenade launchers fitted to the muzzle of automatic rifles, fired at a 45 degree angle from a hip-held stance. On Alice's edit desk, in slow motion, the trajectory of the tear gas canister was exquisite, and many times she made a perfect cut from this to the shot of panic-stricken rioters running, which was always dramatically affecting. Obviously, Tango could not film both the firing of the tear gas and the running simultaneously, so there had to be some substitution along the way. Alice learned to strip in footage from other events on other days.

But while she became adept at dramatizing history, she had never seen it being made.

"Why don't you come along with us today?" the correspondent said to Alice. "The Minister of the Interior is receiving the freedom of Soweto, but we won't get on the news tomorrow because of the party congress, so there'll be no hurry for an edit."

"Unless there's big trouble."

"Then you can head back with the first tape that has anything really newsworthy on it." He smiled at her. "It's up to you. I just thought you'd like to see the real thing for once."

The correspondent was Philip Burley. He was very British in the land of guttural accents and lower-deck manners, but not effete. He was well bred and Cambridge educated. He often wore a double-breasted navy blue blazer. His hair was receding early, but that distinguished rather than undermined his youthfulness. His skin was clear and always slightly red-burnt rather than tanned in the African heat, and this, too, was distinguishing. His manner was informal and approachable without forfeiting status. Most foreign correspondents were witty at the expense of South African politicians, businessmen, sportsmen, technical standards, media practices, menus and much else. Most foreign correspondents considered themselves inherently superior to white South Africans in an arrangement not dissimilar to that by which most white South Africans considered themselves inherently superior to their black countrymen. Philip Burley did not express or imply such sentiments; Alice had always been impressed with his manner toward his staff; he was unlike the men she had known.

They left the office in white suburbia and drove toward Soweto in the crew van with the INN NEWS stickers prominently displayed—a level of protection against ordinary crime and political reaction in particular.

As they approached the municipal compound where the day's event was due to take place, Tony said, "Some days you can just smell there's going to be trouble."

Tango, driving, nodded. The compound was surrounded by a circle of police vehicles and armed white policemen in bush camouflage which they wore for township operations. Handlers with German shepherd dogs stood between them. This was what was required for an event at which the minister of the interior would be awarded the freedom of this city.

The ring of defense secured an area about the size of a football pitch, inside of which moved the police commanders, the press corps and the apprehensive black dignitaries who had been balloted to greet the minister. Just outside the security circle, a rapidly growing crowd of black demonstrators was gathering.

The South African Police had placed in charge of press relations a sandy-haired major who had once been a small town newspaper journalist himself. He had also been an actor in photo-comic books. He wore his camouflage uniform with the collar turned up, aviator sunglasses, and persevered with a comradely attitude toward the press corps, as though he shared much in common with them. Behind his back, the major was the subject of merciless humor, but his faith in the image he had created was cast iron. Perhaps he believed that one day they would see the error of their ways. As the military helicopters carrying the minister approached, the volume of protest from the crowd grew, and the major felt it was time to put the event in perspective for the press.

"Most of the citizens of Soweto support the minister and are grateful for what he has done on their behalf," he shouted over the chopper blades. "These protestors are mostly kids who have been deliberately misled by the banned organizations." None of the reporters wrote that down.

Alice, without a specific job to do, was free to observe what she chose. That afternoon, Alice looked into the faces of two young South African men, the likes of whom she had never come across before. The first was an Afrikaner riot policeman, about twenty years old, enormous and powerful in his camouflage and weighed with spare ammunition, whom she caught looking at her breasts as she knelt down to pick up the notebook she had dropped. She returned the stare, and he did not look away. They looked at each other across a chasm. He kept looking at her as he responded to a shouted order, and fitted a grenade launcher to the barrel of his rifle. At that stage, his stare was merely the return of a challenge. It did not contain what she had seen in that first moment when he had been watching her. Then, Alice had seen in his eyes a combination of lust and contempt that was primitive. It stirred her, frightened her, and she thought, that was the feeling women have had down the ages when the barbarian hordes from across the mountains had come and massacred their men and were breaking into the homes to rape all the women. Finally, the policeman broke the eye contact with an exaggerated sneer, packed with all the resentment the Afrikaner had against the liberal English-speaking fellow white, and walked off.

And later, when the minister landed and the singing and chanting of the protestors was at a fever pitch, she had been standing right behind the ring of police holding the protestors at bay, and she caught the eye of a young black kid. He seemed to her almost maddened in a hypnotic communal fever and when he caught her looking at him, he mouthed at her "Kill you bitch" from five yards away, while a police dog straining on a leash spat foam in his face as it yapped hysterically. That time, Alice had not been frightened but stunned. Couldn't that kid see she was with the press? The foreign press, who so valiantly carried his struggle to the world? She felt an absurd urge to go up to him and explain to him that not all the white people inside the ring of steel were his enemy, but suddenly the kid and all the others had turned and were fleeing, and Alice realized she had heard but not comprehended the soft airy *boof* of the tear gas launchers.

She turned and saw the crew running—whether towards or away from something she did not know. She set off to follow, but was immediately cut off from them by a squad of riot policemen who knocked her to the ground as they surged across her path. She stood up and ran in the direction the crew had gone. She heard an amplified loud hailer, but not the words. Then she was off the public terrain and among the little block houses. People and noise merged around her. She ran straight into a black kid who dropped the rag held to his nose and revealed a wild grin to her. There seemed to be something happening in the yard of the next house so she tried to climb the fence, cutting her leg on barbed wire. She was standing alone at the quiet center of the storm, thinking how useless she would be at reporting any of this, when a completely silent tear gas canister flung itself out of the sky and onto the ground twenty feet from where she stood. The sight of it paralyzed her, even though she had seen exactly that thing in Tango's irreproachable close-focus work. Then the constriction hit her throat and the panic came quickly and overwhelmed her. A large black woman wearing a colorful scarf on her head ran out of the house carrying a large iron bucket, from which she calmly decanted soapy water onto the sizzling teargas canister. It died slowly. Then Philip's hand was on her shoulder, and he was shouting instructions to her on how keep calm, how gasping and panicking only made the effect of the tear gas worse. She vomited as he pulled her away, splattering her own shoes.

Somehow, the crew reformed at their vehicle which was among several still guarded by a detachment of police. Tango drove the crew truck fast and expertly and they found a hill half a mile away where Philip could be lined up in camera shot so that the smoke rising from houses torched in the riot was visible behind him. Philip was disheveled and he had a small wound on his forehead where Tango had accidentally smacked him with the camera when they were piling into the truck.

The shock of the tear gas gone, Alice was on a total high. She sat at the edit desk for four hours without standing up, and cut together Tango's footage into a stark and gripping account of what had happened.

Alice cut from a close-up of the heartbreakingly innocent face of a kid of maybe ten, to twelve frames of the powerful arms on a white cop just as he triggered a tear gas launch, to a long shot of the tear gas canister making its wayward hissing arc across the rickety roofs of Soweto shacks. She buttoned the sequence with a shot of a police dog pursuing three black kids around a corner. Technically, the shot was poor—Tango had just been firing the camera whichever way he was facing—but the unsteady camera and the blur in the focus gave the whole sequence a stab of eyewitness truth. Then there was Philip on the hill, looking like he might have been running just behind those kids, coolly summing up another episode in the fight for the heart of a desperate country. He kept his words simple, with no reference to the wound on his forehead. "This is Philip Burley for INN in Soweto." It was the way Alice cut it together that suggested to the audience that he was lucky he was still around.

"Top of the bulletin," he whispered in Alice's ear as she worked fast and sure and the runner was dispatched to the satellite station.

They arrived at their favorite restaurant in platoon strength, with Tango at the front firmly easing lesser folk out of the way. The proprietor knew them well, knew that Philip's expense account was boundless in this weak currency, and started them with a free bottle of champagne.

That was the first night Alice made love to Philip in his bedroom upstairs in the production house. After midnight the phone rang—the news desk in London wanting a detail for the news anchor's intro to the story, which would lead the morning bulletin.

At 3 a.m., a lion in the zoo in the valley below them started roaring its deep, scarred, pitiful, caged roar. The site for the house was chosen in 1896 because it looked north, away from human clamor of the gold mining operations and across virgin veld. The first occupants would have heard lions in the night as well, but those would have been hunting zebra where a strip of shopping malls and cinemas now stood. Alice lay awake into the coming day. Johannesburg is at 5,500 feet elevation on the central plateau of southern Africa, the highveld, and even in the midsummer, the dawn is cool and refreshing.

If Tango or the producer had been around for that scene, they would have scarcely raised an eyebrow. There's another young woman lying in the bed of a foreign correspondent. She had done the opposite of shooting the messenger, she had fucked the messenger, mistaking him for the heroes he sang of. He had stirred her up with a thrilling dose of danger and real history on the hoof, and then headlined the show himself with a grave and concerned closing summary to the camera. Lying in that dawn, Alice was looking at the past and the future of her own life, and feeling herself at the hinge.

20

Alice woke in the semi-dark when Simon raised his head to check the surf. He stood up with the sleep warmth and slowness in him, yet she could sense his body coming to performance level as he eyed the swell. She got up and went with him, walking with the blanket wrapped around her while he carried his board. While he waxed his board, she rolled a joint with a mild mix of marijuana, so that by the time he was out behind the breakers, she was nicely high without being pole-axed. Just right to slip reality.

Out on the swell behind the breakers he was idle potential. She loved that phase. But then she also loved the first few moments of the ride, the way he paused fractionally while he decided what expression was most appropriate to put on that particular wave, on that particular day, in that particular life. And then into the wave, and the poetry flowed down his legs and into the board and into the sea. Alice thought, what he had that was

103

special was time. Like the fish eagle, he had a mansion of time in the split seconds between changing forces around him, time to re-appoint himself. He tapped art from a wave by placing himself at the point where energy was released in the unfolding of the shape of the water; energy which had been delivered here from deep in the Indian Ocean. It had been happening this way for millions of years but here on this given day, Simon was positioned to expose the energy and display it.

The night before, she had asked him why he had chosen that way for his life.

"Because surfing is of no earthly use," he said. "You can't store it for a hard winter, use it to train mechanics, hang it on a wall or market soap powder with it. You can't zip it over the Internet. It is gone as the wave goes, and you have to make it all over again."

She watched him terminate the ride, drawing the energy back into his body, killing his momentum by sinking the back of the board and turning it around into the riptide that would suck him out again. She heard a raucous bird cry with a remote part of her mind, and there was a delay while her doped mind sorted it as neither seagull and nor fish eagle and rather too loud. Then she looked up and saw a vision of Breakdown flit across the tapestry of dune bush behind her. Adrenaline squirted in her but before she could act on it, he emerged from the bush line, and stood making his bird noise and beaming at her. She was completely confused as to his purpose until he added a few bars of ululation. Then it came to her that this was a greeting to the one who released him from captivity, and she realized that probably no one had taken the trouble, or been able to inform Breakdown that he was no longer wanted as a murder suspect, and that the magistrate and the body were gone and he could return to his former life without fear.

So she waved and started toward him for that purpose, but Breakdown performed a final bow and then scrambled away into the bush, and although she called after him he did not reappear. Soon she heard his bird-like call from far off.

Walking back to the house, she told Simon about it, and he nodded.

"I've seen him watching you."

"Have you? When? You didn't tell me."

"Only once, but I realized what it was. You saved him. He pays respect to you. That's how Breakdown thinks."

"It's a bit frightening. Do you think he's dangerous?"

"I'm sure he's dangerous, but not to you. There's a very direct connection of things in Breakdown's world. The issue of the moment occupies him entirely. You know what happened once? Breakdown helped me collect a whole lot of firewood and afterward I gave him some old clothes. About a month later, I was with a group of surfers who had come down from Durban and we walked past him. He was wearing the clothes I gave him and he was doing his stupid bobbing walk and some of the guys laughed at him and mocked him. They were just being childish and it was just a few minutes. He said nothing, just walked off. I didn't have anything to do with it, but I was with them, and I was the only one in the group he knew.

"That afternoon, I'm alone at home, I hear this commotion outside. I go out, Breakdown is standing on that flat area outside my front door. He's like hopping with rage and babbling some confused language. Now he's got my attention. He proceeds to rip off the clothes I gave him, ripping them to shreds in the process. He gets them all in a bundle, throws them on the ground in front of me, and walks off, stark naked. When I thought this through, I realized it was intolerable for him to wear clothes given to him by someone who had been part of an insult towards him. Even

105

though he had no other clothes at the time, because he'd thrown away his previous rags when I gave him those clothes. And I just thought, that's very pure, and I respected him for it."

"So what did you do?"

"The next day I walked over to where he sleeps at the end of the bay there, and I did the same thing. I shouted and babbled until he saw me. Then when I had his attention I got down on my knees and made like a deep bow, which I thought would mean an apology. And I left some clothes on the ground for him."

"The same clothes?"

"No, different."

"And he wore them?"

"Yes."

That night, awake in the dark of Simon's house, Alice's world was full of the righteous passion of Breakdown. She felt him in the bush around Port Victoria. She walked the house again, silently, as Simon slept. It had become a habit. Every experience was sharp. She wandered at random like a poet, taking up messages at whim. Her mind relished processing the exotic aromas on the breeze, even the stink of discarded bait or fast-drying cow shit. In the middle of the pitch dark night, she would be smack crackling awake, standing in Simon's kitchen dead still for minutes at a stretch, listening to the sounds of the house. She had moved out of the hotel and into Simon's house. She spent a lot of the night awake and slept deeply in the hot afternoons, waking with cool perspiration on her skin.

It was the dreaming that most alarmed her. In Simon's house, in Simon's bed, beside him at night or alone in the afternoons, she dreamed like a burdened laborer with a massive quota to fulfill.

She could be sharp and active in the morning; she could deliberately eat a large lunch and eschew all alcohol, but still the afternoon would bring an irresistible lethargy upon her, the bed like a mother lode magnet. As soon as she hit the bed, the teeming cast of her dreams reached up and snatched her into sleep, pulverizing her subconscious with vivid activity.

When she told Simon about the dreams, he said, "Trust your dreams, for they know who you are. It comes from an old song. Don't know the name of it."

The night after she was visited by Breakdown, Alice was in no doubt that there was in her subconscious a revolution. Her dreams were exquisitely free of the trivia of waking life, always about the real point, even when the real point was a small hurt or pleasure, buried under loads of protocol. The subconscious retains the print of every violation, every glory, and Alice sometimes felt her dreams were an inventory—a rolling check, like the memory check her computer performed each time on startup.

Her eyesight improved. In London she had been experiencing difficulty in adjusting focus between near and far; her eyes seemed to freeze and be reluctant to take in a changed context. Alice had put it down to normal aging, but back in Africa, that disappeared and her eyesight seemed crisp again. She felt quick and sharp and wide open to sensation.

"I can feel my body coming back to me," she said to him one afternoon as they walked. "Makes me realize I spend a lot of time treating it as a stranger. I once asked a psychiatrist how long would take me to get better. And he said, you don't get better, you get different. That may be the only privilege of depression. You get to meet another person within you. The one who isn't such a fuck up."

Alice had learnt that the person who graduates depression and its treatment can never be the same as the person who stood on the far bank of depression, seeking any possibility other than to cross. Depression and its treatment offer one of the few real opportunities for personal revolution. The personality renovation that sometimes comes with anti-depressants can be so profound that the patient has no basis of comparison between the two states—they are different people, and one is not welcome.

So Alice adapted to her medication like a convert takes religion in adulthood. She had bullied her doctor into perpetual prescriptions so that she was now one of the few non-institutionalized patients who had been medicated continuously for many years. Now that she had incidentally synchronized her medication withdrawal with so much other change in her life, there was no control group, and no scientist would have been able to tell her why she was feeling whatever she was feeling. And she *was* feeling.

On a still, close evening, Alice was watching the translucent geckos on the walls near the paraffin lamp in Simon's cottage, marveling that they could have come through the knock-out rounds of evolution so vulnerable.

Simon was massaging her neck; she winced when his thumb found the spot.

"You've got a lot of restriction just here," he said, "around C-6."

"I put my neck out being polite to Philip's boss. It comes back every time we have dinner with them. By the time I get to bed I can't move."

21

When Simon slipped on the rocks, his first reaction was to not believe it. Even the pain was briefly hypothetical.

It was late afternoon. They were collecting mussels for dinner—Alice wearing smelly old gloves and using a screwdriver to dislodge the big ones on the underside of overhangs below the waterline. Simon was mostly attending to her, coaching her, enjoying her enjoyment.

He had been hurrying, that was why. Not on his own account, because if Simon had been hurrying with only himself in mind he would never have slipped. But Alice had been trying to negotiate a short crevice and Simon had been in a hurry to get beyond her and hand her down.

Gravity. To the average person, such an unnoticed force. But Simon knew gravity intimately—it was one of the symphony of forces rolling through the plane a surfer occupies, the forces that adhered him to his board across angle and time, however improbable his kinetic circumstances appeared to be. That same force which held a simple altar to the precise same spot of a church floor for twelve hundred years had uplifted Simon and given him flight. Now it reached up with the unseen hand of a traitor and snatched him off the rocks.

In a vivid action replay, he saw himself gripping a rock corner with his left hand and putting his weight on it briefly as he swung his right leg through and down to a footing below. But the rock was slippery with spray, and his hand slipped and transferred excessive weight to his right.

The polio had affected Simon's right ankle and foot. Through years of surfing he had retrained and tested it until it could do things that ninety-nine out of a hundred normal people could never achieve. Although slightly deformed, Simon's right ankle was a star performer. But the unanticipated transfer of weight made his right foot skate off the rock when it came down. He grabbed at another rock, taking the skin off his palm, but that only created a slingshot effect.

People fall all the time and come to no harm. Babies survive the most amazing accidents. Football players cartwheel through the air after malign tackles, drunks fall out of windows and stumble away, cursing only the women that betrayed them.

Simon fell six or eight feet, at thirty-two feet per second squared, perhaps a bit slower given the resistance of the humid air, landing with the small of his back on a slight protrusion of rock. He retained a clear memory of his head snapping back. There was a moment of anticipating pain.

"Simon?"

Alice had thought he was behind and above her, waiting to come down the crevice after her; she hadn't realized he had tried to get around in front of her. Then she saw him leaning back against the rock in a silly way as though he was playacting being kept waiting by a woman. She grinned at him.

"Come on," she said, "let's go eat these mussels and have dirty sex."

Dom Marais showed up at the Cape Hamilton that afternoon after an absence of several weeks. He told them he had been in Durban, which they asked no more about, it being assumed that was a dagga wholesaling trip. Dom said to Clive that all the beers that night were on him, which they took to imply a successful wholesaling trip. They told him about the dead guy and the unhappy demise of Slipknot.

"Shit," said Dom, "Nothing happens here for five years, then I go away for two weeks and all hell breaks loose."

Then Alice came running off the beach. She was in apparent shock but gave a clear description and they all rushed out with her, except Dom, who set out in the direction of Mama's Bar.

The others were all standing over Simon when Dom arrived ten minutes later, carrying the back door of Mama's Bar under his arm. Simon had slipped into a sitting position, vomited down his shirt, and his head was hanging forward, but he was conscious.

No one was doing anything.

Dom put the door down next to Simon. "Let's move him onto this and get him home."

"You're not supposed to move people with back injuries," cried Alice.

The eyes Dom turned on her were absorbent. "That's in a situation where trained medical staff are on their way. That's not going to happen here."

It was obvious that the trip to the hospital over badly rutted roads would be more likely to damage than help someone in Simon's condition. So, after laying planks under the mattress to make it firmer, they settled him in his own bed. Woodstock was dispatched to Sammy's for medicines.

"Anti-inflammatories," said Alice. "Tell him I want ones with the package insert."

Clive said he would send some booze and food from the hotel. Johnny said he would knock up some rudimentary crutches in his workshop and bring them down. Simon himself was silent, other than to assure them he was sentient, whenever asked.

Dom led Alice outside. "Let's see what happens. If he gets worse, I want you to send for me, okay?"

She nodded, although without any understanding of what Dom might be able to do about it.

"I'll stay the night at the hotel and come by in the morning."

And he walked away, carrying the back door of Mama's Bar under his arm with no more effort than Simon carried a surfboard. When he reached Mama's, Dom screwed the door back onto its hinges, and then walked on to the hotel where he made several phone calls.

Woodstock returned. Sammy did not have anti-inflammatories, with or without a package insert. He had morphine in syringe vials but no sealed syringes, paracetamol and other tablets that he insisted were strong for pain but which were identified only by a long technical name that Alice did not recognize.

She gave Simon the paracetamol and sat in a chair next to the bed. She asked him to count to ten, and he could do that. She asked him to name some of his favorite songs, and he could do that, including some very old ones. He said he could feel her fingernail pressing into the palm of his hand. She traced her fingers on the backs of his big toes, and he said he could feel it.

That was all she could think of to do. He did not complain about the pain, although he avoided all movement and his face was pale and his skin clammy and he perspired in short bouts. He didn't look in danger, except that he didn't look in the slightest bit like Simon. He asked her to roll a joint and she did, and they shared it. She brought a wide necked bottle and held his penis so he could urinate into the bottle. That took time, and Simon winced during the process. They listened to the beginning of Bob's radio show, and Bob wished his friend Simon a quick recovery, and played half an hour of music in his honor, mostly Little Feat, which everyone knew Simon liked.

He couldn't sleep, although he didn't complain of pain.

"Tell me some more," he said.

She turned off all the lights and sat in a chair next to the bed so she could face him and hold his hand in hers. As she talked she felt the wind change on her shoulders, and wanted to ask him if he felt it too. Instead, she talked on.

22

"You should just forget everything from there," says Felicity, Alice's new surrogate mother. Felicity addresses Alice as an adult, probably because her own two sons are already more children than she can handle. Felicity is as thin as her filter-tipped cigarette. Alice watches them move through the day in syncopated harmony, Felicity and her cigarette.

"You start fresh here," says Felicity. "Some time will go by, things will start to seem better. You can stick with me, help me out. We'll be the girls together."

Thus was Alice incorporated into a family of cousins; it was a year since her mother had died, less than a month since her father died. She was eight years old. It had been deemed that Alice would do better in a household with other children, in a place less remote. Leaving her birth home in the big house overlooking the river and the lagoon at Port Victoria, she had traveled north in the Chevrolet beside her Uncle Robbie. They made a seven-hour trip up the east coast of Africa to her new home and her new family. Alice's late birth had muddled the generational structure of her family. Her cousin, Jerry, was twenty years older than she and he would become her father figure. Jerry was the son of one her mother's sisters. She had not seen him since the funeral, and not that much before. Jerry and Felicity had twin sons of their own, Jonathan and Greg, who were Alice's nephews, but a year older than she was.

Jerry worked for the sugar company as an overseer of labor. They lived in a modest company house on company land, and the company cane grew right up to the fence of their yard. When the cane was high it was like being in a lost camp in a jungle, and when the cane was cut, a new scenery of hills and homes and roads suddenly leapt in at the windows, gauzed like ancient oil paintings by the fine mesh of the fly screens.

"You're equal in the family with us here," said Jerry by way of a welcoming address. Spoken to as an adult, Alice was nevertheless there as a child, a waif. At that age, life was made up of days and nights; Alice would get by that way. Watching Felicity, Alice made a subliminal note not to emulate. Felicity's mouth was red. She was pretty but distracted in the manner of someone who has recently experienced a small violence and expects that it might recur. She sought quiet and order. Outside the kitchen window, the tall, densely planted green sugar cane rustled. Felicity was fastidious about the screen doors. Her house smelled of floor polish and fly spray—the floor polish applied by a servant, the fly spray by Felicity herself. She played a lot of long-playing records by British pop artists, which in that context suggested nostalgia for a life she never had. Dusty Springfield rolled out over the sugar cane as Felicity's thumbnail broke the foil seal on another pack of cigarettes. The heat was a factor in everything from food spoiling to divorce.

"You talk to me about anything you need to, okay?" Felicity said to Alice. "Don't be shy, we're the girls together in this house."

But Alice proved to be self-sufficient. She managed the world from a small core: her bedroom a sanctuary where everyone had to knock for entry. Jonathan and Greg were not to see her naked, that was Felicity's edict. There were fights, of course, but generally, her surrogate brothers were tolerant of her, if only because they were totally absorbed in the conflict between themselves. She befriended the household dog, a Rhodesian ridgeback acquired for security rather than love. Alice knew dogs from home and quickly bonded with that one; the dog slept in her room, under the open window. In the night, she lay awake listening to it breathing. Her relationship to the world was feral; she cautiously explored small sections of it. Where she found herself unchallenged, she took possession. Only slowly did she move on to append new territory to her safe zone. She occupied herself with chores for Felicity, and made herself agreeable, and the relatives who came to visit remarked upon how well she had adjusted. The relatives were especially considerate of her, and brought her presents to make her feel accepted. That was what made her feel different. But it was agreed that she was doing fine, all things considered. Concern turned to those demanding attention: the twins conducted life as though they had made a pact that only one of them would survive to adulthood. Through a six-year struggle for nest dominance, Jonathan and Greg pelted each other with food, dead creatures, dog shit, cricket wickets, clay lats, the weighty cast iron miniature cars of that time, and the peculiar slang of white South Africa.

"Don't just sit there with your thumb up your bum and your mind in neutral."

"Go pull your wire, you moegoe!"

Plus a variety of untranslatable retorts derived from Zulu and Afrikaans, all based around toilet activities, masturbation, and shortcomings in sexual performance and intelligence.

Jonathan and Greg tried to kill each other, and they taught Alice to kill as well, beginning with the blue-headed lizards, hiding in plain sight on the trunks of flat crown trees, trusting too much to the camouflage of their mottled skin on the blue-gray bark. Those, she killed with stones propelled from a slingshot, which Jerry cut from a tree branch and trimmed for her with a cane-cutting knife. They graduated to snakes, even the deadly green mamba, which must be stoned from a safe distance. Alice experienced a deep thrill at the killing of a snake she knew to be deadly.

Gradually she took possession of a wider landscape. Her eye came to know the contours of fields of deep green sugar cane stretching away to the horizon and the way the wind patterns on it dissolved and reformed. She came to know the distant sound of the mill running all night in the crushing season, the drone in the night heat and sickly smell of molasses mixed with the breeze from the Indian Ocean coming across the cane.

Feral. Everything about Alice was physical rather than intellectual. She had cheetah-like reflexes. She would destroy all comers at table tennis on the wide verandahs of the company houses. She had a congenital mistrust of contemplation. Not through dullness. Her view was that to think about it was to destroy its essence. Or at least that was how she expressed it much later. But her reluctance to think anything through may have been more appropriately located in Felicity's welcoming words to her.

"You should just forget about everything from there."

They moved house often as Jerry was promoted, always to another company house in the sugar cane, but larger and eventually more elegant houses. If Alice were to look at the photos of those days (which she never did) she would see tea cups and cricket bats and bicycles, hot Christmas lunches on wide verandahs in the middle of scorching mid-summer, the mantelpiece over the unused fireplace lined with cards showing snow scenes, which none of them had ever seen in real life. The colonial society was axiomatically one where social practices were maintained in a context where the forces that created those practices did not exist. Although that eventually broke the practice, it hardened it first. Where Alice grew, the English-speaking, British-derived people were in the hardened phase. All perceptions of quality and rank derived from an increasingly remote understanding of Englishness.

116

Felicity was described as highly strung. She sat and looked out of the window for hours, the smoke from her cigarette dispersed by the small noisy fan that was her only defense against the summer heat. She kept the house clean and her lipstick fresh.

"Let them kill each other there, I'm sure they know how to deal with that sort of thing," was Felicity's remark as Jonathan and Greg were packed off to boarding school. Alice saw Felicity sink into the new quiet of her own home.

Felicity was highly strung for a length of time spanning at least Alice's tenth birthday party (recalled because of the epileptic fit of her friend, Adele) and her seventeenth (recalled because Alice had sex with David Raw in the sugar cane and sliced the skin on the back of her arm painfully in the process). On the eve of both of those parties, Felicity had suffered a sudden unwellness, requiring Jerry to stand in. Jerry was not good with children. He considered his job well done if all of them were still able to walk at the end of a party.

On that sugar cane coast, heat and humidity shaped everyone. There were those, like Felicity, who were oppressed by it and became more and more confined, their days limited to nervous rituals about the house. After Jerry became a manager and they moved to one of the largest houses on the estate, Felicity seldom left the big quiet house, where any intrusion from the outside world was neatly bookended by the clatter of the screen door.

Alice was cared for, but not cherished. The life learning that passes between parent and child in incidental moments—this Alice missed. Practical lessons she got from Jerry who couldn't stand the howls of sibling rivalry coming from his two sons, so taught Alice instead to balance the tension in wheel nuts when changing a flat tire.

Alice's method became to act on impulse or not at all. Notions of play, idle curiosity, trial and error were unknown to her. She would launch herself at the main target without preamble. She often fell back, stunned, wounded. But she was often effective. Her life was full of short cuts, abrupt arrivals, lack of preparation, unfortunate timing, a flair for improvisation. Without ever thinking it consciously, she shaped her entire existence around assessing people for their usefulness and vulnerability to inducement.

Alice had a scar on her lower lip—a wound from a childhood incident she could not remember—which had not been stitched when it should have been because the doctor was a long drive away and the family had been preoccupied with a greater crisis that day. The scar made her lip slightly plump and drew attention. It enlarged her attractiveness. It made her worldly and it made her vulnerable. Realization of the power of these variables came to her incidentally, but she grasped them and turned them into tools. She realized that her lip was more than just a zone of altered sensation on an erotically symbolic surface.

When she was twelve, she had an encounter with the parent of another child who became embarrassed to talk about Alice's lip. Later, when Alice learned from the friend that it was because the parent mistakenly thought the wound had been inflicted by adult violence, Alice instantly comprehended the drama that lay behind things, and the power of that drama. Thus, Alice understood sexuality before she knew sex. She intuitively grasped the underlying power trade, and she knew that power lay in apparently giving it over, but in fact retaining it. At sixteen she was a knockout—good-looking and physically accomplished and all wised-up about the world. The deployment of her sex appeal for social advantage was a natural outcome and a skill at which she became awesome.

White families in the cane lands were of two classes:

landowners and mill employees. Alice grew up among, but not of, the sons and daughters of wealthy sugar farmers. The resentment was always there. The kids of the rich had a gloss, possibly the product of a selective gene pool, but also aided by the accoutrements of the rich, not just the clothes and cars, but the expectation of a good outcome. Exploiting them came naturally. Alice learned the power of her nakedness, the way a lioness knows the weight of its paw in cub discipline. She knew that her nakedness was a weapon, and like many weapons, awareness of its existence was as effective as use. Even when holstered in clothing, Alice's nakedness was the issue on the table in any exchange she had with men, or with women who might be affected by what Alice could do to men.

She learned to tell the needy boys the things they wanted to hear and, like hypnotism, it turned them all smug and slack and manageable. Her hands became skilled.

She left her home with Jerry and Felicity in the sugar on a decision that came to her on a day when the mill smell was particularly putrid and she had been playing her stereo loud and Felicity had asked her to turn it down. Life was rolling along out there in the world while she was sitting in the sugar cane, a life she might conceivably be good at. She had been a lodger in that house, it was that easy for her to go. She could see it hurt Jerry, kind Jerry, the ease with which she gave up the connection, so she spoke some words to comfort him. But those were words over her shoulder; she was already gone, accepting a ride down the coast to Durban where there was the promise of a mattress on the floor of a school friend's apartment. She was eighteen.

She lived in tight circumstances for a few years, but at the time it was almost impossible for a white person in this country not to progress. She was quick and good-looking and on the make. She moved from Durban to Johannesburg and spent two years living in a commune in the suburbs with other young people—working hard then running in a pack through clubs and parties, cars driven too fast and teeth chipped on the poolside at 3 a.m., volleyball on long lawns on Sunday afternoons.

Cared for but not cherished in her adolescent home, Alice did not cherish herself. She used her body as a tool. Her relationships with men always developed precipitously. She would draw them with the appearance of supplication. When the balance of power shifted to her, as it always did, she would thrust the relationship away. Alice's soul had been imprinted with the axiom that the search for love led inevitably to disenchantment, so she sought instead a place to put a lever into a personal arrangement.

That was the volatile young woman Philip first saw playing volleyball on the lawn of the house next to his office, when she was just a runner, and something in him marked her as different, even if only differently desirable.

Philip was from a social sophistication beyond hers. But Alice had plenty of resources. That first morning, she got out of his bed in the upstairs room of the production house, walked through to the en suite bedroom, peed, and left the urine unflushed in the bowl for him to smell when he woke. She was strong and quick and she imposed herself on him like a savage and then left him alone for weeks at a time, giving him time to dwell on whether her appetite for life could go unfed for that long.

Philip offered her the possibility to completely expunge the record of her childhood. She had no clear idea of why it was necessary to do so, she just found herself attracted to the possibility. In return she offered him the lure of emotional risk. They were married in a Devon village where Philip's parents lived. The church was the first Alice had ever entered.

23

"My uncle farmed black people. Like cattle."

The impact of that statement, which Alice made at a dinner party at Philip's boss's house, set the course for her new life.

They had been in London less than a year. A third of that had clipped by in the distraction of appointing a new life. Then her first northern winter came and Alice found herself aghast in a world where the gray sky lay on the roofs of houses for weeks at a time, and night came at four in the afternoon. And the rain. The rain Alice knew in Africa came in massive downpours that raised a din on iron roofs and created savage new watercourses until the cloud was spent or flung away by the wind, and then it would be sunny again. In London, rain did not fall. It hung in the air in a film, the better to defeat umbrellas.

Around Christmas, when the daylight was gone by 5 p.m., she fell into a malaise and wouldn't leave the house. Philip complained that the central heating was running too high and the house had a smell and Alice shouted that the house had a smell because smelly people had been living within those walls for several hundred years, an environment to which she was unaccustomed. She made excuses to avoid dinner invitations and cooked mashed potato four times a week.

"Comfort food," she said.

Philip asked how much comfort she needed and banged out of the house. For as Tango had foretold, Philip's turn in South Africa had made him a little famous. He was going up in television, which means indoors. On the studio set, Philip cast himself as a rugged intellectual with vivid field experience. At the peak of his powers, he felt compelled to get out and display himself. He loved dinner parties, situations where he would be encouraged to display worldly insight from his time of looking down the gun barrel of a revolution.

Around the dinner table at Philip's boss's house, couples paused over their Alaskan salmon and out-of-season airfreighted vegetables, lightly steamed and served in Spanish olive oil and the juice of Israeli lemons. They looked at Alice.

"He was a labor broker," said Alice. "His job was to recruit black men to work on the mines." She raised her hands and placed quotation marks in the air around the word "recruit."

"I lived in the same house. I saw it every day. They called it recruitment, but really, what he did was buy young men from the chief, just like cattle."

Good material, not her own, came to her mind. "In a sense, these guys were the true executives of apartheid. They corrupted the chiefs with financial inducement. They provided the masses for the migrant labor system, one of the absolute pillars of apartheid. My uncle. Just an ordinary guy. His father was from Sussex—not an Afrikaner, not a Boer, not some apartheid zealot. Just a guy making his way in the world. That's why apartheid became so powerful. It had financial incentives."

The other dinner guests fidgeted with their food: Alice's witness was too vivid. She could see Philip understood that—he was trained in providing a coated version of the real world.

"Alice left when she was eight," he said.

"When my father died."

"Alice's father was disabled in the war, so his family had to live with his brother."

"That's what made Alice such a brilliant editor when she came to INN," said Philip. "She'd seen the world behind the news. She had empathy. I believe it showed in her work."

Thus was Alice cast as a refugee of conscience in London. She quickly found herself collaborating with Philip in minute refinements to her personal history. Philip and Alice both knew that Alice had not had a political thought in her head when she walked into the offices of INN in Johannesburg to become a runner and then a videotape editor. Certainly, she had done excellent service in the creation of news items that told the story of the suppression and the revolution. Here in London, they both needed her to have credentials as the wife of a rising political commentator.

She became a spontaneous witness, someone who had something authentic to add, from personal experience, not the remote outlook of a foreign correspondent. She was an insider. That version of Alice reflected well on Philip. He had not been merely an objective reporter of moral sin in that Godforsaken land; he had by courage and example drawn to his flame that escaping, innocent moth and provided her the medium by which she could bear that witness.

Alice joined the library and borrowed books about the history of her own country. That enabled her to weave her personal memory and experience into a larger tapestry. She was asked to talk to local groups and Philip suggested she raise funds for the ANC, but she declined both of those.

It was true that she exaggerated some facets, told some lies, but we all do that as we make ourselves. Essentially, her evidence on the condition of her country was accurate, although it was not her own true story. This functional version of Alice was viable for two years, and she and Philip were happy. Then she had Julia, and the sea changed in her and about her.

"The thing about having a child," Alice said to Dr. Sweet, "is that you start seeing the whole world through her eyes. And you start to get these flashes from your own childhood that you'd completely forgotten, so you're hyperaware of how the most casual remark influences a child, and it becomes very difficult to—

you know—make choices for your child. Which you're obliged to do every day. Hundreds of them. I live in fear of the accumulation of small choices."

"You have postpartum depression," said Dr. Sweet. "It's very common."

"Julia's twenty months. It's not like I've just given birth!"

"That's not outside the diagnostic range. And you have no clinical symptoms that take us anywhere else. So why don't we give you a try on an anti-depressant, and just see?"

Alice declined the anti-depressant, as most people do when first invited to accept a diagnosis of themselves that is freighted with stigma. She resolved to get through it on her own, like a grown-up. She came at herself with logic. She had as a starting point the realization that in moving countries, she had lost an indefinable part of herself.

"You have no horizon here, no wilderness," she said to a mother in the playground, in answer to the perpetual question invoked by her accent. Landscape, as much as anything else, transformed her. Alice had grown up with a sky full of light and a far horizon. In London, she lived under a low gray sky and the horizon was the terrace row across the street from her window. She was seldom at rest, always conscious of the stream of hurrying people vacuumed by the mouth of the tube station. She thought a lot about what Julia was missing by growing up there instead of in Alice's own homeland.

In the anterooms of depression, many strange dances are performed. Dr. Sweet had said Alice lacked the clinical symptoms for an alternative diagnosis, so she developed them. Without reading a single textbook, she reproduced the symptoms of various diseases. A year went by as she tested for numerous possibilities ranging from brain tumor to liver dysfunction to heart disease. In expensive London clinics, they biopsied her swollen lymph glands (benign fatty tissue) and echogrammed her heart, while in laboratories, crews unknown to her labored over copious samples of her blood, urine, and stools. She was neither anemic, nor diabetic, nor many other things that corresponded with her symptoms. Her sense of dislocation and her inability to remember things were not the signs of aphasia or early-onset Alzheimer's. She had had Philip drive her to the Hammersmith Hospital casualty at three o'clock in the morning, waking a neighbor to watch Julia, convinced that any rational person in her state would believe themselves minutes from complete system collapse. And she had lain there for three hours as an efficient but increasingly brusque night staff returned regularly to record negative test results on the board beside her bed.

Dr. Sweet raised the subject again, and Alice finally capitulated to his diagnosis. Anti-depressants were among the most common medications in the developed world. Yet the effects and side effects of an anti-depressant were subject-specific, and doctors could do no more than try to establish that the treatment had been effective to a therapeutic level and that the side effects were managed; beyond that, each patient was on a unique journey, alone.

After a month on anti-depressant medication, Alice thought it was the greatest stuff ever.

"This is who I was actually meant to be," she said, causing Philip no little discomfort by becoming a vocal advocate of the drug. "They should put it in the water supply," she said.

Dr. Sweet's role in Alice's medical management was reduced to ensuring that she did not accumulate a stock of medication for suicide purposes, standard practice. Aside from that, he was happy to award her a perpetual prescription and file her under 'problem solved'.

And certainly, Alice would never again suffer from the depths of melancholy or the phantom dread disease symptoms. The medication clipped the tops and bottoms off her emotional graph. She cleaned the kitchen, the car, Julia's room and the lizard's cage. She bleached the kitchen towels and picked every last microscopic shred of lint from the tumble-dry filter. But that could not remove the source of disturbance.

She found herself awake at two in the morning, lying on the bed in the spare room, slick with regret and anxiety and in a state of mind where she judged herself unqualified for even the simplest role in daily life. She felt like a rejected transplant organ—she was not of the same tissue as this society. She remembered feeling this way as a teenager in the sugarcane. Her method of dealing with it then was to lie flat on her back in the hot bed in the dark room and call on God to simply reach down and switch her off.

"I don't have it," she would say then. "I don't have the means to carry out this life. I'm not getting better at it. Just remove me."

And she meant it, and in those days she still believed in God sort of, so it was a means of dealing with it. But many years later in London, Alice no longer believed that any God was going to give her problems a place in His schedule, and in any case, now that Julia was with her, the switch-off was no longer an option. She had to go through with the thing, by the rules, with a smile, because she could see Julia watching her every minute of the day with an unblinking stare, laying the foundation of her own personality on the model she saw in her mother.

Just once, she attended a depression support group meeting, to please Philip. During the tea break an older man, attractive but ruined, flirted with her like a teenager. When she rebuked him, he took no offence. "That's the great advantage of what we are. Once you accept the label, everything's okay. Personality for us comes down to which batch of chemicals is in charge."

Alice had come to anti-depressant medication at a time of great innovation. Every year something new became available. It became routine for doctors to cycle their patients through the options to find which one worked. By this method, Alice improved. Sometimes she thought of herself as someone who needed anti-depressants as others need reading glasses—a simple corrective. Or perhaps, she thought, she just became better at managing who and what she was. Or both.

Alice became methodical and swam many lengths of the health club pool and had Julia's friends to tea. She trained the flat accent right out of her mouth. She completed a three year correspondence degree through the Open University. She became an enthusiastic, even overbearing, member of the spinning classes at her health club.

Slowly, Alice trained herself to be the person who was required to shut certain doors forever. It made her think that suburban parents were domesticated in much the same way as animals.

24

Waking, the first thing she was aware of was the sound of the surf and for a moment there was pleasure in that. Then she realized the bed was wet. She twisted around to look at Simon. His eyes were open but he wasn't looking at the surf, or at her.

"Simon?" she said.

"I can't move," he said.

She took off in his Jeep for the hotel, but just a hundred yards up the track she came across Dom, walking towards her.

"He's worse," she said. "It's bad. He can't move."

"Is he aware of what's going on?"

"He talked to me, but he's not right. He peed the bed and I don't think he even knows it."

Dom told her to go back to the house and stay with Simon. He got into the Jeep and drove away.

The helicopter turned inland off the sea and flew almost straight over Simon's house. By that time, Dom, Clive, Johnny and Alice had carried Simon up the track from his house to the nearest piece of open level ground, near the village huts. The helicopter dropped down towards them in a tightening circle. Dom had anticipated the effect of this arrival, and had stationed Johnny and Clive on opposite sides of the level ground. Alice had the impression that the helicopter blades sucked people out of the huts and nearby fields. Barefoot kids laughed and scampered in the squall of dust, twigs and plastic bags that blew up as the large machine settled onto the ground.

The medic gave Simon an injection and they strapped him to a stretcher that slid into a bracket inside the helicopter.

Dom took Alice aside. "I'm going to ride up with him, make sure he gets the right people and all that. Okay? I'll handle it. You hold on here till you hear from me."

She nodded. He squeezed her hand and then turned and vaulted up beside the stretcher. The helicopter shook itself to life again, jerked into the air and veered away at an abrupt angle over the ocean. The village children danced. Johnny came up next to Alice as she watched the aircraft shrink in the sky.

He touched her on the arm. "Come on."

She walked away with the men.

PART THREE

25

"Is this Magistrate Mkhize?" said the voice on the phone, the voice of a young white woman.

Mendi, sitting in his stuffy office in the capital, had his mind on lunch and his eye on two young secretaries who were eating their sandwiches in the courtyard outside his window. His curt "Yes" did not encourage a prolonged conversation.

"This is Ursula Wolfe, of the *Daily Chronicle* in Johannesburg. I'm phoning about the inquiry into the death of Martin de Villiers."

"Never heard of him," said Mendi. "You've got the wrong person."

"They just put me through to you because they said you were in charge. The man who was found at Port Victoria."

"That man has not been identified."

"Not formally," said the Ursula Wolfe voice, "but my contacts tell me it's definitely Martin de Villiers. So it's going to be quite a story, and my news editor wants to carry something in tonight's paper. Have you determined whether it was accident or foul play yet?"

In Mendi's clinical opinion, this reporter was sexy. She had a sexy voice. And her impudence was provocative—or would have been if directed at anyone but Mendi.

"Phone me back in ten minutes," said Mendi, pressing hard on the voice of authority.

"I'd really like to get a jump on the other media, so if you can give me something exclusive I'd really appreciate it," said the voice.

"Yes, yes."

"And if there's any mystery, you know what I mean," continued the voice, "my editor says I can come down there and get a color piece. Around you and your investigation."

"We'll discuss all that when you phone me back," and Mendi hung up on her, just to make sure she understood who was in charge.

Mendi gathered his thoughts and then uttered a profanity. He had forgotten all about the naked white man. His recent sojourn in Port Victoria had become, in Mendi's mind, all about and only about, the discovery of Slipknot van den Heever and his unavoidable death while resisting arrest on a charge of attempting to subvert the liquor licensing statute of 1948. As a news item in the media, Slipknot's death had warranted little attention. In a country where stories of past brutalities know no bounds, the death of a retired brutalizer warranted only one day's media attention. But as a legend, the termination of Slipknot had radiated through the wide community of people tied forever to the gallows of apartheid. And through that, a certain glory had come to Mendi, who had been sent, almost by divine intervention, to the hairy backside of the country to pry the tick loose from his hiding place and squash him. His phone had been ringing. Party elders and political leaders wanted to hear for themselves the story of the hated Slipknot's undignified death. It turned out that Slipknot van den Heever had pissed himself in his death spasm— just like so many condemned men had pissed themselves in his gallows. That was how the legend was written, Mendi had seen to it.

Mendi strode down the corridor and into the general office where sundry prosecutors, policemen, secretaries, clerks and people who made tea were killing time until the lunch break.

"Who the fuck is Martin de Villiers?" he demanded, "and why wasn't I told that the white guy from Port Victoria had been identified?

"So he was what, exactly?" said Johnny, his face creased with concentration. He was installing a new gas canister for Clive behind the kitchen of the Cape Hamilton.

"A TV oke, apparently," said Clive. "Like a journalist, but only on TV. One of those guys who has a haircut once a week."

"Gooi us another beer."

Clive sent the can of Castle on a slow arc through the air, and Johnny caught it and popped it and let it foam over his wrist briefly before he tipped it into his mouth. It was a breezeless day. Johnny had fished early and successfully, and left Woodstock with instructions to scrape down every rust spot he could find on the boat and prepare it for painting.

"So the magistrate is coming back?"

Clive nodded. "That's why he phoned."

"So he's going to be pissing about here. What's he going to

find out that he didn't find out before?"

"Probably fuck all."

"Probably definitely fuck all."

"What's the guy's name again?"

"Martin de Villiers."

"Never heard of him."

"I asked Sammy to bring a newspaper from town. Apparently there's a big article about this guy."

Woodstock did not scrape the rust off the boat. It was too hot. He allowed a judicious hour to go by, filling the time by giving himself electric shocks from the 12-volt batteries in the boat. In the army, Woodstock had heard of army servicemen who went crazy in the bush war—"bosbefokked" was the non-technical phrase—being treated with electric shock therapy. He had immediately been attracted to the idea, although his own military service had been one hundred percent combat free. Woodstock found the jarring snap of DC current into his body exciting in the moment and calming in the afterglow. He saw it as a way of going to the doctor without going to the doctor. After an hour or so, Woodstock set off to join Johnny at the hotel. Johnny would ask whether he had done the rust and Woodstock would say he had and it would be tomorrow's problem.

At the hotel, Woodstock joined Johnny, Clive and Bob, who were already drinking. Crushed beer cans that had missed the drum in the corner were lying on the paving around it. Clive handed Woodstock a beer without him asking for it, and marked it in the book. Woodstock's bar and food bill came directly off his salary from Johnny.

"So how the fuck did such an oke end up dead here?" asked Woodstock, when they told him the news.

"Maybe he fell off a fishing boat."

"Johnny fell off a fishing boat, but he's still sitting here," said Woodstock.

It was intended as filial regard, but the precise image inflamed Johnny.

"I didn't *fall* off any fuckin' boat, you little cunt!" Johnny growled. "This ocean here, right here—this particular bit of it is one of the most dangerous currents in the world. It's been in National Geographic. My boat was capsized by a massive freak wave, and if you'd been on it you'd be fish food now."

Bob raised both hands in the air. "I'm sure Woodstock means that despite being capsized in rough seas, you survived, whereas this journalist pussy died just from falling off in a dead calm sea."

"Yeah, well, he's a liberal, it's different."

"Probably a vegetarian."

"Fucken homos," added Woodstock.

"Whatever he was, he wasn't a homo," said Clive, who had by then read the long article Ursula Wolfe had written. The newspaper had feted the dead man because he was one of their own. Martin de Villiers, 48, a graduate of Wits University (MA, Political Science) was eulogized as an Afrikaner who had deserted his origins to become active in the National Union of South African Students, a fully-fledged white liberal from the age of twenty, with a fat file in the Bureau of State Security before he even started his first job as a journalist with the *Rand Daily Mail*.

He had risen quickly through the ranks but never became editor; he was much too slick to gain approval from the sort of people who served on the boards of directors of the conservative mining companies that controlled English newspapers. Instead, Martin de Villiers went solo, made himself conspicuous. Good-looking, articulate and judiciously iconoclastic, he became a standard choice for the overseas news media on the rare occasions when they wanted to show the world that not all South

African whites came off the same production run.

After Nelson Mandela was released and the country started to gather momentum toward pell-mell change, Martin de Villiers deftly re-engineered himself as a socioeconomic forecaster. He provided good sound bites and never failed to remind folk that, as a crusading journalist who had fought apartheid, he had met and interviewed many of the leaders of the struggle, some of whom were currently in top positions, and some buried in the land they had freed.

He won himself a TV show on the renovated state television where he displayed to the nation a serviceable knowledge of the social landscape, plus a good tan, quick wit, smart clothes, excellent teeth, and a flashy Rolex. His was an image known across the country, and if he had washed up on any other beach in the country he would have been soon identified. But not in Port Victoria, and not by Mendi Mkhize, who had a pervasive antipathy to white liberals. Like chickens, they all looked the same to him and were about as interesting.

"I still don't get it," said Clive after they all read the article and conveyed its contents to Woodstock, who had a difficulty with print. "What was he doing here? Why didn't his family or whatever know he was here? Why did no one see him before he turned up dead?"

"Who knows."

"So chuck us another beer, Clive."

26

Clive Gilman had little ambition in life, in fact was quite surprised to have ended up owning a hotel—even such a forlorn hotel as the Cape Hamilton. But Clive could generate some enthusiasm for easy money and easy money was what came to mind when the only telephone in Port Victoria started to ring every twenty minutes. First Mendi Mkhize called and booked five rooms to provide for an as yet unspecified entourage. Soon after, Ursula Wolfe phoned to book rooms for herself and a photographer. The next day, someone booked accommodations for a three-man television news crew, and asked lots of complicated questions about electrical and communications facilities.

Clive called a meeting of the leaders of commerce in Port Victoria. "This is a chance to make some chunky money," he said. "They'll all have expense accounts."

His audience—Johnny Fourie, Mama Xhosa, Sammy, Woodstock, even Bob Peace—didn't really seem to be grasping the bonanza at hand. Clive realized he would have to come up with something more in line with their experience.

"Think of it like the sardine run," he said. Their faces lit up. This was a metaphor they understood.

Once a year, at the beginning of winter, the southeast coast of Africa hosts a spectacular natural event. The prevailing current here is the Mozambique, a warm flow from the equator, which powers southward at some eight miles an hour. But with the onset of winter, cold winds and cold water in the south conspire to create a northward countercurrent very close to the coast. That current is rich in nutrients and plankton, and draws with it feeding and newly spawned sardines in spectacular volumes. Individual shoals of sardines in the current have been known to reach nine miles long, more than a mile wide, and fifty yards deep—a biomass feeding opportunity that attracts sharks, seals, seabirds, skates, rays, the lot. They eat the sardines and they eat each other all the way up the food chain, even to old men who stagger into the shallow surf with leaky buckets and scoop up sardines fatigued and disorientated by continuous attacks from game fish and diving birds.

That was the image that came to mind when Clive said "sardine run" to his fellow entrepreneurs.

"But how do we get them to spend?" asked Johnny. "These are city types. What do we have that they want?"

"That's right," said Sammy. "What will I sell them? They'll bring their own suntan lotion."

"They're going to want clean table cloths," grumbled Mama. "And I got my two sixteen-year-old nieces working for me now. Those girls are ripening by the day. The local men know that if they try anything I'll put poison in their food. But men from the big city? They think God put village girls on earth for their enjoyment. Journalists from Johannesburg? Shit, there could be havoc."

Bob Peace, who had so far sat in the corner, silent in a wreath of dagga smoke, came to life. "If I might make a suggestion. You folks have got to change the paradigm."

"Don't talk Californian here, Bob," Johnny said irritably.

"You've got to think of this thing in a whole different way," continued Bob. "Take charge of the situation and turn it to your advantage. Now, these people are coming to a place they know nothing about. You think they'll see it as a dirty little village. And, if you let them, they will. But you can change that. Have you ever been to Disneyland? Behind all the crap, it's just a fun fair driven by engines and gears. The rest is perception."

"What the fuck is he talking about?" said Woodstock.

"Search me," said Johnny. "I think the dagga finally took over Bob's brain."

But Clive and Sammy were on the same wavelength. Bob got up, walked around and put his hands on Johnny's shoulders.

"Who is this man?" asked Bob.

"Shit, Johnny, watch out," said Woodstock.

"No, this is not the Johnny you know," said Bob. "This is the man who killed one hundred and thirty sharks last year. This is the man who survived in the sea for fifteen hours when his boat was capsized by a freak wave as high as a gum tree and then walked out of the surf. This man is a local legend. That's who the journalists want to meet and who they want to go fishing with, and they'll pay good money for it. Now, that Ladies' Bar of yours, Clive, is that not where the infamous Slipknot van Den Heever was shot dead? Yes! Okay, that spot, that spot where he fell, that should be a shrine to democracy in this country, and journalists should have to pay to see it! Mama—your restaurant on the beach? Forget clean tablecloths, this is an authentic African eating place for locals. You tell the journalists you don't want them there, and they will offer you more to get in and sit in the corner, and they will beg you to bring them the food of this area and serve them just like anyone else.

Bob raised his arm and pointed. "That bay out there. That is where the world's great surfers come and where one of the living legends of surfing, Simon, surfed until his tragic injury earlier this year."

"And the wreck!" said Woodstock.

"Now you're talking," said Clive, suddenly getting it, and Woodstock seemed so astonished to receive what he believed to be a direct compliment on his intelligence from Johnny that he glowed.

"Right!" said Bob. "The wrecks. This coastline is dotted with the wrecks of the Portuguese and whoever and there's unknown treasure out there."

"In fact," said Clive, "we are only living here because we are planning to get the gold off that wreck in the bay."

Sammy shook his head. "I don't think they'll believe that."

"Journalists?" Bob smirked. "They believe bullshit. That's

137

what they're here for. But it's up to you to make a legend for this place."

"This is brilliant," said Clive.

"What about Dom Marais?" said Woodstock, boiling with the need to top his earlier effort.

"What about him?" said Clive.

"You know, the dagga, he's the biggest producer in this—"

"Whoa!" said Johnny.

Bob was shaking his head. "Don't go there, Woodstock."

"But it's true!" said Woodstock.

"Stick with the bullshit. It's safer."

As the meeting broke up, Woodstock headed for the toilet. The heavy ceramic fittings were 1930s vintage, of the type much coveted for retrofitting trendy city restaurants. Hygiene was not a big factor in the Cape Hamilton Hotel. Clive's method with the urinal was to leave it to get smelly, then throw in blocks of pungent purple slow-release disinfectant, and then sluice the whole place down with buckets of bleach and Dettol once a month or so. In the interim, it held an aroma of combined human and chemical components that could knock a sensitive person to the ground.

Using both hands, Woodstock fished laboriously in his pants and duly produced a partially tumescent organ of startling dimensions. In his ironic way, God had blessed Woodstock with an organ that his personality seldom gave him the chance to put to use. At least, not in company.

"Careful with that thing, Woodstock," said Bob from behind him.

Woodstock jumped. The others had entered the toilet en masse; much beer had accompanied discussion of the coming invasion.

"Put it away, Woodstock," chuckled Bob. "Give the poor thing some peace. I saw you pulling your wire in the bushes when you were watching the English chick in her cossie on the beach."

Woodstock went scarlet and shuffled closer to the urinal, head down. "I wasn't pulling my wire! I was winding my watch. It's one of those that winds itself with movement."

"Bullshit, that woman gives you the root, it's okay, you can admit it."

Woodstock couldn't pee. Embarrassment, self-loathing, loathing of the woman washed over him. Memories of his stepbrother, of all the men who had taunted him, washed around him in the stink of the room.

"Piss or get off the pot, Woodstock," said Johnny, "or I'll be forced to piss on your shoes."

Woodstock didn't comprehend his own state of mind sufficiently to explain to himself, let alone the others, how the woman aroused him, but he knew it was not in any way they were thinking of.

"That fucking bitch does nothing for me!" he said.

"Hey, Woodstock. Come on. Use it or abuse it."

"Christ, no, he abuses it enough."

"Oh, yeah," said Woodstock, "I'll use it okay. I'm going to naai that English chick, north and south, and then you'll have to listen to me tell you about it."

"Difficult to tell who'll suffer more, her or us," said Clive.

"Woodstock, you fucken idiot, you just told us the woman does not turn you on," said Johnny.

"I'm not going to naai her because I want to. I'm going to naai her because she deserves it."

Woodstock walked out of the toilet, out of the hotel and into the night. He relieved himself onto the beach sand, and then walked home.

Walking back up the hill after the meeting, Johnny was trying to get his drunk mind to focus. He liked the ideas that had come up at the meeting, and he could see there might be some fun and money in prospect, but Johnny had a problem he couldn't solve.

That morning, he had been sitting on the boat on the trailer, hooked to the truck, waiting for the tide to turn and give him the surf conditions he liked for going out through the breakers. He could take the boat out in just about any condition, and often did. By synchronizing applications and withdrawals of power on the twin outboards, he could switch the boat through any pattern of breakers and leap the foaming obstacles out into the benign swell beyond the point. Some who went with him swore they would never go again, but in most cases that suited Johnny fine. A bit of breaker racing was a good way of filtering unsuitable fishing companions.

But this morning, Johnny had felt uncharacteristically mellow and decided to sit and contemplate the surf for a while. So he sent Woodstock back to the house on an errand and enjoyed a quiet five minutes watching the cycle of slate grays and blues on the surface of the water that preceded sunrise. Then he heard something in the dune bush behind him. He turned and saw there, within the framework of the deep, dense green bush, Breakdown's face. It was visible for a moment, like a rogue frame inserted into a film, and then gone. But in that moment, he saw in Breakdown's expression, a judgment upon himself. Indeed, the momentary frame could have been Moses, not that Johnny was religious, but he was a seaman, and did believe in something bigger than humanity, he just hadn't thought much about what it might be.

He had an urge to call after Breakdown, to stop him and speak to him, and explain how sorry he was for his part in the deceit that had led to Breakdown being held captive, but the thing about Breakdown was you couldn't communicate with him, and shouting after him would quite probably be misinterpreted as anger or dismissal; Johnny wanted to avoid any such misinterpretation.

Woodstock returned then and the moment was gone, but it was lodged firmly in Johnny's mind. There was the possibility of a wrathful visitation from Breakdown which, if it occurred before an audience of the expected media, could be very embarrassing. And yet, walking home in the dark, Johnny found himself more concerned that he might *not* get a public judgment from Breakdown; that Breakdown considered Johnny's transgression to be so far beyond redemption that wrath would be wasted on him.

Johnny had never held himself to any moral standard in the past, which was why he had ended up here with all the other discards and refugees. But on the subject of Breakdown's arrest, Johnny felt bad in a way he had never experienced before. And on top of that, the troublesome magistrate was returning.

27

The day after Simon was evacuated, there was a message from Dom via Clive's phone: Simon was stable, longer term assessments were being made. Alice slept in Simon's bed without him. She fed the cats, who eyed her suspiciously, doubtlessly linking the absence of Simon, whom they loved, with her presence, which they resented. Alice's brain kept rejecting images of Simon in a hospital bed. The Simon she knew moved his body from one position to the next like his cats, projecting his center of gravity along the most efficient route without flourish.

Simon's removal had the effect of restating a question Alice had pushed out of her mind for several days: What was she doing here?

Ostensibly, she was here because her Uncle Robbie had died some three months earlier and quite unexpectedly bequeathed her the house on the hill overlooking Port Victoria. Truthfully, the death had not meant a lot to her, so much time had passed since she had fled her childhood. The house meant little more. But she had seized on the excuse for a trip away from her life in London. At that moment, it felt to her if that excuse for a break had not dropped out of the sky, she might have gone mad. For in recent months Alice's balancing act, stable for several years under the benign influence of anti-depressants, had begun to collapse.

The version of herself that she had acquiesced in for the sake of Philip's position was not stable. Social occasions invariably presented a problem. A year previously, Alice found herself again at the end of a long evening with an empty wine glass and a booking for a hangover and no escape route. As ever, the discussion was the competition for places at the elite private schools, and the ruthlessness of the selection process, and the horror of rejection and failure for both child and parents. The opportunities for one-upmanship were endless.

"It's the anxiety," confessed one.

"I never had that," said another. "I always knew my kids were bright."

"That must be very gratifying for you, you know, considering *you're* not." Alice heard herself say these words, and realized that she had been uttering such things to herself for a long while, as a distraction from the world she had found herself in: an internal satire on the prattle while she swayed there with a rictus smile. But that time the words formed into sound and slipped out of her mouth, like witnesses who would no longer be intimidated.

Of all the facial expressions that resulted, she would

remember only Philip's. It was that of a man handicapped in life by a difficult wife. It gave her a bodily surge that carried her out of the house and to the car and gave her strength to flail against him for the duration of the drive.

"Why do you care more about them than me?" she demanded.

He said nothing.

"It's because you so desperately want to fit in with these people."

He said, "Everyone makes an effort, that's how it works. You've just never got over feeling like an outsider."

"Thank God I'm an outsider. Look at these people, Philip, just really look at them—not at their money and their postcode and their job description. They don't live in real life. They actually talk about air miles. They have no life, only plans about life, fear about life, contingency plans for maintaining standards of life, security. They are tourists in life. Life must have a logo and a little pink umbrella in it for them, and a note at the bottom about who they can complain to if it isn't what they ordered."

Philip endured it. That was his great strength. He was not the most brilliant foreign correspondent or TV anchorman, but he knew how to survive the game. That embarrassing occasion could be put aside because it occurred with minor acquaintances. The one that could not be put aside came later with Philip's colleagues, people with the power to determine his future.

More than ten years had passed since Alice had settled in London. On any given day, it was home to her. Her daughter's accent was posh London private school. In those ten years, Philip had risen but not as fast as some. He never said it, but his way of not saying it suggested to Alice that he felt her depression was the weight stopping them from rising further.

There came a dinner party with a couple they had first met soon after they were married and who had since risen higher. It was necessary for the Risen Wife to make note of this.

"I always remember that thing you said the night we met you," proclaimed the Risen Wife. "*My uncle farmed black people*, you said. It was so refreshingly honest."

When Alice cut her off, there was the flatness of the South African accent. "I'm sorry, I don't understand. How is this unusual to you? You do it every day. You think your relationship with the Polish woman who comes to clean your house is any different? She fights her way to this country against the obstacles of a jingoistic immigration control, language and strangeness, she rolls up at your door and washes your toilet and you pay her an amount that is irrelevant to you but vital to her. In six months or a year when the immigration people turn her out, she will go home to a life of poverty and you'll get a duplicate to fill her place. The rich farm the poor."

That time Philip apologized for her in front of her.

28

Alice had made, as far as she could recall, five visits to her aunts since the first day when they refused her entry. On each occasion, she had gone up with the intention of getting the answer to a certain question, and on each occasion she had returned without asking it. It was a game they played better than she did. She sensed they knew the question, had no intention of answering it, and indeed had spent long lifetimes perfecting not answering it. Distractions, apparently legitimate, often intervened; the aunts' lives were frequently upset by the small events that played havoc with old people.

Once when Alice arrived, they were absorbed in stripping and cleaning the revolver. The previous day, Phyllis had tried to discharge the weapon at a dog rooting in the rubbish bins, but the trigger was stiff and her arthritic fingers pulled the barrel off target. Her shot ricocheted off the cast iron of the slow combustion stove and buried itself in the kitchen door. Failing to make a case that the weapon was more danger than defense, Alice had helped them service it, and even fired off a few test shots herself.

On another occasion, she had arrived to find Johnny working on their ancient Morris Oxford car with the two aunts at separate ends of the house, refusing to speak to each other. That vehicle had only fifteen thousand miles on the clock, almost all of which had been logged on the two-mile journey to Sammy's and back over the latter decades of the twentieth century. The car was garaged beside the house and the space between the house and the hedge was narrow for thirty yards or so, requiring some careful reversing work. The aunts accomplished this with Phyllis behind the wheel, maintaining 4,500 revs and slipping the clutch while taking guidance from Abigail, who waved her arms in the air to assist her sister in keeping a straight course. Over the years, the clutch had become stiffer and Phyllis's muscles had become older, so maintaining a steady crawl speed at 4,500 rpm was becoming more and more trying. On that day, Phyllis allowed her pressure on the clutch to waver, and the car bolted back five feet before stalling stone dead. In the last two inches of that movement, it found Abigail. If she had been a step closer her hip would surely have been shattered, but she was simply popped onto her backside like a toy.

"You hit me with the car!"

"I did no such thing!"

"You've probably broken my hip."

"Nonsense. Get up, you look like Little Miss Muffet sitting there."

They were both in shock. When Alice interviewed Johnny, he said, "There's nothing wrong with the car. The driver could do with an overhaul."

"There's no need to be personal," said Alice.

"Or I could just tell you I put in a new clutch and charge you five hundred rands," he retorted and walked away to his truck.

Now, with Simon gone and her sabbatical from London life expiring rapidly, Alice arrived at the house with a resolution to get things settled.

"I've decided what I'm going to do with the house," said Alice.

It was gratifying insofar as for the first time since she'd been there, she felt she had the jump on them. They watched her silently.

"I'm going to ask you a question. If you give me the answer, I'll leave here and you can live in this house for as long as you live, and I'll not disturb you. If you don't answer it, I will have the house sold, and you'll have to make arrangements to find an old age home or something."

The double act sprang into action.

"Where are we going to find an old age home?"

"There's nothing for hundreds of miles!"

"We'd have to go to the city!"

"That's right," said Alice. "It would be very inconvenient for you to leave here. Very emotionally stressful. And you would find an old age home very difficult. They have to have strict routines there. No gin, I shouldn't think."

"This is just like you!"

"Why are you doing this to a couple of old people?"

"I'm doing it," said Alice, "for the simple reason that you will not tell me what I want to know unless I force you to."

"Don't be ridiculous. Do you think we're hiding something from you?"

"We couldn't hide anything from you. You thought you knew it all when you were still a teenager."

"Tell me," said Alice, "why Robbie left me this house in his will."

Abigail snapped, "You asked us that already."

"And you didn't answer me."

"Yes, we did."

"We'd like to know ourselves."

"You tell us! You're the one he left it to!"

Alice patiently remained silent during a prolonged volley of denials, ending with Phyllis saying, "We can't answer your question, because he didn't tell us, and now you can stop threatening two old ladies in this manner."

Alice had been rehearsing the calm she would maintain during all this.

"I didn't say that he told you. I'm saying you know. I never saw him from the day I left Jerry's when I was seventeen. I spoke to him about five times in those years, and not at all for the last ten years. Then he leaves me his house. You two lived here with him since after World War Two. You know why he did it, and I don't. It's as simple as that."

She eyed them each in turn, confirming her determination. Phyllis stood up. If Alice needed confirmation that she had put her finger on the key sentence in the legend of her family, it came with Phyllis's trembling hand and her refusal to meet Alice's eye.

Phyllis set sail for the kitchen. "I'm not going to put up with this," she said. "I'm going to carve the chicken."

Abigail regarded Alice with a steady eye across her heavy gin glass. "You've upset her terribly. She can't take this sort of thing. It's cruel of you to threaten us like this."

"It's cruel of you to treat me like this."

"How do we treat you? We treat you perfectly well. You were

147

always like this."

"What am I like? What was I like? Tell me."

Here we are, Alice thought. Four decades had come to this room, this day.

"Ungrateful."

"Explain to me what I have to be grateful for."

"You know. People looked after you. Your mother's problems. Then she died and your father died. You always had a home."

"I'm a kid and my family looks after me. Why is this extraordinary?"

Alice could hear Phyllis in the kitchen, mowing through the inevitably over-cooked chicken with the electric carving knife. That implement had been purchased in Umtata by Sammy after Robbie's hands had become too unsteady to carve the roast chickens and beef joints and legs of lamb, and put him in danger of self-amputation.

"Tell me what my mother's problems were."

"You know very well..."

"Actually, I know nothing about it at all, not one shred," said Alice, and as she said it, she realized that, too, was one of the central ignorances in her life.

"And you needed looking after," Abigail pushed on. "And Jerry took you in and they gave you a family with kids your own age in a place where you could go to school, and Robbie sent money that was spent only on you, and you just ran off."

"You know what I hear? I hear a lot about family, and about home, and about what I should be grateful for. I'm missing one word here. You know what it is?"

Abigail may have known. But at that moment, there was a loud report from the kitchen, the sound of a gunshot. Abigail rose from her chair with uncommon agility.

"There! Now you see what you've done! She's shot herself,

too! May the Lord have mercy on you."

But they found Phyllis on her feet in the kitchen, completely frozen over the remains of the chicken, with the electric carving knife blackened and smoking in her hand.

"You're the cause of this!" Abigail was attending to Phyllis, but shouting at Alice.

They detached Phyllis from the burnt out appliance and sat her in a chair. Her face was flushed, but that could have been the gin. Alice pulled the plug of the carving knife out of the wall socket.

"What happened?" said Abigail, massaging her old sister's hands between her own.

"She's sliced through the power cord of the machine," said Alice. "Because you don't have proper fuses in this house—"

"Oh, excuse me, it's your house, maybe you should put in proper fuses!"

"I just looked up from what I was doing," said Phyllis. "I thought I heard you calling..."

"If you wanted to hear what we were saying," said Alice, "you should have just stayed in the room."

"Get out!" shouted Abigail. "Get out of this house!"

"You can't kick her out," said Phyllis in a theatrical drone. "It's her house. She's the one trying to kick us out."

But Alice left anyway, without supper. She knew she should have stayed to calm the two old women and see that they got themselves to bed without heart attacks. But she was in little condition to care for others. Walking away from the house, down the hill in the dark, Alice was reeling in memory unearthed. The sound like a gunshot in that house had instantly found resonance in her memory. Alice saw herself running out onto the verandah and falling down the stairs when the gunshot came. She had cut her lip.

149

Heading back to the Cape Hamilton in the dark, Alice walked fast, stumbling and sometimes blundering against overhanging branches, but she kept moving. Away from the house and the glare of memory.

29

"Who the fuck is Tradition Dube?" said Bob as he walked onto the verandah of the hotel at midday. Clive was hunched over an old manual typewriter, retyping menus with a fifty percent price increase. Johnny was keeping him company with a beer, waiting for low tide before going out to catch extra fish for Clive's freezer.

"You've also had a visit from the magistrate," said Clive with a grin.

"He arrived at the studio last night. Scared the shit out of me. I've got like five kilograms of dope hidden in that place, behind the soundproof boards, everywhere. I don't even know where all of it is. But he was chill. All he asked was if I knew this guy Tradition Dube. I thought he was talking about a recording artist. I said what label is he on? Who is he?"

"Never heard of him," said Clive. "He asked us, too. No one has."

"Maybe I was high," said Bob, "but the magistrate seems to be a lot more chill."

"Yeah, I noticed that, too," said Clive. "He was actually polite to me when he checked in yesterday."

"Why's he here?" asked Johnny.

Clive shrugged. "Further investigation, is all he would say. But he's brought a hunting party."

Mendi Mkhize had returned to the Cape Hamilton Hotel,

accompanied by Detective Henry Dhlomo of the murder squad and three officers trained in special weapons and tactics.

The telephone call from the journalist about the identity of Martin de Villiers had re-engaged Mendi's interest in the events at Port Victoria. There was something off about the whole story and he was determined to know what it was. For his part, Detective Dhlomo's success rate on investigations was not good and his enthusiasm for his job somewhat less than his enthusiasm for a cold beer at midday. Mendi had chosen him for those very reasons. Detective Dhlomo had surrendered command of the investigation without complaint and happily led the SWAT team in making enquiries at all the informal dwellings in the hills around Port Victoria.

Mendi was way out of line, and well aware of it. The death of Martin de Villiers might in due course prove to be a Crime Against a Tourist and worthy of note in the Commission's deliberations, but the investigation of the death per se fell into Detective Dhlomo's domain. Mendi had no real role there. He had even less justification for a SWAT team. But he also knew he'd get away with it. Mendi's stature in the party had risen since the unregretted demise of Zacharias "Slipknot" van den Heever. Daily, Mendi was receiving faxes about serving on new committees and advising on new issues. He felt a whole lot better about the world.

Meanwhile, police investigators in Johannesburg had been interviewing people who knew the deceased in an effort to understand what he was doing in Port Victoria, and who might have wanted him dead.

With the dissolution of his second marriage, Martin de Villiers had learned that, in his case, commitment was a passion killer. No sooner did he marry a woman than she appeared to be transformed overnight into a sexless frump. Moreover, his wives

151

were less enthralled by *him* after they married him. After his second divorce, Martin took a practical approach and kept his affairs with women brief and unconvoluted. He quickly found he was good at that: good at targeting suitable candidates, and good at presenting to them a version of himself they found attractive. That version was, in his forties, of a suave and successful man of the world, with a touch of father figure, offset by ruggedness. Martin was a regular at the gym and was not above topping off his tan while there. In the course of having his visible teeth capped, Martin de Villiers became friendly with his dentist, and discovered that the dentist operated in a similar fashion since his own divorce. The tanned political commentator and the tanned dental surgeon formed an effective alliance and rotated women between them—the dentist's profession gave him access to a ready supply. In fact, Martin had won his gold Rolex watch in a bet with the dentist as to which of them would be the first to bed a certain former Miss South Africa finalist who had her entire mouth veneered in super-white porcelain as part of a forlorn bid to rejuvenate a dying modeling career.

Martin apparently found it all very satisfactory. None of the women managed under that program ever meddled with the categorization of wine in his cellar, which was something he could not abide. While it was a lifestyle that required him to decant his hair restorer into an unmarked bottle in his bathroom cupboard, at least he did not have to share the bathroom cupboard.

Consequently, not many of people knew what was in Martin de Villiers's head at any given time. His intimacies were always planned and mainly physical. But an interview with one Marie Kriel, a personal trainer, produced a clue. While entertaining her in his home some weeks before his disappearance, Martin de Villiers told Marie that he was planning a new book about the liberation struggle. That was not a topic likely to make Marie Kriel go weak at the knees, but Martin mentioned it because he was going to interview that Tradition Dube fellow for the book, and finding him would require Martin to hike deep into the bush. This disclosure in turn gave Martin the opportunity to mention his excellent strength and endurance results in the monthly printout from the computer at the gym.

Police in Johannesburg were continuing to sift through Martin's effects for more accurate information. In the meantime, Tradition Dube was the one clue.

"I never heard of Martin de Villiers," said Johnny. "I never heard of Tradition Dube. A few weeks ago I'd never heard of Mendi the magistrate. People are dropping like flies. This place is becoming like fucken Johannesburg airport. A man can't get a moment's peace."

Dom walked out of the gathering gloom onto the verandah.

"How's Simon?" said Clive.

"He's doing okay. Too early to say."

"You just get back?"

Dom nodded, accepting a beer. "So what's happening here?"

"They identified the dead guy," said Clive, pushing the newspaper report across to Dom, who glanced at it and laughed.

"Shit, that prick. The world is better off without him."

"You know him?"

"Not personally. But he's one of those buggers who made himself famous for being a liberal."

"Exactly what is a liberal?" Woodstock had been reluctant to ask that of his drinking buddies. Woodstock knew of course that liberal was a general term of contempt, like "cunt" or "homo," but he had only the vaguest notion of what it was.

"A liberal is a complicated beast," said Dom.

"Bullshit," Johnny interrupted. "A liberal is just a white man who had polite servants back in the old days, before they took over the country."

"Does he sing or play sport or act or anything?" asked Woodstock.

"No, he just talks on the TV, and interviews people, and gives his opinion."

"How do you get famous for something like that?" Woodstock was struggling.

"You got to understand," said Dom, "that out there in this country—on the other side of those hills—there is a whole new industry called Rich White People's Fears. There's a lot of money to be made in this industry. Security, burglar alarms, all the obvious stuff. But also other stuff. Rich white people want to be told that it's okay to be rich and white in this country after democracy. They lie awake at night worrying about their jobs, their mortgages, pensions, unit trusts, beach cottages, executive car allowances and deductible golf club memberships. Martin de Villiers was the guy on TV who told them it was all going to be okay. He wrote books and he made after dinner speeches and the rich white people went out and bought all these things and they realized that although it's gonna be tough, it's gonna be okay, and they can all feel okay about themselves again."

"Could I get a job doing that?" said Woodstock.

"I don't think so," said Johnny.

"And this is the guy," said Clive, "who ends up dead on our beach?"

"Yup."

"And nobody knows how he got there?"

"Oh, I'm sure there's a bunch of people who know," said Dom. He took a long sip of his beer while all the others waited in anticipation.

"Just because the newspapers don't know, and the magistrate

doesn't know, doesn't mean nobody knows. There's no mystery here. Just a delay of information. There'll be a perfectly logical explanation."

Dom drained his beer. "Where's Alice?" he said.

"Still staying at Simon's possie," said Woodstock.

"I gotta go tell her what's happening," said Dom. He turned to Clive. "Can you give me a few beers to take without having me shot?"

They all enjoyed that.

30

When Alice got back from visiting the aunts, Simon's house was completely dark. She had considered moving back to the hotel, but it was now full of Mendi and his cohorts. She was both nervous and determined not to be nervous. She thought of Breakdown out there somewhere and was not sure whether the thought was reassuring or frightening, despite Simon's contention that he was her self-appointed guardian.

Dom, sitting on the verandah, called out to her as soon as he heard her coming, so she would not be startled.

"I brought some beer," he said, indicating the cooler box at his feet.

She sat down. "How's Simon?"

"Brain-wise, he's pretty much a hundred percent. He knows what happened, he's talking, he's lucid. Back-wise, no change. Which is good news at this stage. They're giving him the anti-inflammatories intravenously, and they're just keeping everything immobile until it settles down and they can assess. The doctor says we have reason to hope for a good outcome, but he won't make any specific promises."

He popped the lid off a bottle of beer and offered it to her. She sat down next to him in the dark.

"You did well to arrange the helicopter so fast."

Dom shrugged.

"I didn't know you and he were that close," she continued. "It's lucky for him."

"I keep life simple," said Dom. "I divide the world up, good guys and bad guys, whether it's the president or the local surfer. The good guys must stick together."

"Still, you can't afford to lay on helicopters for everyone who's a good guy, can you?"

"Simon's brought me a lot of customers and connections in Durban."

"Customers for?"

"Dope. Marijuana. Simon's well connected. Obviously."

"I see."

She let the beer envelop her. It suppressed the aunts and amplified the sound of the insects in the dune bush.

"So we have to talk," he said.

Of course. Dropping by with the cooler of beer. She felt the hit of dread. "You're going to tell me now that Simon's going to be paralyzed for the rest of his life or something."

"Nothing like that. The prognosis I gave you is legit."

His manner was calm. He'd make a good father, she thought. He didn't over talk a crisis.

"The thing is," said Dom. "Simon has a wife."

She said nothing. She was sure Simon had never denied having a wife. He just hadn't mentioned it.

"Not a very serious wife. They've kind of been separated for six years or so, but never aggressively, and never divorced."

Dom seemed quite comfortable with some silence in the dark.

"I'm just thinking," she said, "how he let me ramble on to him about my marriage."

"Maybe he thought you needed to talk about yours. He didn't need to talk about his. It's not unresolved. Obviously you two had something special going on here. He didn't want to spoil it."

"How chivalrous."

"It is, actually," said Dom. "So the point is, I don't know if you were thinking of going up there to the hospital or anything like that—and you were only going off again to London afterwards, you'd probably cause more hassles than it's worth."

She forced accumulating images out of her mind. Dom was right. Yet she hated this brutal intervention; she hated being turned away.

Dom opened new beers for both of them.

"So did Simon tell you all about me?" said Alice.

"Actually, I know a bit more than Simon. I know who you really are."

"Really? That might be more than I know myself."

"I grow a lot of marijuana," he said. "The people around here mostly know that. Some people I supply for free, some earn good money from me, the ones who don't smoke I have other agreements with. Most of them accept I'm good for the community, although you can never take that kind of thing for granted. But strangers? – that's something I have to check out. You arrived here with the magistrate. That was very confusing of you. We didn't know whether you were a civil servant, a wife, a hooker or a lawyer. When it turned out you weren't really with him at all, you became even more mysterious."

"I'm sorry if I frightened you."

"We need to keep on our toes," he said. "You were a good exercise."

"Who's we?"

157

"I have a partner. He doesn't come to town much."

"So, you followed me, and you saw me going up to the house?"

He shook his head. "We just knew you had to go up to the house after we clocked who you were."

She didn't want to ask a question that would contain too much information. But he was onto even that, and smiled at her.

"My partner recognized you. We know who you are. Where you fit in the community. Welcome home. You belong here more than most. If the people around here understood your links to this place, they might make you mayor. Or hang you in the high street. Depending. You could have been a freelance assignment for Slipknot before he stepped on a historical banana skin himself. That's the wonderful thing about this country, don't you think? History lives all around you all the time. You don't keep a weather eye, it up and bites you when you least expect it."

"Who's your partner?"

"I'll let him tell you that himself. If you come up and visit us. We don't have a lot of visitors, in our situation, but you get a visa on account of what you did for Breakdown, which I compliment you on. That took an independent point of view, to do that."

Alice had the feeling she had not been paid a compliment of this gravity more than twice before in her whole life. Dom's huge face was steady on hers. What she felt from him was kindness. She decided to trust that feeling.

"Okay," she said, "I'll come visit."

He stood, drank most of a bottle of beer in one draught, and said, "Take the river path that you took last time."

He allowed her a moment to log the significance of that, which she did quickly; they were on a wavelength now. She smiled.

"Sit where you sat next to the river. Watch the fish eagle for a

158

bit. We call him Madiba, for obvious reasons. We'll come get you there."

He walked off the verandah and the dark absorbed him quickly.

"What time?" she called.

"In the morning," his voice came back.

His movement startled some creature in the bush, and it blundered noisily for a moment before the sea sound covered it.

Alice tried to lock the doors that night, but none of the locks had ever been turned and the salted wet breeze had set them like concrete. She slept poorly.

31

Following the town meeting, Clive hiked his prices and quadrupled his normal expenditure on cleaning materials. Sammy made a special trip all the way to Durban and bought up stocks of items he didn't normally carry. That was a seminal moment for him, a test of the intuitive trading instinct. The foretold visitors to Port Victoria were completely outside Sammy's life experience, but he did not believe them to be outside his intuition for trading, handed down through generations. It was a challenge he responded to with excitement.

Mama Xhosa sat her nieces down and gave them an introduction to sex and discipline that could have served as the foundation for a new religion. Then she instructed them in binding their breasts as flat as possible. For his part, Johnny worried silently away at how he should respond to any market for boat rides, fishing, local exploration or general acts of bush savvy. Of all of them, he was the least carried away with the prospect of a financial killing and allowed himself a good helping of skepticism about it, so he could walk off with a shrug if it did not materialize. He could take it or leave it, he thought. But none of them had catered for Ursula Wolfe.

By stepping out of her three-month-old gun-metal blue Suzuki 4x4 utility vehicle with pale leather upholstery outside the Cape Hamilton Hotel, Ursula Wolfe arced a contact across two poles of a culture that were never intended to meet. She was as authentically South African as Johnny, Mendi, Slipknot or Breakdown, but she was out of her normal range on the doorstep of the Cape Hamilton Hotel in Port Victoria. She was a Johannesburg Northern Suburbs Jewish Princess who should have been sitting on some seat at a catwalk show, or in the business class cabin of an airliner. She belonged in the feathered nest of money at the very tip of that wealth-polarized society, slinking along the roofed boulevards of the shopping malls, storing data for future jewelry whims. But here she was, fresh from a ten-hour drive, maintained in mall condition throughout the journey by air conditioning and a sachet of vitamins and supplements from her mother's nutritionist. In the back seat of her vehicle was a week's supply of bottled water. She strolled through the vacant reception area and out onto the verandah.

"Check it out," yipped Woodstock, an octave higher than the call he had used to announce the arrival of Alice. They all swung around.

"Must be the reporter chick," said Clive.

Johnny's face seemed to instantly swell up, as though he'd been stung. "Chaff her that you're full," he said to Clive, "and I'll offer her to doss at my place."

Everyone looked at him. Johnny had never been known to blatantly acknowledge lust—it surrendered too much power. But Ursula Wolfe had a combination of physical assets that spoke to Johnny. She had a vulnerability that came from her lightbonedness, but also a lushness in the breasts and hips. She had the slightly glandular cast in the mouth and throat that suggested hormonal activity even in idling mode. She was an adolescent deer from the prime extract of the gene pool on the brink of her first breeding season.

"Bangs like a shit house door," pronounced Johnny. "You can see it."

"Every day in every way," contributed Clive.

"And you know she's bloody good at it," said Bob with the wistfulness of a sailor who knows he'll never see his home again.

She pushed her sunglasses onto her forehead and ambled toward the men with a lubricated gait. They sat like a copse of petrified trees.

"Hi there," said Ursula as she reached the table. "God, it's hot here." Through the fabric of her light blouse she caught the front of her bra between two fingers, eased it away from her skin and set it more comfortably. White flecks appeared at the corners of Woodstock's mouth.

"I'm Ursula Wolfe," she said, "from the *Daily Chronicle*. There's no one in reception."

Like a man under hypnosis, Clive introduced himself and then the others. Ursula told them the TV crew was unloading their kit outside. She had driven down in a convoy with them for her safety.

"Let's go and get you all into your rooms," said Clive. "Give us a hand, Woodstock."

The two men walked away with Ursula. Johnny and Bob Peace watched them go. Only Johnny's mouth moved slowly. "I'm going to naai that chick or shoot myself between the eyes," he said, quietly but clearly.

161

32

Alice retraced the path by the river. The walk seemed to take longer than before and she worried she was on the wrong path, but it was just the expectation. She reached the spot where she had sat on the bank of the river, and made sure she was visible from the far bank and the steep hill above it, although she doubted this was necessary. She brought along a bottle of wine—something she would have done if visiting a friend for lunch in west London—and the last two lobsters from Simon's freezer.

Dom came along in twenty minutes, whistling as he walked, so as not to surprise her, she assumed.

"You like to walk?" he said. "Shall we take the steep path or the winding path?"

"Steep," she said.

Alice studied his calves as she followed him up the path. It's not possible for a man in his fifties to be still growing, but sometimes Dom seemed even larger than the last time she saw him.

The steep path was not so much a path as a vertical shortcut, a ladder with rungs of roots and convenient stones and deliberately installed stones. Sometimes they pulled themselves up by branches. She watched his calves working like hydraulic pistons. The climb was short and stiff and propelled them out of the valley basin. Then they hit an elevated plateau of bush where the path was easier again. Shards from childhood were coming back to her—when you're walking in the bush, don't follow immediately behind the person in front of you, leave space for branches to whip back and for startled snakes to slither away. He did her the courtesy of not instructing her on those things.

Instead, he said, "You okay about the Simon thing?"

"I'm dealing with it," she said. "Obviously it was never going to last anyway."

But Alice's skin still knew where his hands had touched her, and where his easy eyes had rested on her. Whatever flowed from that point in her life, it would never happen again. It was done. That door was closed. There would never be Simon or another Simon. This was sealed off from her other world. This was time out of time.

The terrain changed as they reached a plateau that led between two kloofs in the hills. The gradient was much easier, and the bush changed its texture. She might not have noticed but for the accompanying shift in the nostrils.

"Hey!" she said.

Dom gave a chuckle, kept moving. "We grow it in among the bush, so that aerial spotters don't pick it up. It's not easy. We have to encourage it to grow horizontally. We hook it through branches."

He stopped next to a plant, put his massive palm behind its leaf, throwing that distinctive jagged profile into relief. Alice had always thought the leaf looked like the logo for a good-time product.

"*Cannabis sativa*, which I think is Latin for useful," he said. "Zulu name is *nsangu*, Xhosa is *umya*, but we all know it as *dagga*, which was originally a Khoisan word. Truly a cross cultural weed."

"And the rumor is you make a good living out of it."

"We're enthusiastic amateurs. The big guys are mostly in Lesotho—similar terrain to this, lots of sunlight, indifferent policing. Did you know that after international aid and migrant mine workers' wages, dagga is Lesotho's third biggest foreign currency earner? When the world wakes up to the wonders of this plant, it's going to be bigger than aspirin. Let us pray that is not in my lifetime."

They walked on through Dom's plantation. Where the ground was almost flat, there was a clearing, and in the clearing, the house. Dom gave a whistle and two black Doberman pinschers bounded across the cleared ground toward them, radiating ferocity.

They snarled at Alice and circled her with an energy that suggested it was too long since they had last been permitted to take a piece out of someone. Dom made a point of introducing them to Alice and getting them to smell her. He spoke to them in Zulu.

The house was not so much well hidden as well placed. Nine out of ten people who came that far to build a house would have made it conspicuous, but whoever built the house slipped it around the side of one of the kloofs, so that it was not visible from the river or the road, but only to those who had already committed themselves to a climb.

A black man came off the verandah and walked to meet them. He and Dom exchanged a few words in Zulu.

Dom said to Alice, "Meet Lethukuthula Dube."

"Call me Lethu." He pronounced it *Lair*-too.

"Hello, I'm Alice."

He was lanky and presented himself in a diffident manner, but he had something particular that drew her eye. The skin around his eyes was slightly darker than the rest of his face. The rest was brown and shiny, the vibrant look of the Zulu, but the skin around his eyes was an unreflective, dark tone, with a coarse grain. It looked as though something toxic had been thrown in his face, something that had made his eyes wise and sad while the rest of him was boyish. Light disappeared into those eyes and didn't come out again.

"I'm trying to remember my Xhosa," said Alice. "The *thulu* means quiet, right?"

"Peace," said Lethu. "*Let there be peace* is what my mother named me. There was fighting across the hill when I was born." He paused, then said, "I remember you."

She studied his face. He seemed about the same age as her, or younger, but she got no inkling of recognition.

Dom said, "It was Lethu who recognized you when we were trying to work out what you were doing here. When you walked up the gorge, we followed you with the binoculars."

"Where do you remember me from?" she said.

"You lived in the big house, as a little girl."

"I did," she said, "but when did we meet?"

"We didn't meet. I just saw you sometimes. I used to come with my father to do the garden. I used to sit next to him while he dug the weeds, and you were there with those dogs that watched us."

That was so classic a cameo from the old master-servant white-black relationship of her childhood that Alice blushed and turned her head away.

"You used to walk with the man to the river. I saw you there when I was fishing."

"But still, how do you recognize me?" she asked. "I can't recognize people from the way they looked when they were six or whatever."

"We knew you went up to the house. So I thought it was probably you. Then I got you close up in the binoculars." Lethu paused and raised his hand, pointing at her mouth. "I saw you get that cut. On your lip."

"You saw it? I don't even remember it. What happened?"

He seemed to watch her for a moment, as if she were testing him.

"You fell off the verandah while you were running."

She was aware of Dom watching her, so she handed him the

bag she was carrying. "Wine and some lobster from Simon's freezer that I thought would go to waste. We'd better cook it fairly soon."

Lethu made a fire in the small barbecue pit. She went in with Dom to get beer. Inside the front door, an automatic rifle was propped against the wall.

"What is that?" she said.

He held it up under her nose. "AK-47, the manmade scourge of Africa. Up there with malaria and AIDS as a population control device. Millions upon millions of them produced. Unit cost is down there with a paper clip."

"Where did you get it?"

"You can buy one of these for the equivalent of twenty dollars in any township."

Once the lobsters were boiling on the fire, they sat in the shade of the verandah. The dogs lay facing her, watching her, perhaps hoping that her diplomatic immunity would be withdrawn.

Dom produced two large joints of marijuana.

"I'm sure Simon introduced you to our product?"

"Yes, we went and got some from that guy at the radio station."

"Not prime quality then. Bob keeps stuff hidden all over the place and he doesn't know which pack is which, age wise, so I don't give him prime. He doesn't know the difference. In dope smokers, it's the same as with alcohol. You get your quantity market and your get your quality market. There's no point in providing quantity to the qualities, and quality would be wasted on the quantities. Bob's a quantity."

They lit one of the joints and passed it among them. Within a few minutes, the colors softened for Alice, and she slid further down in the old deckchair they had provided for her.

"Can you tell the difference from what you had before?" asked Lethu.

"Right now I don't think I could pick my own child out of a group of three," she replied.

"That's the difference," Lethu said.

"Not really," chuckled Dom. "We'll have to develop your palate, if you stay."

"So are you coming back to live here?" It was Lethu.

"I don't know what I'm doing," she said.

That was the moment it occurred to her that they were getting her stoned as a truth drug, but the truth drug also made her feel that her secrets and wisdom should belong to the world, and anyway, no person should have anything to hide and if they did, they should be gently placed in a situation where they revealed the hidden things, so as to be relieved of them. The sun started to creep under the verandah roof and she reached for the factor 40 in her bag.

"What I've found, coming back after all these years, is that I have two simultaneous lives. Not a past and a present, as I thought."

The sunscreen was more viscous than usual, possibly because of the heat. The joint was passed to her again, and she took a long drag. She rubbed sunscreen onto her nose.

"That's a tiring walk," she said.

She took a siesta on the sofa. When she awoke she marveled that she could fall asleep among strangers here. She walked outside into the mid-afternoon. Dom was sitting on a rock talking to three black women. Lethu was working at a long trestle table on the verandah, parceling a mound of fresh green marijuana into packs of various sizes. He had three old scales, the kind that used cast iron counterbalances.

Lethu nodded toward the three women talking to Dom. "When the crop is in, they come up and make their buys," he explained to her.

"Why do you have three scales?"

"We sell in three sizes. This is just quicker than changing one scale. You want to help?"

She wanted to laugh. The thought of Julia's private school teachers came directly to mind. First graders playing shop to learn how to count and make change. How would Julia's headmistress, Mrs. Fowler, deal with the image of one of the members of the Parents Association packing marijuana for commercial distribution?

"You can do the best stuff. We call it Pitco Tips. So you write P.T. on the packet with the felt pen, like this, see? That's the bud. You get it on the female plant. See the seeds? That means it's been pollinated. Where they grow for business in Mexico they actually take out all the male plants so they can't pollinate the females, and then the buds are always seedless. They call it sinsemillia. But we sell it with seeds. Did you know that when it is under threat, the dagga plant can develop male and female on the same plant?"

Alice did not know that. She imagined that millions of dope heads around the world were oblivious of that. She got lost in the process, sorting plants, stripping off the buds, weighing and packing into packets of three sizes. She wrote P.T. on the packs.

"The leaves around the bud we use for second grade. Other leaves from lower down is for the real lowlifes. The Indians in Durban call it *majat*."

The three women left with their plastic bags and Dom joined Alice and Lethu at the sorting table.

"It takes you a long time to sell," Alice said to him. "It must be like a Middle Eastern carpet bazaar."

Dom grinned at her. "The selling happened in five minutes.

After that we were just chatting. I've got a hundred eyes and ears. That's what keeps us safe here. That's how we knew you arrived and went up to the house and came out crying."

She had to keep her eyes down, on the work she was doing.

"The people who keep us informed, they get their personal dagga free," said Lethu. "They only pay for what they sell to other people."

"Doesn't sound very businesslike."

"The big money is in Durban," said Dom. "We pack up the truck, I make some phone calls, we drive up to the big dealers in the city. Then it's big money, quick."

"What if you get stopped in the truck?"

"It happened once. We had to jump out and run. Lost the whole load."

"Not to mention the truck!"

Dom shrugged. "We just stole another one of those. But the police burnt all our dagga." He shook his head at the recollection of waste.

"You just stole a truck?"

"Toyota Land Cruiser, four-by-four," Lethu said with some pride. "Even got a CD player. Only thirty thousand kays, like new. Air conditioning."

Dom laughed at her expression. "They get a new one from the insurance! They can get a different color. It's like a trade up for them. Wonderful system."

And, at that moment, Alice found the logic impossible to contest. They all worked silently for a while, the aroma of the leaves thick around them.

Lethu glanced at her, caught her eye. "Your father was the man who took all the chief's men for the mines," he said, his eyes on his work. She kept working, too.

"Actually, that was my uncle, Robbie, who did all that stuff.

My father was the one in the wheelchair. He died long ago. Do you remember him? Did you see him?"

He studied her face for a moment, his scrutiny made her want to check for food around her mouth. Then he said, "Yes, I remember him. Sorry."

"Don't be silly. There's nothing to be sorry about. I can see that's a natural assumption. I'm glad we've set the record straight." She was treating it lightheartedly. "They were all just as racist as each other, but I'm glad you understand that my father was not the one who made money out of selling your fathers and grandfathers to the mines. My father was the one who had his backside shot off in the war and ruined all the furniture in the house with his wheelchair."

A few minutes later Alice felt a flush, like she was getting a virus. She thought, too much dope and too much sun and she had a long walk home, so she asked Dom if they could set out. He scanned her face briefly and nodded and went to get her a water bottle for the walk. She packed up her things. She looked at the sky, because she had the feeling she was hurrying to get home before a storm broke, but the sky was clear. Then she thought that maybe an hour spent wrapping dagga in little packages had caused the stuff to be absorbed through her fingers somehow, and that was affecting her.

"Let's go," said Dom. He was standing on the edge of the cleared area in front of the house.

She turned to call goodbye to Lethu and found him approaching.

"Come and work again," he said, teasing her.

He must be my age, she thought, but at times he had the look of a teenager. In a confusion of cultural inputs, she did the London thing and put her hands on his shoulders and touched her cheek to his, both sides. He became paralyzed during the process. Dom's chuckle reached her, and she turned quickly and started walking away from the house.

On the bush path they walked in silent single file at a steady pace. Dom had the stride of a man who could walk to Zimbabwe. When they were on the road that led to the village, they slowed and walked side by side. The sun was below the hills behind them and the light was going fast.

"Go back," she said. "I'm okay. You'll be walking in the dark."

"I'm going to stay over at the hotel," he said. "I've got some people to see here. Do you want to have a drink?"

She had two, quickly. The hotel was unusually busy. She wanted to be out of there, but found she was postponing being alone. But the point came when she could see that Dom was watching other parties, so she left. It took her twenty minutes to walk to Simon's house. She cleaned her teeth and lay on the bed with her clothes on. She felt chilled, though the evening was sultry.

She woke just before dawn. A light breeze came off the sea, driven by the coming sun, carrying for Alice a whole new version of the world. A version similar, in many ways, to the old one, but quite different. And the thing she couldn't get over was, when she saw the new version, it was instantly more plausible than its predecessor that had reigned long and undisturbed. She was simultaneously in shock at the new shape of her life and at how she had never spotted it. The face of the crocodile hidden in a child's drawing.

Alice walked out of the house onto the beach sand. She walked the beach into the dawn, raw in the world, her skin removed, feeling every message like an alarm. A few words from Lethu had burned a lifetime's protective coating right off her.

33

Family legend is one of the most corrupt of human institutions. Walking the beach in that pre-dawn, Alice prepared herself to cut up the quilt of who she was and rearrange all the little patchwork pieces. If her past was different than what she had thought, did that make her a different person? Was she still the same collection of molecules that had set out from London only a few weeks previously? She was pretty sure her body, ever a more reliable witness than her mind, was giving her an answer in the chill of shock. Alice was physically frightened of what was immediately ahead of her.

Alice knew the legend of how the two people she had always called her parents had met. It was the first Saturday of June 1930, Clairwood Racetrack. Len was a racehorse trainer and stabled his horses there in the winter racing season. Even in the winter it could be humid and muggy.

Len regularly walked his string of horses to the beach, where the soft sand was benevolent to the jarred legs of thoroughbreds that had been raced too hard too young. Walking the horses flank-high into the warm seawater was also thought to be therapeutic, although the riders had been reluctant since two horses were lost to sharks. Thirty years later, the local council would install shark nets to prevent the loss of valuable holidaymakers from Johannesburg.

That Saturday was a race day at Clairwood. Len arrived on his Norton motorcycle on a mission to bet on a horse, not his own, but one which he knew had been prepared for a betting coup on that day. He saw a long-boned, winsome woman, wearing a deep red dress. A tall young woman, she was standing alone on a crowded racecourse, striking, yet diffident. She did not know that she was about to meet for the first time the man she would marry, but her attitude was that of someone who was ready to do so.

What he did not see was that the young woman had few resources of her own other than what she was: young and attractive. Her father had deserted the family years before and she and her mother were living on the kindness of family members.

Eileen's father left forever when she was a child, striking her life with this condition: she had always been isolated against the background, unconsciously she chose that, just as she unconsciously chose the red dress, the precise shade of which said not so much *notice me,* as *help me.* It was an irresistible image to Len, a man of twenty-five, deep through the chest, built for rugby, accustomed to resolving life with energy. He had a cliff of a forehead and deep set eyes. She saw him smile and her body made that small intuitive rearrangement of itself, which held his eye. He was the kind of man who could stroll over and introduce himself to a woman he did not know, and she was the kind of woman who would have high regard for such an accomplishment.

So they converged, two young strangers. Uncountable permutations might have arrayed from that moment, and each would have been true. But only one did. If they could have known what they were setting in motion they might have recoiled, and each begun to look again for another encounter with less fraught outcomes.

Len knew how to look for pedigree in a horse. His patrons at that time were not rich, and he did not have the funds to buy the best horses, so he had to choose smart. Before he bought a horse, he would pore over its pedigree, assessing the implications for speed and stamina contained in the breeding and race records of its progenitors. Then he would conduct a detailed examination of the actual animal in its physical attributes. If he was getting some speed at the price of temperament, he liked to know that. Only when he was satisfied that he knew all that could be known about a horse's body, spirit and pedigree, would he consider bringing it into his stable.

But he made no such examination of Eileen before choosing her to be the mother of his children. Neither did she of him.

He had come to the course on his Norton motorcycle to bet on a horse. But the encounter with Eileen made him late and the betting window closed while he was in the line. Eileen and Len stood side by side as the horses came charging past the finishing post. The horse Len had wanted to bet on was hampered in running by a tiring front-runner and finished third. To Len, that event was blessed: here was a woman who had interrupted him from placing a bet that would have been a loser. A star-crossed woman.

Len demonstrated his suitability as a companion and protector to that young woman by giving her expert, inside advice on which horse to put her money on in the next race. Eileen was accustomed to making a little money go a long way, and anyway, she had come to the races for the social component, the horses were of no real interest to her. So she hesitated to bet. Without further consultation Len lent her five pounds of his own money, placed the bet, collected the winnings, deducted his initial five pounds and gave her the profit. Success made this transaction gallant. Perhaps if the horse recommended had been touched off by a fast-finishing outsider—as many would be in the future—Eileen's intuitive selection process may have proceeded along another channel. But on that day, it seemed to her that he would be able to do that all his life. She had chosen him as her life's mate before the last field of the day came bowling home down the straight.

They married without preamble and lived in Durban. Len was young, fit and able. He moved up, acquiring wealthier patrons. Through his contacts with wealthy racehorse owners, he was branching out into other businesses, dealing in scrap metal and buying land. Those were the legendary days. Anything was possible. The country was still, in many ways, a frontier society.

Often when Alice was a child, she would lie for hours next to Len on the bed, looking at old photos from the horse racing days. There were two black and white photos mounted in a black sheet of cardboard. One photo was from the photo-finish camera. The other showed her mother posing with the horse after the race. Under the photos, a cursive inscription in gold lettering recorded that the horse's name was Bridgescorer. The owner was recorded as Alice's mother, the trainer, Len.

Len and his brother Robbie were not close. Robbie, the oldest child, was burdened with expectations and responsibility. Dogged. Then twin sisters, Phyllis and Abigail. Finally Len, the youngest brother. His place in the sibling array became risk - taker. He was stronger, more courageous than his elder brother. Robbie chose a business, unglamorous, and worked hard at it. Len threw himself into the world and the world appreciated him. Len and Eileen spent what they earned, gambled, saw their money go on broken down horses and land speculations predicated on developments that had gone elsewhere. That had not troubled Len because he always assumed he would have his strength and enterprise for many years to come. In those days, you could come from nothing, no pedigree, no advanced education, and conquer the world.

They came out of corrugated iron shanties on the side of small roads connecting distant places. It was the age before specialization. One man's career could encompass bridge building, racehorse training and diamond prospecting. They would go two decades without seeing a doctor and then die as if shot while running. In two generations, you could plough a furrow straight through the fertile middle of the twentieth century, go from the corrugated iron shack to a house with a clear blue pool and a Chevrolet parked outside and kids who would travel overseas. But along the way, you had to survive the war in Europe.

In that country at the foot of Africa, English-speaking people of British extraction like Len described themselves as Europeans. In those days, things were not yet "black" and "white." The country was still part of the British Empire, but the white people who ruled the country found themselves divided on the issue of the war. When the white Parliament decided by a narrow majority to declare war on Germany, many Afrikaners were opposed, and some who declared their support for Hitler found themselves interned for their trouble.

There was no conscription in that country. Everyone who joined up to fight did so as a volunteer, and Len was among the first. He was trained for a period and then put on a ship in Durban which sailed up the east coast of Africa. The colonial forces were deployed in the desert campaign. It was still Africa, geographically, but it was about as abstract a field of conflict as could be conceived.

Robbie, working away at his business in Port Victoria, a place even more isolated then, felt no compunction to go and fight a war, which was, in his view, extremely unlikely to touch him. He was making money, living a life within his control. He built a fine house at the top of the hill overlooking Port Victoria. It seemed to symbolize his influence over the place. All the people in the area were beholden to the tribal chief, and the chief was beholden to Robbie.

In North Africa, in July 1941, Len's newly arrived company of white Africans won a game of barefoot rugby against their counterparts from New Zealand. That night, as they scooped the fine desert sand from their ears and the corners of their eyes, orders came through from Montgomery's headquarters for them to be moved. Len carried his canvas pack and his .303 rifle to an open-backed Bedford truck and sat down among the members of his platoon. He never stood up again. An hour later the truck drove over a landmine. Thirty-one of the thirty-two men in the truck were killed. Only Len survived. Shrapnel driven upwards by the blast minced through the backs of his legs, his buttocks, rectum and large bowel. Small pieces were discovered and removed from various upper regions a year later. He was taken to a hospital in Cairo where he floated in the zone between death and survival for several months. He spent a further period building up his strength for the journey home and, having done that, he spent a year waiting—no hospital ships were being run down the east coast of Africa because German U-boats were decimating Allied shipping.

After being shipped from Cairo to Durban, Len was taken into the hospital there, and Eileen moved in as well, so she could be instructed in the methods of caring for her husband. That routine involved three aspects: massage to keep blood flowing in the feelingless and motionless legs to avoid gangrene; care of the wounded areas to avoid infection; and regular evacuation of bodily waste by enema. Eileen did those things for her husband, week in, week out, from 1944 to 1967, and one would think that such a service could win forgiveness for anything. But they had no income, so it came down to this: Len, together with his wife Eileen, would live under Robbie's roof in the big old house on the hill above Port Victoria. Robbie had never married. There was a severity in him that repelled intimacy. After he had started to do well, his twin sisters, Phyllis and Abigail, equally unmarriageable, went to Port Victoria to live with him. As she thought about that, it struck Alice that those arrangements strongly suggested a family pattern of inability to make links outside the family, but there was no longer any objective witness left with whom to check that.

From then on, in that house would live two men and three women, with only one of the women being a wife, and she not the wife of the head of the household. Into that house would be born a child, named Alice, who would be told lies for her own protection.

34

Alice was standing outside Sammy's shop when he opened the door for business. She shied in surprise and spoke quickly, as if pre-empting an expected assault.

"I had nothing to do with locking up Breakdown, you know," he said, blinking.

"I know that," she said.

"The men who got him in there—Johnny and Clive—they didn't like it, either. They were just doing what the magistrate made them do."

She nodded. "I heard that, too. I need cat food."

"Oh!" he said, "of course."

He was packing it for her when Mendi's large frame filled the doorway. He held them a moment with his most authoritative look.

"Do either of you know Tradition Dube?" he asked.

By then, this question had been put to every living person in the community except Breakdown. Mendi had even instructed Clive to phone the hospital in Durban and get a nurse to ask the surfer if he knew Tradition Dube. But no one knew him.

35

"Why didn't you tell me?"

Alice had banged on the door until Phyllis appeared in her dressing gown. When she said that Abigail was not up yet, Alice told her they would talk in her room. When Phyllis told her to come back at lunchtime, Alice said they would talk now in Abigail's room, or she would have the two of them turned out of the house by the end of the week.

The two old women watched her like birds. Without time to prepare for the day, they looked like living remains, scraped from the surface of an accident.

"Tell you what?"

"You always want to know something."

"Curiosity killed the cat, you know."

She waited until they subsided completely before speaking again.

"Why didn't you tell me..." her voice caught and she had to pause. "Why can't you just tell me that my real father was Robbie?"

"Well, really!"

"We heard you went mad in London. Had to go to the psychiatrist, didn't you?"

"You were always, always the cause of trouble!"

The fact that tears were swelling in her eyes seemed to make her aunts only more indignant.

"And look at you now! You come here and frighten the wits out of us at the crack of dawn!"

She sat at the three wooden steps, which led from the grass to the verandah at the main entrance to the house, looking down the slope to where the lawn ended and the thick bush began. This had been the world to her when she was two and three. This was where she had laid with the Alsatian dogs, watching for moles in the lawn. This was where she had tripped and cut her lip. She realized now that her aunts could never retract the fiction around her birth. The luxury of admitting such things did not exist for them. And, in a way, their confirmation was superfluous. The new version of Alice was up to her.

Imprinting. The word came to her. That's what the anthropologists called it. A creature removed from its biological parent directly after birth will imprint on the next large warm accommodating beast it finds, and take it as parent. That happened even across species. It had happened to Alice. Told that Len was her father, treated like a daughter by Len, she had built herself in that frame. Now she was jerked out of the frame and forced to look at it.

She walked the house, falling through layers into the well of her childhood. Memories traveled on small sounds and displayed themselves on surfaces.

The ground floor of the house had been adapted for a wheelchair. The bedroom equipped for her father's needs had French doors opening onto the verandah. Sometimes she lay there on the bed beside him and he read to her. Not the children's classics that Alice had pressed into the ears of her own child, for Len had zero tolerance for two things: fiction and religion. So Len read to his daughter from the *Farmer's Weekly*, *Duff's Turf Guide*, and the *Stud Book*.

When she fell asleep there sometimes, her mother would leave her there, switching off the lights. And Alice would be left next to the man she thought was her father—half corpse, half man—and listened to him breathe. In the hospital, they had told him that one of the many risks he faced was repeated chest infections because he would spend so much time prone. So Len had made breathing his specialty, and as his increasing wheelchair mobility put bulk muscle onto his chest and arms, the top half of his body became like a powerful engine. He learned to breathe deeply and rhythmically, creating a trance-like state for both himself and the child lying next to him in the darkness.

Wide awake in the dark, she would watch for hours the pattern of the tree silhouettes on the wall. On summer nights, the French doors would be left open and the sounds of the bush would be funneled into her ears.

Lying next to her guardian father and his massive chest and his rhythmic breathing, she would hear the squeal of something caught and killed out in the bush that flowed down the hill to the river and the sea. The dogs would lie on the verandah, just outside the door, and she could hear them breathe, occasionally lifting their heads to a noise. Some nights, Alice had poured herself silently off the bed, crawled along the floor to the dogs, and lain among them. In the morning she would bring her father tea, slow-stepping barefoot on the paving as she concentrated on the level in the cup. He would use those hydraulic arms of his to push himself into a sitting position and sometimes she would see the pain riot across his features before he could erase it.

Len's wheelchair became a creature of the house in its own right. As his white, bloodless legs withered, his chest and shoulders and arms expanded from the exercise of propelling himself about in the wheelchair. Increasing areas of the grounds were adapted so his wheelchair could pass—ramps installed and pathways concreted—and Len wheeled himself to the stable where Robbie's two horses were kept. With assistance, he could get all the way to the flat crown tree on the far corner of the lawn, where the family often took Sunday lunch overlooking the lagoon and the ocean. From the waist up, he was a fine looking specimen with a full head of black hair, and his tall, slim wife stood behind his wheelchair when visitors arrived.

The lone child in that big house on the hill above Port Victoria, Alice lived in heat and sweat and succulent tastes and things that she would only later learn were wondrous. A few swings of a broomstick handle would knock from the tree six avocados, each large enough to feed two people. When the fruit trees produced, they produced in obscene quantities: guavas, mangos, martingulas, mulberries, rough-skinned lemons, which Alice learned to peel and eat with salt. All that was normal life to Alice when she was three and four and five and six in the big house on the hill above the Umzimvubu River on the east coast of Africa.

Len occupied himself managing the accounts of Robbie's business, and he did that with a dedication that surpassed all need. He not only provided a comprehensive office service, he sought to perfect it, reduced its cost and improved its efficiency. He re-used paper meticulously. Unneeded documents were torn neatly in half and the reverse side used for notes. Pins and paperclips were recycled from documents received. Len taught himself to type and generated all invoices, letters, and suchlike. And, using an upright and high-speed block capital handwriting, he completed the many government forms associated with Robbie's business.

Len had all but surrendered the life he used to know, but a couple of times a year, shreds of that old life come to visit him. Alice remembered it as a kind of circus. Sometimes they came alone, but mostly in groups of two or three or more. Men from Len's past life. They were all men, men without women, and they all sought Len, not Robbie. They were the survivors of the war, and they came to find the man in the wheelchair, the gambler they had known who trained horses and played rugby and who was now hoarding paper clips and filling out forms. They were making a pilgrimage to the unlikely survival of one of their own. They were the survivors, but not untouched. They carried the noise of shattered lives about them.

They were men who were missing parts of their bodies and much besides. Anyone with all twenty digits intact and functional was an exception. Amputations were common. Shell shocked jockeys who could not ride any more, their hands shaking and their timing gone. A drunk, a former ack-ack gunner, his hearing forever overlaid with the stutter of gunfire, who fell in love with the voice of the operator on the party line telephone and called her up continually, playing her Gene Autrey's "A Bridle Hanging on the Wall" at distorting volume.

Men who had come to pay homage and who brought gifts, the stuff of the world beyond the barrier of hills: a record player and a pile of 78s, a bag of Springbok biltong from South West Africa on the far side of the continent, a kaross, which was a bedspread of meerkat skins from the Karoo. Those gifts were not particularly appropriate to the needs or wants of Len or his household. They were simply what the visitors had in their lives. When they were drinking, surplus military flares whooshed up into the night sky and sent the hadeda birds yelping away over the valley.

They were scrap metal dealers and borehole diggers and truck drivers. Industrial men. They ranged across that big country, shooting animals or riding them or farming them, building bridges over rivers or damming them, planting forests and cutting them down and digging deep holes in the ground to get metals or water out. They could fix cars and pumps and never saw a TV set or a doctor. They smelt of wet timber, railway sidings, hillsides of dripping wattle, sugarcane, coal, gold and manure.

They parked their old cars on the lawn and drank in the middle of the morning and were elaborately courteous to the women of house. In the long afternoons they slept on the verandah. They came to see Len. Robbie and the aunts withdrew to the sidelines, and looked on silently.

Alice could only recall one occasion on which Len had left the property at the top of the hill. A plan had been hatched to get him down onto the beach, some talk about it being good for him. There were two men visiting, living in the rooms above the stables. They manhandled Len out of his wheelchair and into the back of Robbie's Chevrolet. They drove down to the dunes, manhandled Len again out of the car, and laid him out on a blanket. Then they pulled the blanket along the soft sand of the path through the dunes and down onto the beach. There, advance plans had been made for a party. A fire was burning in a pit. Other friends, making a surprise visit and staying at the hotel, emerged with gifts. Bottles of whisky were opened. There were a dozen lobster and a sugar pocket full of oysters to start with, and then meat to be cooked on the fire. The sun dipped and the talk turned to beloved racehorses, animals that had lost when they should have won, robbed by bad luck and bad timing by poor jockeys, horses brave and true. Alice and her mother were the only females on the beach, and Alice sat in the crook of Len's arm as the light went and she listened to stories from beyond the hills of a changing world. Those visitors came to see Len as an act of friendship, as a mark of respect, but also as a pilgrimage of nostalgia. For Len, trapped in his condition in his wheelchair, was a monument to the world they knew before the war. Beyond the hills, the country was changing, and none of those men was suited to the change.

By the time they were ready to leave the beach, all the men were drunk, and they loaded Len back into the Chevrolet with less care. Alice saw the voltage of pain across his face, and the look he gave her that made it their shared secret.

Decades later, Alice sat on the verandah and tried to decode for herself what her aunts would not or could not tell her. Where had she been conceived? When Eileen and Robbie were engaged in the sexual act that brought together the sperm and egg that would be known as Alice, where had they been? She couldn't say. She could say pretty much where the man she called her father would have been, because Len's physical universe was proscribed by the paths his wheelchair could take: the ground floor of the house, the verandahs, the path from the side door to the stable, and the big table under the big tree. He would have been somewhere on that grid, which he occupied for twenty-two years.

How did Robbie and Eileen reach a stage in their exchanges around a close-knit house where such acquiescence might even enter her mind? Alice could not imagine a dishcloth going missing in that house without the aunts noticing it. And that made her realize she could not imagine the thing at all. She was prevented or protected from understanding what had happened in that house by the flawlessness with which Len had loved her.

A jarring version of her childhood snapped forcefully into focus, that the one true and natural thing had been Len's steady love of her. Everything else was unnatural: the eyes of adults upon her, the way they treated her, treated each other, the elaborateness of the theatre they created around her. She felt it now, like a blow, so that it pushed air out of her in a gasp as she stood in the kitchen of the big old house, aged thirty-eight, with the material of her life chaotic around her. Then it snapped away again. She thought: this is what it's like to have a nervous breakdown.

Alice walked out of the house kitchen and across the verandah. From the lounge, the eyes of the aunts watched her, she could hear their eyeballs scratching in their dry sockets as, with the last of their lives, they tracked her progress across the map of her own. On the lawn, in the sun, she stopped and turned back to the house, her eyes drawn to the upper verandah which formed an L along the north and east sides of the house. The verandah was now protected by wooden shutters, which could be folded away to edges. But Alice remembered that there had been no shutters when she was a child. She remembered long white calico drapes, which could be drawn against the sun, but were most of the time tied in groups so they made a succession of white wineglass shapes. And Alice remembered that when a storm came up quickly the wind would get the drapes before the aunts could, and stream them out and whip them, and the ends of the calico became frayed.

On very hot, still afternoons, the drapes might be drawn against the sunlight. Alice could remember such an afternoon when she and Len had been at the stables. Len would talk to Alice all the time; no opportunity for the passing of information was left unused. At the stables, he would tell her about the appropriate food mixes for horses. Racehorses in training got lots of oats, but a racehorse that came off the track had to be got off the oats as quickly as possible, or he would kick the stable yard to smithereens. Len would tell her stories from a tapestry of legend from his racing days, tales of snapped stirrup leathers that made the difference in a driving finish, and a filly that wouldn't perform because her owners' wife wore cheap perfume to the saddling enclosure and gave her respiratory problems, and a jockey who fell dead right out of the saddle at the starting tapes because he was an undiagnosed diabetic on a rigorous weight control program. Len explained the handicapping system to Alice in detail and why a horse's odds shortened when people bet on it. Len made lots of predictions about the world of which he saw ever less. He told Alice that scrap metal dealing would be the big industry of the future, taking apart the machines that men had made and recovering the constituent elements. He said land was the way to make money. He said any fool could make a fortune digging boreholes. He said Alice should become a doctor. He loved the Goon Show, the BBC shortwave radio service.

The book of things Len did not tell Alice was also ample. He said nothing about his time up north, the military, the desert, the accident, the injuries, the pain, the hospital, the trip back or his life there. And she never asked.

From the verandah there was an excellent view of the stables, and Alice had looked up to see her mother standing there, with the drapes drifting around her in a soft offshore breeze, the same breeze that Simon loved for surfing. Alice had waved at her mother and had been disappointed not to see her wave back before she was enveloped by the drapes.

Alice went back to the house, mounted the stairs and folded back the shutters. The upper verandah had a good view of the stables—a controlling view of the property, in fact. She could stand in the shadow there and see everything. The master bedroom—Robbie's bedroom, opened onto that verandah, as did two other bedrooms, at present occupied by the aunts, and presumably in Alice's childhood, although she realized that she didn't really remember. The house had been thus divided: Robbie and his twin sisters slept upstairs, Len and his wife and their child downstairs. Not that Alice had been banned from upstairs, but that there had been little reason to go there. Her life had been fully catered for downstairs. It looked as though little had been touched in Robbie's bedroom since his death. The bed was made. There were his hairbrushes on the dressing table. Alice opened the wardrobe: his clothes were still there. Alice reflected that those clothes would fit Breakdown well, but she knew there was little prospect of getting Breakdown to pull on another man's clothes again in a hurry.

So was that where she was conceived? Had Eileen drifted up

the stairs while Len was at the stables or under the tree or trapped in his cripple's bed downstairs? So, what was Len doing at the precise moment that Robbie and Eileen fucked? What was he thinking? What were the aunts doing? What time of day was it? It seemed inconceivable that all those interested parties would have suspended awareness to the degree that Robbie and Eileen could have acquired even the time necessary for a brief and businesslike exchange of body fluids, let alone the tremulous event that she had in mind. So perhaps they had made a trip somewhere in the car, or had been down on the beach alone, or simply slipped into the bush at the fringe of the lawn, a membrane that could rapidly transport you from civilization.

Endless unanswerable questions arose from every new thought, a chain reaction of small emotional earthquakes in her. She knew the answers were probably unknown in the living world, and thus unobtainable. Alice's life from there on would be determined not by what happened that day, but by what she thought happened and how she lay down with those thoughts.

The man who had raised Alice as his daughter had once ridden motorcycles and played rugby barefoot in the desert with other soldiers waiting to go to the front. Alice wondered what he had thought when his wife had brought him the news that she was pregnant. That man must have lain in his cripple's bed and changed himself into the man who would raise her, the child, as he had.

Africa being what it was, unexpected death was not as unexpected as elsewhere. And certainly, Alice's mother had died an African death. Once Alice had reached an age where she did not require constant watching, Eileen had taken to walking on her own. Along the beach, through the bush, along the river, even in the river where the density of bush on the bank made it easier to wade through the water. The walks became longer and longer, and Eileen could be gone from the house from mid-morning to dinnertime. She became something of an expert on the local topography and a figure of note among the local black people, who walked the same paths. Many times Alice had wished there was someone who could give witness to those days for her, and tell her what the walks were about and whether they changed her mother.

The day Eileen did not return, they had not even missed her. She had only been gone a few hours, and it was only mid-afternoon on a mild day when a squad of local villagers issued onto the lawn in front of the big house. The oldest male among them came forward alone. He hesitated to encroach onto the verandah, and instead called to the domestic servant in Zulu. He said he needed to speak with the Mkhulu Mlungu—the white father. After a long interval, Robbie came out onto the verandah wearing the slightly irritable face he donned for those who approached him directly about their family problems, instead of going through their chief. The black man kept his eyes down and moved from foot to foot as he gave the news to Robbie.

Eileen's body was never returned to the house, and Alice was told nothing until that evening. A snake, probably a green mamba, had bitten Eileen. The mamba's bite is severe but not always fatal, provided anti-venom is administered, but Eileen had been on her own and far from home. It had been some hours before two black women had come along the path where she was found. Alice could recall the many times she had told other people that her mother had died of a snakebite and how unexceptional a death that had been. School children, teachers, parents of friends, boyfriends had all accepted it. It was one of the ways to die in Africa. Only in Britain had Alice found people who considered that manner of death to be bizarre.

Alice never saw her mother's body. Eileen was buried near

her family home some hours' drive away. Alice went to the funeral with Robbie and Abigail and Phyllis and moved among aunts and uncles and cousins on her mother's side that she seldom met. Then she returned to the isolation of the house above Port Victoria. She always remembered that Robbie had seemed to understand that she needed something concrete to fix that death around and he gave her that by taking her on a long walk down the river to the spot, he said, where her mother had been found. Robbie told her that, terrible as Eileen's death might seem, Alice should not let it give her an exaggerated fear of the bush, or even of green mambas, which avoid human contact wherever possible. He walked her along the path and told her he had no idea how her mother had had the misfortune to put the green mamba in a position where its only option was to strike, but Alice could be sure it was the sort of accident that no one could have prepared for or avoided. They sat at the edge of the river for a long while and saw the fish eagle arc down and take a fish, and Robbie implored Alice to appreciate the beauty of that event, and she did.

36

The purpose of Mendi Mkhize's first press briefing, held on the verandah of the Cape Hamilton Hotel, was to tell the press there would be no press briefings. Watching from the sidelines, Clive was convinced again that something crucial had changed in the magistrate. The TV crew—from the same channel that had hosted Martin de Villiers's weekly show—consisted of a dogged-looking white female producer, a black cameraman and a white soundman. The writer and photographer from the *Sunday Times* both looked like near-retirement folk who would welcome a slow story.

"This is Detective Dhlomo, who is handling the investigation," Mendi said.

Detective Dhlomo waved amiably, and Mendi continued. "First I want to tell you that we believe completely in press freedom. You have complete freedom of movement, you may report anything that you see here, and I will trust you to do so fairly and impartially. But let's be clear that you are here of your own choice. We did not invite you. We do not court publicity. Our job here is to determine what happened to Martin de Villiers, not to provide you with material. When the investigation is concluded to our satisfaction, I will tell you the outcome and answer any questions. Until then, I do not want you asking me to report progress, to speculate, or to comment on your own views. I do not want you to attempt to interview me, any of my officers, or anyone that you see us questioning. The rule is we will not interfere with you if you do not interfere with us."

To Clive, the whole thing was beautiful music. As if reading from the script provided by the Port Victoria Chamber of Commerce, Mendi had suggested to the press that there could be fascinating material released at an indeterminate moment in the future, but nothing in between. Having come all that way, they could hardly head back immediately. They would have no choice but to hang around for a few days with nothing to do and money to spend.

Ursula Wolfe took down Mendi's every word in her crisp shorthand. As much as she had looked like a mall babe out of water the day before, at that moment she was a professional reporter, and apparently a good one. She was a product of a closed-knit Jewish community and she was looking for a controlled rebellion. She might have chosen college in America or good work in Israel. She chose journalism, possibly because it enabled her to infuriate her parents without leaving home. The news editor at the *Daily Chronicle* was pleased to have Ursula Wolfe passing across his vision on a regular basis, but he was apprehensive about being responsible if such an obviously inappropriate specimen were to get mangled in the grimy machinery of newspaper life in Africa. So he aimed her at a succession of cushy slots—women's page, entertainment, celebrity interviews—and she persistently tried to find stories that would give her something more. She knew she was a protected species, but she had no intention of cruising through that period of her life. If there was a big story in Martin de Villiers's demise, she intended to get it all to herself.

"How long do you think your investigation will take?" Ursula asked Mendi.

"More than a day and less than a lifetime," said Mendi, deadpan.

Ursula's shorthand transcription of that ended only a moment after his last word. She made no judgment on it.

"Can you at least give us a daily update on progress?" asked the *Sunday Times* reporter.

"No," said Mendi. "That is all." He nodded and left the room.

The *Sunday Times* reporter glanced around forlornly. "So are we just supposed to hang around and do nothing?"

Clive entered, leading Keshla, who was balancing a large tray of drinks.

"Who wants a beer?" said Clive. "On the house."

"It's only ten-thirty in the morning," said the severe TV producer.

"Got to adjust for the climate, hey," said Clive. "You don't want to get dehydrated. Now let me give you some thoughts on what you could do while the magistrate wraps up his investigation. There's plenty of stuff you could look into for local color. We have an ace ski-boat fisherman, Johnny Fourie, who is available to take you out. He's actually survived in the water for over twelve hours when his boat was capsized—but I'll let him tell you that story. Anyway, he'll have lots of insight into what might have happened to the unfortunate Mr. de Villiers in the water. And did you know that it was in this very lounge that the legendary hangman Slipknot van den Heever met his end?"

The assembled press corps hesitated only momentarily before falling upon the drinks.

37

Alice sat on the point where she had first seen Simon surfing. She longed to talk to him about everything that was happening to her, and sitting here was the best substitute. Just imagining him on his board on the water soothed her. When she thought of him that way, it wasn't Simon surfing, but Simon prone on his board, in that in-between contemplative time, the waiting and watching and maneuvering.

Along the beach came Johnny and Bob Peace, leading a brown heifer with a rope tied around its neck. They detoured slightly to greet her.

Bob asked, "You thinking about Simon?"

"Yes, I am," she said.

"We all do. Simon's good people."

"What are you doing with that animal?"

"Doing a spit-roast for the visitors. Just bought it from the chief down the beach there."

"Mama's going to slaughter it," said Johnny, "and do a little ceremony for the people. Give them some entertainment. Then we slow cook it all afternoon, get some lobster for starters, have ourselves a party."

"They got nothing to journalistic about, seeing as the magistrate's only got one clue—that's going nowhere. We gotta entertain the folks."

Alice gave a conspiratorial grin. "And make some money out of it, though."

"That too," Johnny acknowledged with a wink. "They're suckers with money. It's our duty."

"Other people's money," said Bob. "All on expenses. No one's getting hurt."

"Also a couple women among the reporters, I heard?"

"One babe," said Bob, "and two has-beens."

"Meaning they're your age?" Alice said.

"Women from the city go for the outdoor kinda thing, don't you think?" Johnny was deferring to Alice's judgment on the matter.

"I do," said Alice.

"For sure. Those game rangers at the larney parks, where they get rich Americans and Germans, you know, those guys they get so much—" Johnny stopped stone dead, his vocabulary completely failing him.

"Pussy?" said Alice.

Johnny flinched momentarily, then grinned in comradeship. "You know then," he said.

"It's full moon and all," said Bob.

Johnny threw his head back and gave a howl like a wolf. The heifer regarded him with curiosity.

"Good luck, boys."

"Hey, you can come, if you want," said Johnny.

"Be good for you. You're looking a bit down."

"Worrying about what to do about that old house?"

She stared at Johnny. "You know about the house?"

He shrugged. "Everybody knows everything here. In the end."

"Except who killed the dead guy," said Bob.

"Yeah, that's a tricky one."

"Those two old broads. Got to admire them, I guess."

Johnny dropped down on the rock facing Alice and looked her straight in the face. "Your problem is," said Johnny, "you got to work out what you are."

Alice immediately got one of those snapshots of herself from the remote camera through which she sometimes took a view of her life. She was sitting on a beach in the backside of nowhere with a condemned heifer, getting life skills counseling from a washed up drug-addled deejay and a violence-prone beach bum fisherman who smelt of bait and alcohol and gearbox lubricant.

"That's why Simon is so sorted out, that's why Dom is so sorted out, they know what they are," said Johnny. "You don't."

"How do you know I don't?"

"If you did, you wouldn't be here."

"Yes, I see what you mean," said Alice.

"You worry too much," said Johnny.

"Take responsibility for too much stuff," said Bob.

"You like Simon. You should take some guidance from his way of life."

"Look at Simon," said Johnny. "Simon just rides the wave, you see what I'm saying? He doesn't try and make the wave. He doesn't try and change the wave. He doesn't try to tell the wave how it could be different or better. He just takes the wave and makes something out of it—art, or something. That's why he's so beautiful to watch."

"It's more than that," said Bob. "It's like that thing, you know, wave and particle. You can't be both."

Alice studied Bob's face, but he appeared to be as clean of irony as the heifer, which also appeared attentive.

"You know about wave and particle?" Bob prompted her.

"Not a lot," she said.

"Me neither, but I understand the main thing, and well, the main thing is, you can't be both. You can be wave or you can be particle, and the great thing is you get to choose, except you can't choose both. The wave travels through—the particle is the thing it travels through. One is energy, the other is matter. At the one moment, you can tell which you are."

"That's a different kind of wave," said Johnny. "Different but the same."

"Exactly," said Bob. "Happiness comes from accepting the wave. Riding it."

"You get it?" said Johnny.

"I'm not sure," said Alice.

"Just say what you think."

"I think you two guys could be the last old hippies on the planet."

"Hey, there are worse things to be," said Bob.

"Yeah, and you know, probably from like a university point of view we're talking shit. But you also know we're right," said Johnny.

They set off again toward the hotel, with the agreeable beast strolling along the beach sand between them, requiring no guidance from the rope.

38

Woodstock was in a transport of indignation.

"Jesus F. Christ! I've had fuck knows how many drinks at this hotel, and every single one of them has been written in that book, and at the end of the month more of my pay goes to Clive than to me!"

News that Clive had given the journalists a round of free drinks astonished not only Woodstock. It demonstrated a commitment to enterprise previously unknown in Clive. Spend to profit. Woodstock didn't get, or care to get, that aspect.

"You got to understand, Woodstock, I give them the first one free because it makes them want more. Then they pay for those. It's just business. It's what you learn in hotel school."

"So why don't you give me the first one free?"

"Because he knows you're going to want more anyway, you stupid cunt," said Johnny.

Woodstock knew there was discrimination against him somewhere in there, he just couldn't mount a verbal depiction of it. Clive saw that a diplomatic move was required. He popped the top of an ice-cold one and handed it to Woodstock.

"I tell you what, Woodstock. Every day while the reporters are here, your first drink is free. There's number one. We're all in this together."

Woodstock's eyes swiveled around suspiciously. "What do I have to do for it?"

"Zip," said Clive, "Just be yourself."

Woodstock could remember indignities and beatings going back to the reformatory of his childhood, but he could not remember anyone actually giving him something without strings attached. Then he flattened the beer in one draught.

If Clive had taken the trading aspects of the press invasion seriously, Bob Peace had been no less diligent in applying his concept of legend building for Port Victoria. By nine in the morning he was on the verandah, holding forth to any available audience. It was an uncommon opportunity to diversify his talents. After all, it wasn't that different from being a deejay. And his station as a radio celebrity, however minor, lent credence to his pronouncements. He depicted the death of Slipknot van den

Heever as a classic tale of just desserts. He painted a picture of Breakdown as a mystical savant-beast who talked to the birds and fish and lived by a code beyond the human plane. In fact, the full extent of Bob's legend making talents only became apparent when Ursula accosted Johnny on the verandah.

"Are you Johnny Fourie?"

"That's me."

"Is it true you were in the water for twelve hours after your boat was sunk, and then walked up the beach to your own funeral?"

"More like fifteen hours."

"Aren't there a lot of sharks in this water?"

"You have to know how to deal with sharks. They sense fear. You don't have fear, they go eat something smaller."

"Wow! The waters are dangerous here, huh?"

"Coast is full of wrecks. Some of them are hundreds of years old, some are from last year."

"There's one in this bay," said Woodstock.

Johnny gave him a frown. He didn't want Woodstock contributing to the conversation. Too much margin for error. Johnny held out his arm to Ursula. On his wrist, he wore a hand beaten bangle.

"This is made from brass I stripped off the wreck in the bay here. I beat it myself. But this brass was originally beaten by some artisan in Portugal in sixteen-voetsek-something."

"Wow," said Ursula. She took Johnny's thick, muscular, scarred wrist in her delicate fingers and rubbed the smooth brass. She seemed to weigh his wrist as if it were the measure of the man. She turned her brown eyes on Johnny. "I would die to have one of these. Could you get some more of that brass and make me one?"

A process then took place in Johnny's skull whereby all the

normal brain fluid was drained and replaced with testosterone. The world beyond Ursula, Ursula's eyes, Ursula's flat tanned tummy, and Ursula's potential gratitude for the bangle, ceased to exist.

Although Johnny was supposed to be in charge of the slaughtering of the agreeable cow, he heard himself smoothly telling Ursula that they would have to ride out through the choppy breakers immediately while the tide was still low, anchor the boat above the wreck, and he would dive down and get her treasure. Then he would take her up to his house and use his oxy-acetylene torch to work that brass into any form she chose. Ursula declared the proposition to be both romantic and brave.

Woodstock looked out at the surf. "Shit, I dunno, Johnny, I scheme it looks a bit dicey out there today."

"For you, yes," said Johnny. "Not for me."

The unsolicited contribution from Woodstock actually added value to the product, but Woodstock had to be silenced quickly, so Johnny took him aside and briefed him on handling the preparation of the cow for the evening barbecue. Then he warned him to shut his mouth on pain of having the shit kicked out of him six ways.

Johnny and Woodstock got the boat ready for launching while Ursula attired herself in a swimsuit that appeared to use static electricity to adhere itself to the wearer. The sea conditions were indeed marginal and the ride out through the breakers even more daredevil than Johnny would have liked, but there was no doubting its value once they had made it. Ursula took off her T-shirt, which made Johnny grind his teeth unconsciously. She seemed to be cooperating in the thrill of the adventure.

Beyond the breakers there was still a strong swell. Johnny was no great athlete, but he had a survivability, a resolute buoyancy. He was from the same mold as his nation's rugby players who could walk away from mayhem alive, despite the fact that their digestive tracts were full of partially digested animal fats and their livers were under siege of persistent alcohol abuse. Like old Bedford trucks, they went on normally until they dropped stone dead; there was no gradual decline. Most importantly, Johnny knew those waters, and his own abilities, and the area of overlap of the two. The thing to watch was that Ursula's flat brown tummy didn't cause him to forget where the boundaries of that overlap were. Though he was always up for bar room bravado, on the actual ocean Johnny lived with a keen awareness that heroes die young.

He anchored carefully. He explained to Ursula that the location of the old Portuguese wreck was often hard to fix—it seemed to move and was periodically completely covered by sand. Two years prior, Johnny said, he had brought a bunch of paying customers out there to dive the wreck and they couldn't find the bloody thing.

But Johnny wasn't too worried about exactly where the wreck was. For in fact, Johnny already had in the pocket of his baggy fishing shorts the hunk of brass that would be fashioned into Ursula's bangle. Years ago, Johnny had pulled a four-foot length of brass off the prow of the sunken vessel and there was still plenty of it left next to the fireplace in his house. While Ursula was changing, Johnny had walked up to his house, snapped off a ruler length section and pocketed it.

Of course, Johnny could have simply told Ursula that he had some of the brass surplus in his house. But in ten years of beer chats with Bob Peace, Johnny had actually learned something about women that was going to be useful: drama is everything. In this case, fetching a piece of brass from his house was nowhere as effective a seduction as plunging into ocean and returning with the dripping prize. Ursula was never going to be able to see more than three feet into the water anyway, there was always suspended silt in the active water.

So all Johnny had in mind was a couple of submersions in the water, a bit of routine exercise prior to breaking the surface of the water with her treasure held high, like that hand in the fairy tale that comes up holding the sword. He was completely sideswiped when Ursula asked for a snorkel and flippers.

"You can't come in!" he said.

"I'm a very good diver," she said. "I've been trained in Mauritius. I swim two miles every week at the Health and Racquet Club. I bet I can hold my breath longer than you."

For a moment Johnny was completely without an idea on how to handle this. He spat a fat gwellie onto the glass of his mask and rubbed it in silence. That gave him precious time to think. Then he looked at her.

"You testing me?"

"What do you mean?"

"Well, I am the captain of this vessel. I am also a licensed recreational operator. We come out on the boat and then you start asking for things which you must know violate the rules and the insurance."

When Ursula looked around as though assessing whether such a vessel would qualify for insurance, he stood up so that his large chest towered over her trim torso.

"This is not the Health and Racquet Club, baby. As for Mauritius, that's a fucken coral island, they don't have surf. It's smoother than my bath water. You have Zambezi sharks at your health and prancing club?"

"You told me you bring divers to this wreck!"

"But that was not what we agreed on this trip. This trip is for me to get you some brass. In conditions like this, I cannot have the boat unattended. I cannot have both of us in the water at the same time. I cannot have you in the water at all because you haven't signed the liability waiver!"

"Oh, okay, I guess I can see that."

Johnny was hugely pleased with himself. It was probably the first time he had used words like "unattended" and "liability" in the same year, let alone in the same sentence. It all sounded so professional. And Ursula's tone had become so obedient, and Ursula's neat little bellybutton was so sexy, and he was so in charge.

On the shore, Woodstock knew none of those blissful feelings. Clive was busy with other preparations and Bob Peace refused to help, so Woodstock was left on his own to slaughter the heifer. In principle, there was nothing difficult about it. Men talked about slaughtering animals all the time, the details were taken for granted. The beast had simply to be moved from its present state, which was chirpy and interested in the world around it, to one where it could be skinned and cleaned. Johnny had given him hurried instructions to take the heifer out of sight in the dune bush and shoot it behind the ear.

The animal proved cooperative and allowed itself to be tied to a tree while Woodstock went off to fetch Johnny's revolver. He loaded it and returned. The heifer, which had lived close to humans all its life, had fretted while left alone in a strange place, and had wound its lead rope tightly around the tree. When Woodstock got it unwound, it butted him in gruff remonstration, causing him to drop the revolver in the fine sand. Woodstock swore and kicked the animal on the leg. It roared with surprise and sprang back against the restraint of the rope around its neck. Woodstock's difficult hands were not good with delicate motor movements like tying knots. The heifer jerked itself free, pranced a few paces and stopped. It studied Woodstock apparently to assess whether he was going to continue with that behavior or revert to being agreeable. Woodstock didn't like the look. He was already at the outer limit of his capacity for problem solving, and something in that look suggested that the animal was the brighter of the two parties present. Woodstock wasn't good with weapons, animals, death or responsibility, and he seemed to have got them all on one plate. He retrieved the revolver and spun the cylinder to dislodge any sand. The noise spooked the heifer again and it rapidly removed itself a few paces further and shuffled warily. Woodstock's only training for the execution was the movies, where when anyone fired a gun at some other person, the other person fell down dead. Woodstock pointed the revolver in the direction of the heifer and depressed the trigger spasmodically. The deafening report removed all doubt from the heifer's mind and it took off down the beach in the direction of home. Woodstock pointed the weapon at its vanishing backside and pulled the trigger again, but the cylinder jammed on the residual sand and would not rotate. Woodstock uttered every profanity he knew in rapid succession and set off after the beast.

39

In all the excitement, few people noticed a dusty van that came down the road from the capital. Mendi was handed a parcel. He took it up to his room and stripped off the courier company's plastic packaging, threw the waybill into the bin and found a pile of papers. He sat down and started to read. An hour later he sent down for room service. He kept reading.

Alice was walking through the deserted village at sunset when she noticed that the breeze was bringing her occasional snatches of human noise from the beach. She met Sammy, who was walking home, looking aggrieved.

"Stay away from there," he advised, frowning. "There's going to be trouble tonight. There already has been trouble, fucken Woodstock. It's not even dark yet, and Johnny's had five beers. Everyone knows that's the danger limit."

When Alice walked onto the beach below the hotel verandah, she could see the party had a dangerous edge. A pit had been dug in the beach sand in which a cooking fire was burning. Suspended above it was what Alice assumed was the carcass of the beast she had seen earlier, on a spit. The spit, supported on two inverted forked sticks sunk into the sand, could be rotated by handle. Sections of the carcass were covered with aluminum foil, which reflected the flame light. Further down the beach there was a second fire, more of a bonfire, which seemed to be purely for effect. Speakers from the hotel had been run out onto the lawn on extension cords and delivered a bass-heavy version of Bob Seger's *Night Moves* out into the humid, smoky air. There was a metal bath with beer cans and chipped ice in it. There were blankets and pillows and tables.

There were about forty people, all the locals, all the visiting reporters, Mendi's entourage, including his SWAT team, who were wearing some or all of their camouflage uniforms, and had their automatic rifles nearby.

Looking for someone to talk to, Alice picked Clive as the man most likely to be in the sane range.

"You'll sell a lot of beer tonight," she said.

He only frowned. "It's not ideal. The meat is hours behind schedule. So everyone's gonna be totally pissed before they eat anything. I don't like it."

"Why didn't you start the meat earlier?"

He gave her a look. "Fucken Woodstock," was all he said.

Ursula was dancing on the beach sand. She looked stoned.

Around the fire a dozen men watched her with eyes that reflected the flames. Watching those men was Johnny. And watching everyone was Dom, off to the side, casting a large shadow. The brass bangle on Ursula's slim arm flashed in the firelight. It looked hastily beaten and heavy, like a device to prevent an animal from straying too far. In her trance-like state, Ursula presented a vulnerable yet provocative figure. But none of the local men did more than look. For with the bangle, Johnny had put his brand on Ursula and the local men all knew that any attempt to elbow him off the prize would be met with instant and extreme violence. Whether the outsiders—the SWAT team soldiers and media people—comprehended this was an unknown factor that added to the thrill of observing.

Alice circled the crowd to get to Dom. "What brings you down the mountain?" she said.

"It's a party. I like a party."

"Of course you do. You're known for your gregariousness. You have a pattern of seeking out blathering drunks for company."

"In a small community, one shouldn't miss the collective events. It keeps you in touch."

"That makes more sense. So where's Lethu?"

"He's even less gregarious than me."

"Nothing to do with the fact that the magistrate is combing this whole area looking for someone called Tradition Dube?"

Dom had his eyes on Ursula. "I don't see the connection."

"Lethu's name is Dube."

Dom smiled indulgently. "It's a common name. Like Smith. You should know that."

"You're telling me there's no connection?"

"You met a man called Lethukuthula Dube. They're looking for a man called Tradition Dube. If you were in London and the police were looking for a Mr. Archibald Smith, would you go into the police station and tell them you know a Mr. Terence Smith?"

This man's life skill, thought Alice, is that you never know where you are with him. Dom took a joint out of his pocket and lit it. He offered it to her. She hesitated. "I think I want to be aware of what's happening tonight."

"That's why I'm offering it to you."

She smoked the joint with him. Five minutes later, the world ordered itself perfectly.

Two ten-year-old kids, recruited at short notice from Keshla's kraal, struggled down to the beach from the hotel, carrying additional crates of beer.

One of the journalists asked if the meat was ready yet. The carcass of the beast revolved slowly on the spit, tended by the cook from Clive's kitchen. He shook his head.

"Hey Woodstock!" came Bob's voice from somewhere in the dark. "Maybe you need to shoot that thing again. Maybe it's not quite dead yet."

"Go fuck yourself," said Woodstock.

Woodstock felt electric with awareness of how conspicuous he was. Ridicule had followed him all that day as the story spread.

He had chased that fucking heifer all the way along three beaches and finally caught up with it on the steep incline on the north shore. He had shot it once in the hindquarters and it rolled back down the incline onto him, roaring and kicking and pissing and bleeding. The two chaotic life forms, Woodstock and the heifer, untangled themselves in the beach sand with Woodstock receiving a shattering kick on the shoulder in the process. He got to his feet, found the revolver and shot the animal again in the neck. The only effect of that was more noise. He shot again and its eye exploded. Grinning waiters from the hotel helped him carry the carcass back so that Mama could clean it. That was why the meat was late, and why Woodstock was humming with danger signals no one saw in the firelight.

Mendi occasionally glanced down at the party from his room on the second floor of the hotel. Illuminated in the firelight, the scene was like something on a drive-in movie screen. He could see his SWAT team drinking and knew they would be foul with hangovers in the morning. Mendi liked a good party as much as anyone else, but he was preoccupied that night. He turned back to his reading.

The *Sunday Times* writer said, "Look at this, here we are. It's on occasions like this that I think there is still a great future for this country. We have everything, if you think about it."

"When I was young," said another, "black and white would never have sat around a beach fire together."

Everyone warmed to the theme.

"We've just got to get a few things right, and this country can really steam ahead."

"Africa is just waiting to be developed," said another. "It could be a powerhouse."

There were nods and murmurs of agreement, but into the silence that followed, Dom's voice intruded.

"The last thing Africa needs is development."

"Have you got this old fashioned idea that black people should carry on living in their pretty little mud huts forever?" said Ursula. "That's so racist!"

Dom ignored that. "You know what the greatest blessing on Africa is? Malaria. Can you imagine what the bushveld would be like without malaria? They would make it into fucking Disney World! Malaria keeps the Donald Trumps and Calvin Kleins out of Africa. Africa is on this planet as the ballast against the bullshit that too-rich humans think up to amuse themselves."

If they disagreed, no one said so. Dom's monologue had an edge to it which, when combined with his size, discouraged dissent. Alice watched Johnny Fourie switch his eyes away over the ocean, completely silent, as if waiting for some weather to blow over.

"Africa needs to be wild," said Dom. "It intuitively defends itself. Africa repels civilization like the immune system throws off a virus. Africa's natural state is brutal and savage and unfair and undemocratic and to enjoy Africa you must understand this and love it for this. You know what Africa's got right that Western civilization will never understand? The individual is unimportant. To ants, there are no individual ants, just ant-ness. This continent is the same. No time for small tragedies. Every day animals and people die in extreme pain here. Vultures follow starving children whose parents have been hacked to death in vendettas that go back before gunpowder."

"Shit," said the *Sunday Times* photographer, who was completely whacked on dope and thus more lucid than he had been in ten years. "Sounds like someone stepped on your dream somewhere down the line."

At that, Johnny cast a wary eye at Dom, as if fearing an eruption, but Dom just gave a lopsided grin and stood up, dusting the sand off his pants.

"You're right, I'm talking complete shit. Means it's time to go home." And he walked off into the dark without further ado.

"Weird guy," said one.

"He really shouldn't smoke that stuff if it's going to make him so irritable," said Ursula.

"I'm sure I recognize that guy. Did he used to be famous for something?"

"He just looks like you recognize him because he's so big."

Clive, obviously concerned that Dom's downer had killed the party before all the alcohol was sold, cranked up the music and encouraged dancing. Ursula dragged Johnny to his feet and made him sway on his two stiff pylons in the sand while she skipped around him.

Watching Ursula and the men watching her, Alice was suddenly gripped by the idea that it was her responsibility to rescue the child. Alice felt she knew the type well—a pattern of behavior that was innocently provocative, a schoolyard tease, a mall babe. Such a place in society was known and accepted and catered for in the rules, but in this place, the rules were not known, much less enforced. Alice caught Johnny's eye, and he seemed to read her mind. For with a bizarre gesture, he slowly wagged his finger at her, a warning, she was sure, not to interfere. And there was a logic in that, too. She was there in the heart of a continent that was entirely predicated on the survival of the fittest. In the executive game parks of that country, overseas visitors sat in Land Rovers and watched predators kill and eat their prey every day. They took videos of it. And the handsome game rangers lectured them on the need not to interfere in the natural process, so that if they came upon an orphaned leopard cub, they were not allowed to rescue it and feed it, but had to leave it to be killed by the hyenas or the wild dogs, as was its fate. Johnny's wagging finger was telling Alice to leave Ursula to her fate, which she had undoubtedly chosen.

Alice got to her feet and wiped the sand off her clothes. She made noises about leaving and took a route past Ursula, as if to say good night. "Are you okay?" Alice said to Ursula as quietly and nonchalantly as she could. "Do you know what you're doing?"

Then she looked in Ursula's eyes and saw the flat, calm look of a creature that knew exactly what it was doing. It reminded Alice of looking in the mirror when she was nineteen, when she had known exactly what to do with men.

"I'm fine," said Ursula with a grin.

"Good, okay," said Alice, "I'm turning in."

She made her way across the sand and was halfway up the stairs to the hotel when Johnny's voice reached her.

"Hey, Alice! Sleep tight, hey!"

She raised her hand, and other voices followed Johnny's. She felt a strange comradeship. Then she slipped into the darkness.

40

She knew he was there as soon as she came out of sleep. Instinct, smell, pheromones; something. She was instantly awake and completely still. Even her eyelids were cautious as they opened enough to let her see the room around her. The full moon was giving her enough light to see the figure approach her bed. Strangely, she experienced no squirt of adrenaline or panic. She lay there in the kind of shock that sedates a giraffe as it watches itself being eaten alive by lions.

The figure was short and stocky and Alice was immediately reminded of the Zulu mythological figure known as the *tokoloshe*, a rancid beast the size of a garden gnome with a prodigious penis, which lurked under beds and impregnated impure women. A more realistic identification was confirmed when she caught a ray of moonlight off the sea through the gap between his bandy legs. Alice realized she was lying alone in Simon's house in the middle of the night—and Woodstock was standing over her.

Woodstock was beyond anywhere he had ever been before. He had taken out his personal pain on animals a number of times in his life. He had looked deeply into a cat's eyes as he slowly and methodically crushed its windpipe, ignoring its claws raking into his wrists. But his fear and his shame had always prevented him from venturing into this territory with humans. But there he was with Miss Smelly Pants. He was confident that he was stronger than she was, but he had a large stone in his right hand just in case she needed subduing. He was standing there, absorbed in what he was feeling, a mix of sexual expectation and bowel-moving relief and ringing in the ears. If Woodstock had had any appreciation of religion, he might have taken that state as heavenly. It was indeed glorious, and indeed his due, after the searing pain of the day.

Late in the afternoon, Woodstock had been left to clean the boat after Johnny's wreck-dive, and he had calmed himself with two jolts of battery power. But the party had soured his mood again as he watched the happiness of others. Then Alice arrived and Woodstock had suddenly known that that night, with substantial distraction provided, was the night. On this wild night no one would miss him, or think about her, or be in any condition to do anything about it.

While she lay there, she was completely in his power. She had kicked a bare leg over her cover and he had seen the line of moonlight all the way from her ankle to the waist of her underwear. He swayed on his misshapen legs. Woodstock's entire database on the female body and sexuality came from the pages of porn magazines. He had never touched a naked woman, and the complex notions involved in the act of sex were as inaccessible to him as quantum physics.

She saw him stir. She could hear his breathing and there was a catch in it that brought to her the first flush of fear. That triggered the adrenaline and ended her trance. But she thought the only thing she could think: if she screamed enough and loudly enough and wildly enough, she might just scare him. So she came bulleting up off the bed, screaming, "Get out of here! Get out of here!" She spun away from him, fearing to make contact, as though his very touch was toxic. Her foot got caught in the sheet and she stumbled as she ran for the door. He hurled the rock at her and hit her a glancing blow. It deflected her off course as she ran and she hit the doorframe heavily. He pounced after her and she kept screaming, "Leave me! Leave me alone!" She had one thought: if she could make it out the door, she might outrun him in the heavy beach sand. As soon as she felt the power in his gristly hands, she knew she would win no fight with him. All the pain of his life was in those hands and they bruised her instantly as they made contact. They were the hands of a human constrictor and she felt a wild helplessness that had no reference in her life.

But abruptly Woodstock gave a howl of pain and released her like a spring; she fell away from him with the impression that he had gone spontaneously berserk. He howled and contorted himself and a moment later she saw that something was devouring Woodstock, something dark and quick and completely silent and much more powerful than he. Woodstock and his predator crashed across the room and there was a dull noise as Woodstock's skull was propelled against the wall. He fell still. The shadow stood upright and kicked Woodstock, woofing the wind out of him. The shadow moved and caught the moonlight and it became Breakdown. Alice's ears were ringing and when she stood, the blood deserted her head and she had to kneel quickly. She reached up and switched on the light. The first image to resolve in the searing brightness was Breakdown spitting out onto the floor an unidentifiable chunk of Woodstock.

Breakdown shook his head wildly at the light and she snapped it off again and sat trembling on the floor as he dragged Woodstock's body out of the room. Halfway through the process, Woodstock recovered consciousness and scrambled away from Breakdown like a kicked dog. He made a noise falling off the end of the verandah and was claimed by the night. Breakdown stood in the middle of the room, listening to Woodstock blundering away through the dune bush. Then stillness descended on the house, and on Breakdown. He mumbled something to Alice, who said only "Thank you."

He raised a hand in a salute to her. Then he left the house without a sound.

Alice lay for a long time where she was. She quivered with a creature-like fear of making herself known by moving.

41

The next morning Alice could hardly have been in a more vulnerable state of mind, but she was still angry with herself when Mendi trapped her so easily.

He arrived early; Alice had just finished putting Simon's house to rights. There had not been much blood, although it had got into odd places. There was a shattered vase, which Alice had been using for flowers that she picked on her walks, and a snapped lamp stand. The substantial portion of Woodstock's ear that Breakdown had ripped off with his teeth and spat onto the floor presented her with the biggest problem. She was detained by wondering if it had any burial rights, but decided that it didn't and picked it up with some newspaper and walked knee deep into the sea and threw it as far as she could. That was biologically sound, she felt.

Mendi was lawyerly as he sat in the chair opposite her on Simon's verandah. He had left Detective Dhlomo out of the interview—the man had probably needed his sleep after the night before. Mendi spent some time composing his first sentence.

"Lethukuthula sent a message to me yesterday, with Mama's boy. He said I should come to see him today and that you would show me the way. Naturally, he doesn't want to come into the village."

213

Alice knew instantly he was attempting to trick her.

"Your method is clumsy," she said. "Several obvious queries come to mind, such as why doesn't Temba take you himself?"

Mendi's grin was delighted. "What you mean to say is, who's Lethukuthula?"

She took it in, and grimaced.

"Lethukuthula Dube may or may not be able to shed light on the death of Martin de Villiers," said Mendi. "To find out, I must interview him. You will take me to him, or I will tie you up in so much red tape that you will never leave this place."

She believed him to be quite sincere.

He produced from his pocket a piece of paper and handed it to her. "It's an order of the court compelling you to take me to the place of residence of one Lethukuthula Dube."

"This is just a piece of stationery you've filled out in your room!"

"That's right. I am a magistrate. I can make a court order." He stood up. "I'll wait while you get ready, but please be quick."

"Look, I've still got cleaning up to do. Can't I meet you at the hotel in an hour?"

His smile was complimentary, as though he was pleased she was playing the game with some intelligence.

"I don't want you sending anyone ahead. Five minutes."

42

As a concession to the difficulty of the climb, Mendi removed his tie and donned sensible shoes. But he kept on his dark slacks and his long-sleeved lounge shirt. Detective Dhlomo resisted being woken, and Mendi hadn't tried too hard to overcome his reluctance. The SWAT team, who hadn't had any real swatting to do since their graduation, treated the exercise like the invasion of a hostile neighboring territory and fanned out around the path, their camouflage gear blending into the bush. It was impressive until their collective hangovers met the steep side of the hill.

Mendi and Alice walked together where the path permitted. But once they got into the serious climb, she moved out ahead of him because she was fitter and could maintain a pace, and his shoes were not ideal for the terrain.

She was going fine until she realized she was lost. She thought the route was simple, but there was a difference between looking at a hill and being on a hill in thick growth. She had been on the path—or a path—too long, she thought.

"We'll cut straight up the hill here," she told Mendi, and he passed the command to his men, who groaned.

They struggled for fifteen minutes until she caught the tang of dagga on the breeze. Alice was walking ahead of the others and as they reached the lip of the plateau, she felt a subtle resistance at stomach level. She stopped and looked down and saw a strand of fishing line across her path. She stepped back. She glanced back; the others were well behind her and hadn't noticed yet. She tweaked the line cautiously with her fingers and could see it stretch away in both directions, through the trees. Alice was conscious that a great deal lay in the tension of the line between her fingers. Behind her was an unpredictable military force; ahead of her were two men with at least one AK-47 and a lot to lose.

"What's wrong?" Mendi called, closing in behind her.

"Just waiting for you to catch up," she said. She tramped heavily on the line and caught it with her boot and took forging steps ahead, dragging the line until there was no resistance and then stepping over it and walking on.

Alice had no way of judging the competence of the soldiers.

When she had been young in this country, the army was all white and extremely active. For twenty years, the white government was convulsed by the notion that it was going to be fighting a communist threat on several fronts and had developed a versatile and effective fighting machine for that mission. Adopting the strategy of the United States, they elected to fight the communist threat in other people's countries, and poured men and money into Angola, Zimbabwe, Namibia and Mozambique.

When the "unrest" of the domestic liberation struggle came to a boiling point, the army was recalled and deployed in black townships where it was ineffective in putting down resistance, but totally effective in becoming recognized around the world as a brutal organ of suppression. Meanwhile, the leaders of the liberation struggle recruited thousands of black citizens who fled their home country as exiles and sent them for military training in central Africa, Cuba, and Eastern Bloc countries.

For a number of years, the clash between those two armies was expected with dread, but in the end, liberation was achieved without those forces ever meeting in any significant contact. When the first democratic government came to power, neither army was keen to cooperate in a joint force. Those who had supported the old white government went into commercial practice as security consultants, private investigators, debt collectors, nightclub bouncers, Truth Commission witnesses, weapons dealers, and movie stuntmen. Those who had been trained to overthrow that old government took early retirement and became politicians or policy consultants, after dinner speakers and business moguls.

Alice suspected that the remaining armed forces of the first democratic government were those who didn't have the wit to get themselves sorted out in that manner, the ones least suited to be left in charge of the country's defense, arsenal and training of new recruits. The net result was that the nervous young men who rode shotgun for Mendi's judicial field trip were likely to have certain critical gaps in their expertise in addition to severe symptoms of excess alcohol consumption. However, pretty much everyone in that broad land knew how to fire a weapon. Office secretaries wearing sports bras and docile suburban mothers with tomato sauce stains on their jeans set off to indoor shooting galleries where they donned earmuffs and blasted away at targets with automatic pistols they had received as gifts from their lovers. So even if the SWAT team members had only a rudimentary training in abseiling, helicopter borne assault, hostage negotiation, appropriate force and target recognition, they probably all knew where the trigger was on their R-1 rifles, an assault weapon manufactured locally under license from Belgium.

Such a rifle might be the ideal defense against a high speed Doberman Pinscher, especially if a person waited until he saw the whites of its eyes. The SWAT team did not employ that method, however. The soldier who first spotted the dogs coming through the bush at high speed was already severely dehydrated and exhausted, not to say pissed off, and approaching a hallucinogenic state. The image of the dog triggered in him a cognition event that compressed into one reflex all the fear and loathing that had built up between black people and guard dogs in the nation. He thumbed off his safety catch and emptied his clip in the direction of the dog. His comrades, assuming themselves to have been lured into a cunning ambush, flung themselves on the ground and emptied their clips in an arc between ten o'clock and two o'clock ahead of them, as they had been trained, more or less. That generated more noise and cordite smell than the dogs were comfortable with (Dobermans are essentially bullies—they seldom proceed with an equal contest), and they spun around and ran back to the verandah of the house and crawled under the table.

217

Mendi and Alice, acutely aware they had an even chance of being shot in the front or the back, buried themselves into the hillside in a manner that Alice would remember with a certain nostalgia in her docile old age.

The SWAT leader's later report would note that 416 rounds were fired in the assault on the suspect's suspected hiding place. The firing lasted several minutes. Decades later, hikers passing that way would find bullets embedded in the trees over a wide area and wonder what unrecorded massacre of the liberation struggle took place there.

When the silent alarm had been triggered some minutes before, Dom had thought it was likely to be Alice blundering through the cordon again and had run after the dogs, whistling for them to come back. When the sound of several military weapons on full automatic reached him, he turned and ran back. Lethu was already on the verandah with the AK-47.

"Who the fuck is that?"

"I don't have a clue," said Dom, "but we aren't going to win a shooting match with them. So hide the fucking weapon."

They scrambled, throwing the AK-47 and spare ammo together with packaged and unpackaged dagga into plastic bin liners. That was thrown into a hole covered by a trapdoor in the lounge floor. It would never beat a professional search, but Dom and Lethu's security strategy was geared for theft rather than law enforcement.

They were finished in good time. Dom had locked the two dogs in a room and he and Lethu were sitting on the verandah and paging idly through old magazines when Mendi led his squad up the open area in front of the house.

"Get anything?" inquired Dom.

"I beg your pardon?" said Mendi.

"I thought you might be going after the klipspringers. Good venison if you hang it right. That's not the ideal weapon for them, though. You need a clean head shot."

"Dom—" said Alice.

"I'll handle this," said Mendi. "I am Mendi Mkhize, the magistrate for this area. I'm warning you now that I'm investigating a murder so don't start any bullshit with me." He directed his gaze at Lethu. "Are you Lethukuthula Dube?"

Everyone watched Lethu. He had the stillness of a man who has his own God.

"Yes," he said.

"Have either of you ever met or spoken to Martin de Villiers, the man who was found dead on the beach here?"

Dom replied, "We had a visit from a guy called Martin de Villiers a few weeks ago. Is he the guy who turned up dead?"

Mendi eyed him. "Are you telling me you didn't know?"

"How should I know?"

"You never saw the body?"

"I didn't even know there was a body until after it had been taken away. We don't go into the village much. Ask anyone. So what happened to Mr. de Villiers?"

"Mr. de Villiers came here to interview you for a story," said Mendi to Lethu.

"Mr. de Villiers—" began Dom.

"I am speaking to Mr. Dube here, not you. The dead man came to see Mr. Dube. It's Mr. Dube I am interviewing at the moment."

"But it was Dom who spoke to him," said Lethu. "I didn't speak to him."

"Why not?"

"He contacted us through a friend. He never came here. Dom went to see him. I never saw him. Dom told him I don't speak

219

English."

Mendi turned on Dom. "Is that true? He speaks English perfectly well. Why did you say that?"

"Are you interviewing me now?" said Dom.

"Yes, I'm interviewing you, and I'm asking you an express question. Why did you lie to Mr. de Villiers and give him the idea that Mr. Dube does not speak English when he does?"

"Because when Mr. de Villiers acquired information about how to contact us in a dishonest way, I considered him to be someone who may not have Lethu's best interests at heart. So, until I had more information about Mr. de Villiers's motives, I deemed it to be useful to make life a little difficult for Mr. de Villiers."

Mendi considered for a while and then said, "If you will give my men refreshments, we can sit down and talk about this."

Mendi's small army sat out under a tree fifty yards away where they would be out of earshot. Dom delivered drinks to them. Alice brought four chairs out onto the verandah. She could hear the dogs restless behind a closed door. As the four of them took their seats around the verandah table, she observed that Mendi was calm.

"I don't want to have to climb this fucking hill again," said Mendi. "I want to go down this hill today knowing only two things. So we are not going to even mention that you are growing more illegal dagga here than the rest of my province put together. And that you have knowingly withheld information that would have concluded my investigation long ago and saved us from that platoon of rats down in the hotel. And the many other things you're guilty of that I'm sure I would find if I looked. We are going to sort out just two things here today. The first one is, what happened to Martin de Villiers?" He put his eyes on Dom and Lethu. "Tell me," he said. "Tell me everything. Tell me what you

220

think happened to Mr. de Villiers."

Dom shrugged. "You wanna know? I'd say he slipped off the rocks while fishing. Not the first to do that, not the last. He was a keen fisherman. He brought his own tackle all the way from Johannesburg. I can tell you where he was staying—at a campsite a few miles up the coast. If you go and look there, I'm sure you'll find his kit and his car and everything, but not his fishing rod."

"Why did he stay up there? Why not here?"

"That's where I meet my buyers. I don't do business close to home. Dealers who want dagga know to meet me up there. They don't know where I live."

"What's dagga buying got to do with anything?"

"De Villiers tracked us down through people who knew people and heard that we were growing dagga. So he knew the best way to get face to face with us was to come as a buyer. He was pretty smart in that."

"So you met?"

"Yes, and he told me he knew that Lethu lived with me and he wanted to interview him. So I told him I would discuss it with Lethu, but it would take a few days. And he said that was fine, he was gonna catch some fish. And he asked me about good fishing spots."

"You said you didn't trust his motives. What were you talking about?"

"Martin de Villiers," said Dom, "is a somebody. A celebrity. He has written three books about politics and whatnot in this country. He has his own TV show. His training is journalism. Journalists don't have their own lives. They process other people's. Good people, bad people. To carry on being famous and well off, Martin de Villiers had to write about other people. Martin de Villiers has to have other people's lives the way an abattoir has to have cattle."

In a corner of her mind, Alice wished she could have produced an image such as that while trying to convey to her own husband what it was about his profession she found distasteful.

"And he wanted Lethu?"

"He carried on about what a story Lethu has to tell and how he's looking forward to telling it for him. I told him I very much doubt that Lethu wanted to be part of any story, Lethu wants to live his life quietly down here and leave the past in the past. Then Martin de Villiers said to me that he was going to write this story anyway. And he said that it would be better for Lethu to cooperate in the story so that his side could be clear. He said that people who didn't cooperate in stories ended up losing out, because they didn't get their point of view across.

"I said why doesn't he just not write about Lethu. And Martin de Villiers said to me that wasn't possible. He said we couldn't stop him writing it. He said the public had a right to know this story, and it was his duty to write it. And he said he had written a synopsis and signed a contract with his publishers and got an advance, so now he had to do it. That's how these guys work. He even had the title all ready."

Mendi smiled and said, "Those the Revolution Forgot."

That was the only time Alice ever saw Dom look surprised.

"That's right. How did you know?"

Mendi said, "This synopsis was delivered to me yesterday. Investigators who are looking into de Villiers's death from the other side sent down copies of a whole lot of papers from his office."

Alice could see that Mendi was pleased with the impact of that.

"And did he write about me?" said Lethu.

"Let's come back to that. First, I want to get your evidence completely straight in my mind. I have let you know now that I have other sources of information about this case that you were unaware of. So, let that be a warning to you not to try and bullshit me. I ask you again, Lethukuthula Dube, did you meet this man de Villiers or have anything to do with his death, or know anything about it?"

"No," said Lethu.

"And you," said Mendi to Dom. "You met this man, you had talks with him, you told him where to fish. Nothing else? No half-truths, please. I want now anything that might explain his death."

"I met him once in the campsite at Lusungeti. I'll give the names of two people who will confirm that, as long as you promise not to harass them about other things. After we had talked about his book, he asked about the fishing, and so I drove with him in his car to show him where Bird Rock is, so that he could fish there later. Then I came back here. Two days later, I went down there again to tell him Lethu wasn't going to cooperate with him, and he wasn't around, so I didn't worry about him anymore."

"Was his car there?"

"I didn't see it, but I didn't particularly look for it. People said they hadn't seen him. I left a note for him with the campsite manager. You can ask him for it. That was the end of the story as far as I was concerned."

They waited while Mendi studied his own hands for a while. Then he looked up at Lethu. "You are really Lethukuthula Dube, who ran the street committees in Etingting township?"

"Yes."

Mendi gathered more detail on his own fingernails before saying, "It would be a great honor for me to hear your story, for I have heard many versions of it over the years, and it would give me satisfaction to have the original."

Lethu said nothing.

"You see," said Mendi, "I think that the contents of Martin de Villiers's office will be held as evidence for as long as the file on this case remains open. Which could be a long time. That evidence may even become lost. As time goes by, de Villiers's publishers are going to lose interest. I don't think that book is ever going to be published."

Alice smiled. She had come to admire the magistrate.

"I will tell you," said Lethu. "Can you send the soldiers away?"

"Of course," said Mendi. He turned to Alice. "They could escort you down as well."

"If Lethu doesn't mind I would like to hear his story, too."

43

At midday, most of the cast from the previous night's party were sitting on the verandah of the Cape Hamilton, treating their hangovers with further alcohol when news got around that Mendi had been seen leaving early with his SWAT team and Alice.

"So do you think she actually knows something about this de Villiers guy?" said Clive.

"Naa," said Bob. "That magistrate probably just wants to impress her."

"Alice isn't mixed up in anything," said Johnny. "Alice is a good chick. I like Alice."

Everyone had noticed that Johnny was strangely mellow that morning. Heavy nights usually left Johnny with headaches and unresolved violent impulses, but that morning he had the disposition of a wide, slow river. Everyone wanted to ask, but no one dared. Ursula had not been seen all morning.

Sammy came onto the verandah, carrying a packet of medications, which might prove useful to people with the symptoms of alcohol abuse.

"What happened with Woodstock?" said Sammy. "I was coming back from upriver, early, and there he was walking on the road out of town. Carrying an old portable radio. I stop to talk, maybe he needs help, I see he's had some kind of an accident, his ear is half torn off, he's got blood all on him, he looks like shit."

Everyone looked at Johnny. "Don't look at me! I ain't seen him since the party."

"I asked him if he needed help," said Sammy, "and he spits at me. So, I drive on. He keeps walking up the hill. If he's planning to walk to the capital, he's picked a hot day for it."

"He's gone forever," said Johnny.

"I don't think so," said Sammy. "He was only carrying that radio."

"That's all he's got. And I've never heard him listen to it."

"That shit with the cow must have finally popped his rivets," said Clive.

"Do you believe in that reincarnation shit?" said Bob.

"Like in a previous life you were Errol Flynn and before that you were Cleopatra."

"Yeah, the bit I'm talking about is where you pay for the sin of a previous life—"

"Karma," said Bob.

"That's what I'm talking about. I scheme Woodstock did something really, really bad in a previous life, because he sure has been dealt a kak shift this time around."

"Well, he's not getting any better—in a spiritual sense, I mean," said Bob. "So he's probably going to have to go through it again."

"Shit, can you opt out of the loop?"

"I doubt it."

"Sure you can. Reincarnation only happens to people who

believe in it. Stands to reason."

"I doubt that Woodstock believes in it."

"Shit, would you, if you were Woodstock?"

"I guess not."

"Woodstock's a fucken waste of white skin," said Clive. "Good riddance."

But Johnny wanted even Woodstock to enjoy his mood that day. "Woodstock had problems, you know, that we can't understand. I feel sorry for him."

"Shit, you gave him enough hidings, you didn't feel sorry for him then."

"Hey, I was his employer, I had to keep order. That's not personal. I hope something turns up for him."

44

When they sing the songs of this land in years to come, Lethukuthula Dube's will not be among them. He told his story in complete form to an audience of three that afternoon in the sun on the hillside above the Umzimvubu River, and it was carried away by the river and those three people, who may have told it again in various forms, but as the tale of a mythological figure.

Martin de Villiers had been quite right—many revolutionary heroes are forgotten. Revolutions are the sum of a multitude of actions, many unrecorded. Heroes bloom in the moment, play their role and are ploughed back into the ground.

Lethu was born half an hour's walk from the lagoon at Port Victoria. As a child he had known much that Alice had known: the lagoon and the river and the perfect arc of the fish eagle and the slow play of one day into another. The way the hills faded into one another and made the barrier. But he had known it from a

226

perspective quite different from Alice's. Lethu was born in a mud hut. In the first few years of his life, the only white man he saw was Robbie, who visited all the villages in that area. Robbie shaped Lethu's destiny the way he shaped hundreds of lives in that area.

Men like Robbie existed in rural areas across the eastern half of this land, white men with contracts to ensure a steady supply of black labor to the gold and diamond mines far away on the highveld. Robbie supplied three mines in a group on the west rand—one of the first areas to be mined back in 1890, and thus with the deepest mines. The mine bosses had Robbie on a contract and he in turn had the chiefs in his area on a contract, although in the latter case, nothing was written down.

Mine operators had fixed ideas about the native laborers. They believed that certain tribes had certain inherited capabilities and were suited to different skills on the mines. Some tribes were considered not as brave as others and not suited to underground work. Some were believed to be good with woodwork and given shaft-propping jobs. Mozambiquans were believed to be smart enough to be drivers. Xhosas, like those from around Port Victoria, were believed to be tough and fearless and sent to the rock face in the deepest mines in ten-hour shifts a mile underground. Such a man could spend thirty years of his adulthood alternating the darkness of the mineshaft for the darkness of the dormitory compound, and little thought was given to his welfare unless he fell down.

A portion of the mineworkers' wages found its way back to their families in the remote rural areas. So Robbie could tell himself that he provided the economic lifeblood to the area. But Robbie would also reward the chiefs directly, in proportion to the steadiness of the flow of young men to the labor recruiting center. The chiefs' wealth was in direct proportion to their cooperation in providing labor. Their wealth could be seen in the size of their cattle herds and the provision of building materials and other prizes. Robbie harvested young men from the villages along that stretch of the coast. He was not the first. By the time Lethu came along, that process had shaped the entire society.

When the men were stripped out of the communities, their structure changed. The villages became places of women and children. The communities lost their land skills and the purpose around which their society had been built. They became dependent on the mine wage—what portion of it reached them. That money mostly ended up with the traders who sold them things—white and Indian traders. When the men of the villages returned on holiday, their eyes were changed by the darkness of the mine pit and their interest in the land was gone; they talked of strange places and strange things. They would be introduced to their own children and make their wives pregnant again and head off on the train for another eleven months. Until finally they came home for the last time, after their lungs and their spirit were gone and the mine had spat them out like the overburden that was stripped off the precious metal.

When Lethu got to school-going age, his father, who worked in the mine as his father had before him, decided that it was time to break the cycle. He took his son to live in the black township near the mines, where he would grow up within reach of another world, and an education. So Lethu left the rural landscape behind and went to a city divided into black and white, rich and poor, privileged and oppressed, and found himself on the wrong side of all those equations.

At Lethu's school there was little schooling. It had been written—and Martin de Villiers may have written it himself if he had lived to complete his book—that leaders of the revolution sacrificed a generation of school children and their education to bring the liberation struggle to critical mass. But that was too simplistic. The generations of black children who were at school in the 1970s and 1980s found themselves on a promontory in the history of the country, and that prominence was created not by themselves but by the events that came before them. It unfolded thus—destiny, if you like—and the only control they had over it was how they superintended their own valor and personal justice, and for many even that level of personal control was not possible.

They were the generation on the crest of the wave of change. It was children who had grown up just like Lethu who were shot on the first day of the Soweto riots. It was children like Lethu who were in the crowd that was tear gassed the day Alice was in Soweto. It was children who had grown up just like Lethu who hurled the Molotov cocktails and shouted the slogans and took the rubber and hard-tip bullets of the police force. It was children who had grown up just like Lethu whose lives were later chronicled in stage plays and films. Mostly they were nameless and stateless. Lethu had no home, no place, no route, no future. In 1985, he found himself in Etingting township—so named because the nights there were full of the sound of ricocheting bullets.

It was a poverty stricken place washed by many violent currents. It was poor and overcrowded and badly planned and completely neglected. Migrants from across the country and beyond washed up there. All governmental control had ceased except for the occasional pass through by a military convoy, which had nothing to do with community policing and everything to do with subduing the politicals.

In such circumstances, self-government springs up. In black townships across the veld, which was layered over the deep gold deposits, government passed to committees of residents. They varied greatly. Some were effective and benign. Some were effective and vicious. Some were just. Some were not. Among other things, they held trials of everyone from petty thieves to suspected police informers. The teenagers of the street committees made up government each day and enforcement was carried out according to the temperament of the mob. An unstable mix of good intentions, vigilantism, political dogma and the bravado of youth shaped their direction.

Lethu found himself the leader of a street committee that imposed law in Etingting. He had become something of a local legend because he was unusual in his quiet voice. He was seen to be something of an elder. He was eighteen years old.

"That was when I first met Dom," said Lethu. "He was working in the clinic in the township. I went there once for treatment. I'd been hit in the chest by a rubber bullet at close range. During a disturbance."

"Are you a doctor?" Mendi said to Dom.

"No, I was just a volunteer."

"Dom had got some money from one of the NGOs to start an outreach program for the clinic. He was the one who made it possible for us to go there without the police coming in and arresting us in the clinic."

"I remember something about that," said Alice. "It was a story that came up for consideration but was nixed by the producer. Not enough people dead. Wouldn't make the evening news."

Mendi chuckled and gave Dom an uncharacteristic slap on the arm.

"So you were once a do-gooding white liberal, huh?"

Lethu laughed. "He can't deny it. But I cured him of that! I made his program—what's that word the guy from the NGO used, Dom?"

"Untenable."

"That's it, untenable—I love that word. It's such a gentle and civilized word for the fact that I fucked up Dom's program and Dom's life and changed everything. `I'm sorry, Mr. Marais, but your position has become untenable!'"

"How did you do that?" said Alice.

Mendi had clocked Dom just right. He had been an idealistic young white citizen of the country, looking for something he could do that would help to solve the problem and salve his conscience. The most radical of that type resisted being drafted into the army and exiled themselves outside the country's borders. A few young white men and women even joined the liberation movement overseas and returned as undercover operatives. Most ended up trying to find a position in ordinary society from which they could do something. They worked for trade unions or joined NGOs that built black housing, trained black teachers, or generated research papers that were used to lobby the government for change. They raised money from concerned donors overseas and successful companies at home. For the most part, they were dismissed as softies by the ordinary white public and as useless liberals by black political leaders.

Dom had heard that rioters injured in confrontations with the police never went for treatment in hospitals or clinics because the police were known, or rumored, to make a sweep through such places after there had been trouble. Most of those useless liberals had a cause that touched them personally for reasons unknown or unexpressed, and so it was with Dom. It horrified him that young people should be cut off from emergency medical treatment. So, he started the long process of gaining support and raising funds. Then he secured the involvement of a senior government official who had the will and status to influence police policy. And he succeeded in creating at the Etingting township clinic, an emergency treatment center that was inviolate by the police and where treatment was given without any personal record being required. He not only did all that, but he got the local people to have trust in the system. For a short while.

It was the season of the peak of inhuman violence in the townships. A season resembling the Bastille days of the French revolution, when in the body of a just uprising, a heart of madness took over and started to devour itself.

One day when Lethu was not present, a man was brought before the street committee on charges of being a "traitor"—an informer to the white police. There was no greater crime than that: an accusation easily made and difficult to deny. Informers who were found guilty were "necklaced"—a car tire was forced down over their shoulders, trapping the arms, and they were doused with petrol and burned to death in public.

It was a day on which the street committee was hungry for blood. Armored police vehicles had been touring the township for two days, bulldozing the crossroad barricades of burnt out stolen cars, which were the most visible symbol of street committee control. They had raided two homes and taken out suspects for questioning—a euphemism for beating. One of the suspects detained was Lethu himself, which was why he was not present when the committee was convened.

He was released at midday and walked through the township of shacks and wood fires and corner businesses run from cardboard boxes to the vacant area where his committee met behind the scarred row of converted containers that served as an infant crèche. If he had arrived a few hours earlier, things might have gone differently. But even when he was a hundred yards away, he could hear the tone of the baying and shouting that chilled the bones of the innocent and guilty alike.

Lethu came upon the scene when the convicted traitor was already in the grip of the tire, writhing and screaming. Two teenaged boys were preparing to douse him with petrol. Others were striking matches and waving them in the face of the convicted man: that was the time of breaking him, tormenting him, trying to get him to confess, incriminate others, lose his bowel control, die of shock.

But the shock came to Lethu, as he recognized the convicted man and knew at once that man could never be a traitor. He rushed to intervene and unleashed a cascade of human behavior that most would never see, and those that had prayed they'd never see again. A mob is volatile and intemperate; a mob deprived of a prey in the thrall of consuming it explodes even the code of the mob, which is to protect its own. Lethu denounced the comrades who had made such a judgment. In that way, he authored his own death warrant. In trying to save the convicted man, Lethu became prey himself. Allegations against him sprang to life simply from his actions—if he was trying to save a convicted traitor, then that was evidence enough that he himself was a traitor. The fact that he had been absent from the trial on account of being in police custody itself became suspicious—was he really in custody, or in collaboration?

As Lethu quietly told his tale on the sunbaked hill above the Umzimvubu more than a decade later, his audience shivered with recognition. Mendi knew only too well the forces that could drive the revolutionary spirit down those self-consuming dead ends; Alice had seen the same kind of madness on the face of the youngster who had mouthed "kill you, bitch" at her in Soweto as a police dog tried to bite his face off.

Lethu had been carried on the flood of the mob's passion from street committee leader, to accused, to convicted collaborator in a matter of half an hour. It was decided that he should watch the other man die as part of his judgment. So he was bound and held. The petrol was poured and finally the convicted man lost control and howled like an animal, and the matches

233

were thrown and the air-rush from the ignition blew briefly in Lethu's face, followed by the acrid smell of the burning rubber. The convicted man writhed and staggered a few steps before collapsing; the mob danced around him like children at a bonfire, their faces full of zeal and satisfaction. No sooner was the blackened figure motionless than they turned on Lethu, their appetites refreshed, already two skinny boys rolling a tire toward him across the flat sandy lot where he had, for a short season, been their leader.

Lethu heard a muffled report and looked up and saw the snaky trail of a tear gas canister arcing toward him. The police helicopter had seen the black smoke from the burning rubber tire. Three armored vehicles were approaching, white soldiers sitting on their roofs, firing tear gas and laughing. The mob howled with indignation. There was no time to necklace Lethu, so they tried to kick him and stone him to death in the few moments available before the armored vehicles were upon them and the rubber bullets were flying. The soldiers were quite unaware of having saved Lethu's life, they simply did what they were briefed to do— move through the area and break up the riot, removing all evidence of necklacing as soon as possible, for such things did not play well on the TV news. Lethu's limp body was collected as part of that operation, and when it was found to be alive, was delivered without ceremony to the gate of the clinic. It was Dom who had opened the gates of the clinic and carried Lethu inside.

Lethu survived the beating, but the trouble started when word got out a week later that he was recovering in the clinic. If the mob needed proof that he was a collaborator, there it was—he had been saved from necklacing by police intervention and was being treated in the clinic by white liberals, who no one ever really trusted anyway. Within hours, the clinic was besieged. The soldiers were called to protect it and their diligence in it was much reduced by the fact that it was the very institution from which they had been banned.

From there, it took twenty-four hours for Dom's program to unravel. A program that had neither the support of the police nor the trust of the community was indeed untenable, not the least from the point of view of its financial backers. But, by then, that was the least of Dom's problems. Dom knew that if Lethu walked out the front gate of the clinic, he would be dead within an hour. The whole area was galvanized by the event. Any rational reconsideration of Lethu's status was impossible. Comrades from other areas were coming to the township, looking to be at the focal point.

"I remember all the talk of it," said Mendi. "In the counsel sessions of the UDF. It was one of those things we wished we could get control of but knew we couldn't. There were a lot of those."

So Dom put Lethu, still severely ill, into the back of a medical supplies delivery vehicle and shipped him out of the clinic. He took him to his own home in the suburbs. Three weeks later, when Lethu was medically stable, they set out for his home village. Behind the barrier of hills, in the land where he had known the peace of childhood, Lethu sought the oblivion he needed. Dom, out of a job and out of a purpose back in the city, stayed to see him through the early stages. They had a friendship growing. They did a lot of dope. It cost money and the quality was variable. So they started to grow their own. Neither of them ever left.

"So where does Martin de Villiers come from after all these years?" said Alice.

"Writers keep files," said Dom. "They never forget anything. They keep phone numbers. They look in other people's diaries. They make connections long after everyone else thinks the line is dead. He knew people who are lifelong friends of mine."

"He knew more than that," said Mendi. "In the notes I got, he had done an incredible amount of research into Lethu's background. He'd been to the mine offices and looked up the details of Lethu's father's service, and his home. He even wrote to the old guy who used to be the labor broker here, and tried to find out where Lethu might be living."

Lethu's eyes found Alice's, but they said nothing. Mendi laughed. "You know, the message I got at first was that this guy's girlfriend told the police in Johannesburg that he was going to tell the story of someone called Tradition Dube. So I went around this Godforsaken village for days asking about someone called "Tradition Dube." Then the investigator phones me and says the girl says she meant his name was traditional, meaning a black name she couldn't remember or pronounce."

Mendi and Alice made their way down the hill together. They had to keep moving, because Lethu's story had carried them late into the afternoon and it would make life very difficult to be caught by the darkness while still in the bush. But once they reached the road, they could take the last section of the journey in the warm gloom, with the sound of the birds contesting for night perches in the trees and the cicadas polishing the air.

Walking beside the magistrate, absorbing the night, Alice said, "You have made a judgment of Solomon."

"Thank you," he said.

Then the light went as though turned off at the switch and they had to stumble the rest of the way home.

45

On the morning of her last day in Port Victoria, Alice rose early and set off toward the old house. She chose to walk along the beach and take the shorter, steeper path up to the house; her legs were stronger than they had been a few weeks before and she relished the challenge. She crossed Simon's bay and clambered up over the rocks at the far end. As she came into view of the next bay, she saw down at the shoreline a surfer waxing his board. He had Simon's build and Simon's sun-bleached hair and Simon's bow-like muscles working in his back. But he was not Simon. He was, she saw as she approached him, much younger. He looked up and saw her and she saw him glance toward the headland, where now she saw his truck parked.

"Hi," she said.

"Hi." His smile was easy. "Cool spot."

"It is," agreed Alice. "When did you arrive?"

"Late yesterday. Killer drive."

A young woman got out of the truck and came toward them. She wore a baggy top and a bikini bottom that showed long tan legs.

"Where did you drive from?" asked Alice.

"Cape Town," he said. "You live here?"

"Used to," said Alice. "I'm just a visitor now."

He nodded, his eyes slid away to the surf.

"Ask her anyway," said the other woman. "She might know."

He clearly didn't think so. "No, it's just there's a guy we're looking for. A surfer we heard was living along here somewhere."

"Simon Scully," said Alice.

It was a pleasure to see the way he responded to the name.

"Where is he?"

"He's in hospital in Durban. He had an accident."

"In the water?"

"No. Nothing like that."

"Oh. I'm sorry for him. I hoped he would show me the local layout. I've got a laptop in the truck with the geo's for the area and so on, but there's no cell phone link down here so I can't download any weather and stuff. It would have been good to have someone who knows the local layout."

"Well, I can tell you he never surfed this bay," Alice said. "He said the shelf is too close here. He surfed the next bay south. Because of the current, the surf curls into the bay from the north and makes a kind of circle, so the rip out is right up against the north side behind me here. I just came across now, it's pretty good this morning—about three feet. You better get out there before the onshore gets up."

His grin acknowledged everything she had said. "Thanks," he said.

Alice said, "Simon preferred a longer board than you've got."

The surfer nodded. "Some of the older guys do."

"Excuse me," said the girl. "I hope this isn't rude, but we slept in the truck the last two nights and the hotel looks pretty basic, and do you maybe have somewhere we could wash up?"

"Sure," said Alice. "Simon's house is on the south side, overlooking the bay. It's open. I fired the boiler before I left, so there should be hot water."

"You okay that we go in while you're not there?"

She nodded. "I'm just going for a walk. I'll see you later."

46

Mendi stood before the press contingent with an attitude of gravitas. Detective Dhlomo sat beside him, smiling with the

238

achievement of a good result. Clive and the waiters had been sent out. Mendi waited until he had everyone's attention. He noted Ursula's sharp pencil poised above her fresh reporter's pad.

"We are here because a man died," said Mendi. "The fact that he was a well-known man should be irrelevant to you. But of course, it cannot be so. So all I ask is that you treat the information I give you now with respect, and do not try and make any more or less of it than it is."

He stopped. A beat later, Ursula's pencil stopped.

The night before, Mendi thought a lot about what Alice said to him on the road in the dark on the way home. And what occupied Mendi's mind for a while was that he didn't think he had ever been paid a compliment by a white person before, or indeed ever heard of such a thing passing from a white person to a black person in that country. That was not necessarily because such compliments were never due nor never paid, but because a compliment between races that was completely devoid of subtext was a difficult thing to achieve in that country.

But Alice had truly laid upon Mendi an unqualified compliment and it made him think. Mendi realized that he would never achieve the high political office of which he had dreamed, yet through the tangle of events he stumbled into there, he found his own life. Moreover, he had taken possession of his own country and found it unexpectedly familiar.

The night before, he thought of his grandchildren.

"The cause of death of Martin de Villiers cannot be established with complete certainty," Mendi told the journalists. "However, I have uncovered sufficient evidence to point to a conclusion which satisfies me personally and the requirements of the law. My report will conclude that Martin de Villiers died as a result of falling off the rocks at a popular fishing spot known as Bird Rock. This is death by misadventure. There is no evidence of foul play or mystery. Mr. de Villiers was a well-known media figure, but he was also something of a sportsman. He came down here, on his own with his fishing tackle, and took a cabin in the campsite a few miles up the beach. He asked advice about suitable local fishing spots. Every fisherman knows you have to ask the locals where to fish. Bird Rock is known to be good because the water is deep immediately off the rock. For the same reason, it can be dangerous. The fact that Mr. de Villiers's body washed up in the bay just off the hotel here further supports this conclusion. The currents in this area are strong and dangerous and variable. If Mr. de Villiers entered the water at Bird Rock, it is quite likely that his body could have been carried to these rocks."

Surveying the faces of his audience, Mendi could see they were disappointed. They had come all that way for a big story and had ended up with a sad little death. He needed to toss them something to keep them happy.

"On an informal note, I would just say that I have observed most of you making excellent effort to get to know the local area, and as the responsible magistrate for this area, I would like to say I was pleased to see that. But perhaps there's a lesson here. Mr. de Villiers died because he got out of his depth. Despite much advance, many parts of this country are still rugged and wild, and not to be confronted by the inexperienced. Perhaps Mr. de Villiers's death will be redeemed to a degree if it reminds us of this. That is all. There will be no Q and A."

47

Alice told the aunts they could remain in the house as long as they chose. She walked out of the front door, locking the safety gate behind her helpfully, but really to discourage Phyllis from following her out for a last farewell.

She stood on the verandah for the last time.

She remembered that day and yet she didn't. She remembered much of the inconsequential detail. She remembered how hot it was, how the flame trees were seeding and their seedpods like big boats were cracking open under the hot sun and releasing the weightless seeds into the air. She remembered Len's eyes, the softness of his voice contrasting with the pain in his face. She remembered running off the verandah when she tripped and cut her lip. She was running to call the adults sitting down under the tree. But she had to mix her raw memories with information acquired later to make sense of that day.

It was a Saturday. Her mother had been dead a year, during which time life proceeded in a way that was both just the same and quite different. Len had been poorly lately. In Alice's memory, decline came abruptly for Len. However, she realized that probably there was a build-up period that was hidden from her young eyes—a concealment aided by many factors. Len had a high tolerance for pain and discomfort and symptoms that others would have taken to a doctor. Len had enveloped his disability and pain and multiple indignities in a routine that was seldom referred to except via a few essential code words. But Eileen's death had forced him to open the circle of indignity to his sisters, who at that point had to nurse him. Alice hadn't understood the implications of that then.

It was a Saturday and Robbie and his two sisters were sitting out under the tree having lunch with two men from the mining company who had come down on business. Len had not come out because he was not well. Alice didn't like sitting out under the tree with all the adults while Len was inside alone, so she went in, collected the *Duff's Turf Guide*, and went to lie next to him in his bed and talk horse racing to him. He gave her that soft smile, but she could see he was in pain. When her weight moved the mattress, he winced. Years later, she would be told the septicemia was already rampant in his body, making every nerve end an alarm.

He asked where everyone else was. She told him they were out under the tree, having cold meats and potato salad and drinking gin, lime and water.

"Alice," he said. "I want you to do something for me."

Alice would do anything for the man she believed to be her father, the man she had imprinted on.

"I need you to do this thing without asking why and without telling anyone else. It's between you and me, okay?"

"Sure, Dad."

"I need you to go into Robbie's office, where his desk is, in the top right hand drawer there's a revolver. I need you to bring that to me."

Alice did that small chore for the man she called her father because he couldn't walk, and could not fetch something from Robbie's office for himself. He thanked her, and told her to go out and sit with the others. Alice had walked out of the room. In the corridor, her eight-year-old mind was starting to tell her that maybe another adult should be consulted on her father's request. So she started to hurry. By the time she hit the verandah, she was going at top speed with not much of a thought in her head. Her bare foot clipped the post at the corner of the stairs down to the lawn and she tumbled down them with a cry that brought the adults running up from under the tree. When Alice lifted her face out of the dirt, it was bloodied from the cut in her hairline and the slice out of her lip. She was yelping and people were telling her to be calm. While Robbie was trying to hold her still to get a good look at her lip and decide if it should be stitched, the sound of the revolver firing ripped out of the house. So Alice never had her lip stitched and carried the scar by which Lethu recognized her.

48

On the way back, she saw the replacement surfer out behind the line-up. He saw her and raised his hand. She waved back and stopped to watch him take a wave. Then she walked up to Simon's house to get her things.

The girlfriend was drying her sun-bleached hair.

"What do you do?" Alice asked her.

"Varsity," said the girl.

"You two could use this house for a while if you wanted. I know Simon would want you to."

"Really? What about you?"

"I'm leaving today. Holiday's over. Going back to England."

"Did you emigrate?" asked the girl.

"Kind of," said Alice. "I married an Englishman. I have a daughter in school in London."

"We're often wondering about all that. Like everyone. Whether it's worth starting anything in this country, or we should just leave."

"The waves aren't too good in England," said Alice. "Not to mention the weather. I'm going to tell Johnny you're staying here. There are no keys. When you leave, you let him know, okay? You can find him most evenings on the verandah at the hotel."

"Okay," said the girl.

"Feed the cats," said Alice.

Now she had to keep walking. Away from Simon's house and away from the beach. Away from any discussion about how, when and why to leave this country. Alice had been flung from the land of her birth by forces she did not understand, then or now. Some people are gifted with coherent stories to their lives. They find themselves riding in a caravan of shared beliefs, upward trends, national identity, united families, good fortune that can be easily interpreted as just reward. That is how they can feel their lives slightly larger than they are. Alice's story was in tatters, it seemed to her that she had lived the first half of her life in a country that didn't exist, then or now. She had a collection of memories. She had the scar on her lip and the feeling in her stomach when she saw the scars in the doorframes of the old house left by Leonard's wheelchair. Leonard—not her real father, but the man who held that place in her—had been obliged to remake himself to survive, years of pain and indignity less than a grain of dust in the wind of history. It was the same for her, she realized, she had to go back to London and make herself a place in the world, plank by plank, so that Julia would never feel the way she did now.

On the day she had first driven into Port Victoria, Alice had parked her rental car behind the Cape Hamilton Hotel and had not touched it since. The battery was dead and Johnny had to be summoned to jumpstart it. During the wait, Mendi approached her.

"I hear you are driving back to the capital now?"

"Yes."

"Will you give me a lift? It will save me traveling with those drunken soldiers of mine."

"Sure."

On the verandah of the hotel, Clive was popping the first beers of the day for his reduced circle of regulars.

"I don't know what he was talking about," said Clive. "Shit, I've done a lot of fishing up and down this piece of coast, and I've never heard of Bird Rock being particularly good."

"Fishermen keep secrets."

"Until they've had a beer or six."

"The magistrate said that locals advised him to go there," said Bob.

"What locals?"

"At Lusungeti."

"Who, that slapgat who runs the camp there? He couldn't catch a sardine out of a can. And he only gets drug addicts and surfers staying there. There's no fishermen there."

Johnny nursed his cold beer as he listened to all that. He was watching the white caps on the waves, deciding whether to go out in the boat that day.

"Have you been onto Bird Rock?" Johnny said.

They both shook their heads.

"It looks like a spot that might be good for fishing, because it points out into the current, and the water's deep there. That's why the birds stand there, because they can see into the water. That's why it's called Bird Rock. But no local ever goes there because they know about the blowhole. There's a blowhole that comes out just behind Bird Rock and when the tide is coming in it can fire a massive spray up that blowhole and soak the rock, not to mention making a helluva noise. So, you're standing on the rock in all this bird shit, now it's soaking wet, you're pretty much guaranteed to slide off into the water. Then the rip from the blowhole will suck you out in a minute."

"Wow," said Bob.

"Shit," said Clive.

That account made the death of Martin de Villiers much more real for them than the magistrate's report.

"It's bizarre that anyone would send him there, then," said Clive.

"Maybe he just went. Saw it, thought it looked good."

"Maybe. Maybe not," said Johnny. He still had his eyes on the horizon. Bob got it first.

"Whoa! Are you saying...?"

"I'm saying zip," said Johnny.

"So somebody suggested he goes there because they know it's dangerous?"

"Who?"

"Like who! That's a tough one. For three weeks the magistrate can't get an answer. Then he goes up the mountain to see Dom and comes back and announces that de Villiers died by accident fishing off Bird Rock."

"That's amazing," said Bob. He pulled his roller and dope bag out of his pockets and started to make the first joint of the day. The others watched him for a minute.

"Chuck us another beer, Clive," said Johnny.

Bob took a puff of his joint and offered it to the others.

"So Dom Marais just conned that magistrate like that?"

Johnny stood up. "I don't think that magistrate is as stupid as we think," he said.

"You mean you reckon—"

"I'm going to take the boat out," said Johnny, standing. He arced his empty beer can accurately into the mouth of the drum at the corner of the verandah and turned to leave.

"What you going to do without Woodstock?" called Clive. "You wanna hand with the boat?"

"No, it's okay, I'm training up Breakdown," said Johnny and stepped off the verandah.

"Shit," said Clive. "Did you know that?"

"I didn't know that," said Bob.

"That Ursula chick sure changed Johnny's outlook on life."

"She could change anyone's, mine included. Shall I roll another joint?"

So Alice and Mendi drove up the difficult road out of Port Victoria side by side again, as they had arrived. At the top of the hill, it was Mendi who said, "Let's have a last look."

They stopped and got out. It was high tide, the lagoon swollen. The surf was choppy and irritable. Simon was missing nothing that day, Alice thought. The mussel pickers were combing along the rocks, harassed by tendrils of foam and spray. She thought of Breakdown, and for a moment felt his eyes on her.

Mendi said, "Thankfully, I won't see this dump again."

"You never know," said Alice. "Someone else might get murdered."

Mendi shuffled slightly, and then smiled almost shyly. "Actually, I have had some good news. I have been promoted. I am moving to the Justice Department in Pretoria."

"Oh, that's fantastic," Alice said, and her smile was genuine. "I'm really happy for you."

"And you?" he asked. "Will you be back?"

She had to turn away from the sea then.

"No," she said.

They got back in the car, and the empty road drew them away across the barrier hills.

--oOo--

About the author

Patrick J. Lee grew up in South Africa, where he worked as a journalist and screenwriter. He spent several years in England before moving to the United States in 2004.

He is also the author (under the name P. J. Lee) of the crime novel *The Flies of August*, set in Connecticut.